My Mechanical Romance

ALEXENE
FAROL FOLLMUTH

MACMILLAN

First published in the US 2022 by Maple Press, York, PA, USA

First published in the UK 2022 by Macmillan Children's Books
an imprint of Pan Macmillan
The Smithson, 6 Briset Street, London EC1M 5NR
EU representative: Macmillan Publishers Ireland Ltd, 1st Floor,
The Liffey Trust Centre, 117–126 Sheriff Street Upper
Dublin 1, D01 YC43
Associated companies throughout the world
www.panmacmillan.com

ISBN 978-1-0350-0817-9

7 9 8 6

A CIP catalogue record for this book is available from the British Library.

Printed and bound by CPI Group (UK) Ltd, Croydon CR0 4YY

For Henry

||||||

one

CATAPULT

Bel

Family lore has it that my dad wanted to name me Joy when he found out I was going to be a girl. My mother insisted on Isabel, having already established a taste for saints' names, but thanks to my inability to pronounce the letter *S*, it got shortened to Bella. Then, because I hated that and refused to answer to it, it shrank down to Bel, which is ultimately a testament to how compromise leaves both parties unsatisfied.

To my dad's credit, I'm not a joyless person. Like most people, there are things I love in life—cheese, being right, the beautiful rarity of a well-timed clapback—and things I don't. The top of that second list? Team sports, being asked what I'm doing with my life, and the faint but harrowing sensation that something critical may have slipped my mind.

"Oh man, I forgot it was catapult day," says Jamie, surveying her kingdom from our lofty perch at the top of the quad. "First project of the year—so cute! All the little Physics babies squawking around like tiny frightened birds…love that," she soliloquys, powder-blue nails tapping the can of her dystopian-flavored LaCroix. "Where's yours, by the way?"

Hmmmm. Crap.

Okay, so I *know* the catapult project was probably (definitely) in the syllabus, but in my defense, there was a huge essay due in English last week and I have a quiz this afternoon in Statistics plus a group project in Civics, and anyway, it's really not my fault my grasp of time is so flawed. Aren't there a million different scholarly articles about the impact of academic stress on teens or something? I'm pretty sure I could find at least a dozen if I really put some effort into researching. (I won't, but it's a valid thought, right?)

"Isabel Maier," prompts Jamie, who is unfortunately still here and not part of a distressing dream I'm having. "Your silence is highly suspicious."

"Uh," I say, cleverly.

Spoiler: I do not have my catapult. Primarily because it doesn't exist and secondarily because no miracles have occurred in the last thirty seconds. The only thing currently springing to mind is a very unhelpful slew of obscenities that would cause my mother to make the sign of the cross and then ask me where she failed as a parent. (Hot tip: that's a rhetorical question.)

"Hello?" Jamie says, waving a hand in my face. "Bel?"

"I'm thinking," I tell her, glancing down at my phone screen.

Woof. Class starts in fifteen minutes.

"Excellent," Jamie says doubtfully. "Promising start."

Like all girls who get told they talk like a grown-up from age six, Jamie Howard wants to be a lawyer. Her career goals involve wearing high-powered skirt suits in Manhattan while barking orders at her associates from a corner office littered with ferns. She's the sort of girl who stalks around campus with determination, practically bowling over anyone in her path, and who laughs *much* too loudly at anything she finds funny. Luckily, I have been one of those things since she was conscripted to guide me through transfer student orientation six weeks ago.

"Do you have any, like—" Hm. "Tape?" I ask optimistically.

"What?" says Jamie.

"Tape," I repeat. "Do. You. Have. Any?"

"Bel, I can hear," she informs me, "and not that you've asked my opinion on this, but I don't think any amount of tape is going to help you build the catapult you so obviously forgot to do."

"Allegedly," I correct her. "*Allegedly* forgot to do, and is that a no?"

"Of course it's a no. Who carries around tape?"

"I don't know, some people," I say, groping for the strap of my backpack where a more carefree version of me tossed it below the table. "Don't you carry around a mini stapler?"

"Yes, obviously," sniffs Jamie, "but seeing as I'm not a postal worker or currently enrolled in kindergarten, I don't have any use for tape."

"You're literally not helping," I point out.

"I'm literally not trying to help," Jamie replies with a breath-taking lack of shame. "You do realize this project is, like, *half* your semester grade, right? If you get a zero, that will reflect very poorly on me."

"Okay, now you're really not helping," I inform Jamie. "And considering I'm in a crisis, you could stand to be a little more upbeat."

"You're right, sorry—if you get a zero, that will reflect very poorly on me!" Jamie singsongs.

Marvelous.

For what it's worth, even I initially assumed that Jamie's interest in me was because she takes *all* of her extracurricular responsibilities this seriously—like, to a possibly insane extent. It's unclear why a person actively gunning for valedictorian would choose to hang out with someone who doesn't even own a day planner unless it's a matter of professional courtesy. But seeing as Jamie's still "checking in" with me every day without fail, I think we took an unexpected turn into genuine friendship somewhere between following each other on Instagram at orientation and baking cookies with her grandma last weekend.

"Okay, well, not that this technically changes anything," I say, doubling back on the only option I can conceivably extract from my brain, "but for the record, I don't want the tape. I want the container."

Jamie looks at me blankly.

"You know, the plastic thing that holds the tape?" I attempt. Nothing. Nada.

"Okay," I sigh, "I have fifteen minutes to fix this and zero time to explain it to you. Can you just be helpful, please?"

"Probably not," she says. "Maybe try the office?"

Oh good, great, I'd love to start my afternoon by asking one of the illustrious Essex Academy for Art, Science, and Technology administrators for tape, having narrowly survived an interrogation just this morning about whether I've scheduled some sort of career assessment with my counselor. I sensed an underlying hint of suspicion from them, which I didn't think was fair. Very few of my answers were lies, so I could definitely be doing a lot worse.

But considering my options are either this or the inevitable lecture from my mother...

"Ugh," I say, wheeling around to aim myself in that direction.

"Good luck!" Jamie shouts after me.

Yeah, sure. Because luck is definitely what's missing from the equation.

At my old school, which was admittedly a sham, there was none of this fussing about whether or not people had taken the SATs or chosen a course of study, and don't even get me started on college apps. Branford had about four AP classes and either you were smart and took them (like my middle brother, Gabe) or you didn't care about school so you messed around all day until baseball practice (like my oldest brother, Luke).

This school, on the other hand, is like a weird laboratory for startup CEOs. It's private, per my mother's insistence, and despite being less than ten miles away from where I used to spend all my time, Sherman Oaks is definitely no Van Nuys. When it comes to the lovely little armpit of Los Angeles that we call the Valley, you can feel the tax bracket changing while you sit on the 405.

So yeah, I'm not particularly jazzed about visiting the Essex Academy mothership. Thankfully, my phone buzzes before I get very far.

Jamie: lora just got here
Jamie: she says to try the library?

That's better, considering it's the closest building to where I'm currently standing. Viva Lora! I veer off my current trajectory and pop inside, where the stars have smiled on me despite my vulgar language and probable blasphemy. The main librarian is currently helping someone understand the finer details of the Dewey decimal system, so I snatch a deck of tape from the counter and make every effort not to draw attention to myself as I flee the scene of the crime and head outside.

I pause at the edge of the quad, recalculating. Okay, ten minutes, what do I have? A pen, great. That's actually more miraculous than it sounds. A rubber band. A water bottle.

Hm, that's a thought.

"Are you done with that?" I ask some passing kid in my periphery. He looks up at me in terror, so I'm guessing he's a freshman.

"This?" he echoes, holding up the bottle of Smartwater he's just finished.

I may have only been here for three weeks, but I'm still a senior, so I give him a somber upperclassman nod. "Single-use plastics are like, extremely irresponsible," I tell him, because that's the sort of thing that makes people around here feel guilty. "I'm just, you know. Recycling."

Unless he's some kind of hoarder of empty water bottles, he should let me have it. Slowly, he offers it up to me, still looking like he thinks I might bite.

"Thanks," I say, and then pop over to the recycling bin at the base of the quad. Hopefully the freshman isn't watching as I withdraw two more bottles (gross, I know, but my mom's an ER nurse who loads me up with hand sanitizer—it's fine) and unscrew the caps.

I step back with all four bottle caps in my hand, bumping into someone as I turn.

"Watch it," says the voice belonging to the body I've just collided with.

His name's Teo Luna, which I wish I didn't know, but unfortunately everyone here is in love with him. A pie-in-the-sky sort of love like applying to Stanford, since he's the incredibly loaded son of some tech god. Obviously at this school full of mutants they don't have a normal prom king character like my brother Luke, who drinks a lot of protein shakes and has one of those loud, megawatt smiles to complement his pectorals. Instead, their version of a heartthrob takes a full load of AP courses and looks like he's probably vegan "for the environment" or whatever.

Sure, Teo Luna is captain of about eight hundred science-y things that typically win stuff and he's got those Internet Boyfriend curls to go with his perma-tan, so I guess that's appealing in a hipster kind of way. In my opinion, he could stand to take the arrogance down a notch.

"Beggin' your pardon, sir," I say, briefly cosplaying as Oliver Twist after smacking directly into his chest. He frowns, adjusting the Essex soccer jersey he's wearing in place of his usual senatorial button-down, and in response I bob a curtsy.

"Ooooookayyyy," he says, deliberately drawing it out and turning with a roll of his eyes.

Gross. Bye.

Seven minutes. Eight? Okay, more like five. The deck is nearly out of tape, so I pull out what remains, offer my silent apologies to the Essex Academy recycling initiative for my abominable waste, and wrap the rubber band around the empty roll, breaking off a bit of plastic to hold it steady. A little finagling with the plastic pen cap and a few bottle caps later, I've got a thing that looks vaguely like a duck on circular legs. The base will keep it upright, and the rubber band will work like a slingshot. It's a miniature take on a catapult, but there was no size requirement. All it has to do is work.

Do I have time to test it?

Bell rings, so that's a no. We'll just have to call this a Hail Mary.

(On the bright side, a Hail Mary of any sort might actually please my mother.)

Jamie: so?? are you totally screwed??
Bel: not yet, mon ami
Bel: not yet

TEO

It appears to be catapult day once again. Not my favorite Physics project from last year, but definitely better than anything I've had to do for any other class. I'll take building something from scratch over a reconstructed literary analysis any day of the week, which is why AP Physics was the first thing I signed up for going into senior year.

Besides, I didn't *have* to use the full two weeks we were given for the catapult, but there are high expectations for me at this school. To me, every detail is crucial, which is why I made sure to earn every point of that A+. These new catapults…Well. Not to be a dick, but these look terrible. I think I just saw a junior walking by holding a catapult made up of 80 percent paper towel rolls and 20 percent inadequacy.

Disappointing. If I absolutely *have* to recruit a new team member this week, I'd like it to be someone capable of an interesting design. By the looks of it, though—

My phone buzzes in my pocket, interrupting my thoughts.

Dash: are u seeing this

He's sitting four seats away from me like he usually is but sure, fine, let's text. I glance around to see what he's talking about, but I have no idea.

Teo: seeing what

"Luna," says Mac, the AP Physics teacher, and I groan internally. He's technically Mr. MacIntosh if a vice principal ever decides to wander over to the science quad for some reason, but I think he finds it highly amusing for us to refer to him like the Apple computer. It isn't as entertaining as he thinks it is, but after three years working with him in robotics, I'm essentially immune to whatever Mac finds hysterical. It's like 87 percent puns.

"Must I remind you no phones?" he says, arching a brow. "Put it away."

I turn to glare at Dash, who shrugs. *Be respectful*, he mouths loftily to me.

Sometimes I hate him, I swear.

"All right, we're going to stick with kinematics today," says Mac, projecting his iPad screen onto the board with today's warm-up exercise. Mac loves drawing this cartoon character he calls Chad who does all sorts of terrible things to his friends; dropping anvils on their heads from the tops of buildings, for instance. We only have to figure out the math, but I think it's fairly obvious Chad has some unresolved issues. Probably from childhood.

Today, Chad's throwing a ball at someone: velocity, distance, acceleration, time. There's a reason this is a warm-up. I put pen to paper and scribble the equations with approximately the same level of attention I'd use to tie my shoes.

"Teo," hisses Dash, tossing a ball of paper at my head. "Hey. Teo."

I ignore him. Dash's real name is Dariush, but none of us had any patience for that in first grade, hence the diminutive. I like the way it means he's something moderately unfinished: *Dash*. You dash to the cafeteria line. You put a dash between words. It just takes up space, annoying you in class and slowly deflating your will to live.

"Ma-*te*-o," says Dash, hands cupped around his mouth. "Teo. Hey."

"Dash, Jesus, *stop*—"

"Done, Luna?" calls Mac, and I look up. "Great! Draw it on the board," he says, gesturing over his shoulder with his chin. He gives me a look of conspiracy, like he and I are both in on my punishment. I wish I could tell him that being best friends with Dash is already punishment enough.

As I rise to my feet, Dash points at someone. Jamie Howard? She's frowning at her page, looking lost. She's...well, she's super smart, I'll give her that, but she's more the type to win an essay contest or talk about Shakespeare or something. She doesn't like math or science and considers it, quote, "banal." I think she's just here to cushion her GPA for Stanford. Next to her is Lora Murphy, who's in robotics with Dash and me (and most of the class minus Jamie, who's too busy with Mock Trial or Model UN or whatever liberal-artsy thing she's doing), and in front of Lora is—

Ah. Dash is pointing at Neelam.

Okay, so for the record I don't have a problem with Neelam Dasari. Am I generally better at circuitry than she is? Yes. Does that have anything to do with some sinister patriarchal collusion between Mac and me? No. Not that any of that stops Neelam from giving me a dirty look every time Mac and I talk about what video games we're playing over the weekend, like it's somehow a plot twist that Mac backed the team's decision to make me the driver for this year's bots. She seems to think that makes me some sort of nepotistic brogrammer, when in fact it's a matter of professional expertise.

Anyway, the point is Neelam's somehow got my sketch for the new fifteen-pound bot I designed over the summer and she's completely dismantling it in plain sight—proving I'm not the only one lacking devotion to our warm-up, by the way, which apparently Mac hasn't noticed. Who's benefiting from favoritism now, huh, Neelam? It's not like that sketch is the final design or anything, but I'd appreciate her not being a total dick about it. It's the little things.

I start copying my equation onto the board when I see someone step into the courtyard outside our classroom window. It's Ms. Voss, the Bio teacher (she has one Physics class due to overflow this year or something) talking to the new girl, who I just ran into by the recycling bins. I haven't figured out the new girl's name yet—we don't have any classes together—but she's genuinely the weirdest person I've ever met. I don't even think she's doing it on purpose; I honestly think she's just *like* that. Today she's wearing a super long hippie skirt and a necklace made of tiny spoons.

"Okay," I say, stepping back from the board. "Finished."

"Nicely done, Luna," says Mac. "Looks good."

Of course it does. "Thanks."

Neelam gives me another look as I walk past her desk again. This time she curves her arm around the page, as if I don't know perfectly well what she's doing. As far as I'm concerned, she can make all the proposed changes she wants. Dash will take my side, and so will Emmett and Kai. Ravi does whatever we tell him and Justin's basically useless either way, so really, it's not like I have to worry much about what Neelam thinks. She doesn't make a secret of hating me, and likewise, I've given up on trying to make nice with her. It's not like she's some sort of tragic outcast or anything, either. She has plenty of friends—I'm just not one of them.

I sit down and glance out the window while Mac starts explaining the finer points of my work. It's only the third week of school, so nothing interesting is going to happen in the curriculum for at least a month. Mostly I'm concerned about tryouts for the robotics club, which are happening on Friday. I personally don't think we need anyone new, but Mac won't let us get started in the lab until we hold the tryouts. (Something about fair shots and opportunity, blah blah.)

Unless some freshman grew up on an oil rig or a naval ship, adding a new person to the team means the headache of me having to give yet another course on Welding 101. Being captain for both robotics and soccer is hard enough without being enrolled in six AP classes *and* working on my application for early admission to MIT, plus people are definitely expecting me to be social. I know it's on me to handle the stress of adding someone new to the team, so needless to say, I've been dreading it since school started.

Ms. Voss seems to be taking the new girl to task outside, which distracts me for a moment. Not that I care, but Ms. Voss is really strict, at least from what I remember of freshman Bio. I notice that Jamie Howard is looking out the window as well, and after a second or two she surreptitiously slides her phone out of her pocket. I think she's friends with the new girl; she's her Transfer Buddy or whatever it's called. I don't keep track of Jamie's extracurriculars, which is pretty much all of them. Maybe she's texting to ask what's going on.

My mind wanders again, this time back to the New Girl. Who starts at a new school their senior year? That sucks. Granted, I feel like I've known everyone here since I was in diapers—and *they* all know me—so naturally I can't wait to go to school across the country and meet someone new for a change. But doesn't she have friends? A life? I joke about hating Dash at least 53 percent of the time we're together, but still. Better that than having to make a new Dash.

"—ocity of the ball, Luna?"

I realize Mac is waiting for me to say something.

"Hm?" I ask, snapping out of my distraction.

"What factors did you use," Mac repeats, "when calculating the velocity of the ball?"

Oh. "Speed, distance, time." Cakewalk.

"Thank you for being so kind as to grace us with your mental acuity, Luna," says Mac drily. "Anyone else want to weigh in on Chad?"

I guess she's not *not* hot.

(The New Girl, that is. Ms. Voss is, like, forty, so definitely not her.)

"Okay, let's break into groups of four," calls Mac, clapping his hands. "Go ahead and get after it."

Easy. It'll be Dash, Emmett, Kai, and me. Across the room, Jamie has no choice but to let Justin join her group with Lora and Neelam…Yikes. Bet they wish they had one more girl in this class right about now.

"Did you see it?" asks Dash, elbowing me as I drag a stool out from under the lab table.

"Ouch—*yes*, Dariush—"

"It's not like they're not valid ideas," says Emmett, whose mother wants him to date either a nice Chinese girl or Neelam. Depends who becomes a doctor first, according to his mom, because none of us know how to explain to her that nothing we do is remotely related to medicine.

"Have you actually heard these supposedly 'valid' ideas?"

Kai snarks to Emmett, dropping his books onto the table. He and Emmett both have insane parents whose obsession with their grades is matched only by the obsession with who they'll eventually marry.

"No," Emmett mutters defensively, "but I'm just saying, they *might* be—"

"Okay great, but this isn't a matter of opinion. Teo and I designed it that way *on purpose*—"

"Get to work, boys," says Mac, materializing again to shush us. "Focus. Got it?"

"Sure," I say.

Outside, Ms. Voss and the New Girl disappear just in time for me to offer a cursory glance over the lab Mac drops in front of me.

More velocity! Joy.

Just another day at school, like always.

two

TROUBLE

Bel

S o," says Ms. Voss. "Your catapult."

"Ummm…yes?" I say, deciding to play innocent. I've learned it's always best not to try and guess what's about to go wrong. It's like how you shouldn't tell a cop how fast you were actually going when he pulls you over, just in case. Or something. (I don't know, Jamie told me that.)

"Okay, Isabel, listen," sighs Ms. Voss, which is never a good sign. There's nothing quite like a little bit of manufactured intimacy—*Listen, we're all friends here!*—to make something feel inevitably dire, and only my mother calls me by my full first name. "I think you and I both know there wasn't as much effort on this project as there could have been."

"Oh, um. Well—"

I break off, and then, rather than finishing the sentence, I just… coast to a stop. It seems like the only logical thing to do, really.

For whatever reason, Ms. Voss gives me a weird, lopsided smile.

"What sciences did you take at your last school?" she asks me. Weird question, but okay. "Bio and Chem?"

"Are you asking me or telling me?"

Ugh. "Sorry, telling you. Bio and Chem."

"And how did you do in those classes?"

"Oh, um. I got As in both."

"But you didn't take any AP sciences?"

"I'm...not really into science."

"What about math?"

I frown. "Did I take math, you mean?"

She gives me another half smile. "Yes. Which math courses have you taken?"

"Um, Algebra and Pre-Calc. I'm in Calculus now."

"How'd you do in those courses?"

"I got an A- in Algebra? I think." Sophomore year was weird; I had a loser boyfriend who got me grounded at least four times before I finally broke things off. "But I got an A in Pre-Calc."

"Are you in AP Calculus now?"

"Um...no, just regular," I say. (This is weird, right?)

"So you're not into math, either?" she asks me, and I think she's...joking?

"I guess not," I say, sounding incredibly unconvincing.

"Ah," remarks Ms. Voss, before thankfully moving on. "So tell me, Isabel, have you given any thought to what you want to major in?"

Oh god, not this question. Can we go back to talking about my grades? At my old school, I was considered one of the good ones— aka, one of the ones whose parents did not have to be called on a regular basis—which afforded me the privilege of being blissfully overlooked.

"Well, I'm thinking about studying..." What will make her leave me alone? "Architecture? Sure, yeah, architecture," I say blandly. "I like, you know. Art and stuff."

"Art and stuff?" she echoes.

"Well, um—" Remind me to file this in my dream journal under nightmares. I mean, what am I supposed to say? Nobody I know has "hobbies" or "interests" or does anything beyond "hanging out," which usually involves eating free chips at restaurants or sitting in a parking lot and talking about why doing stuff is dumb. I'm sure Jamie has a speech rehearsed on all the philanthropic reasons why she wants to be pre-law, but it's not like I *loooove* communing with the elderly or any other form of community service we're supposed to crave in our free time. I mostly get yelled at for making a mess when I leave my pencils out or told to go away when I'm trying to borrow my brother's tools. (My mother thinks I have a problem with fidgeting—in reality, I just do whatever I can to stay out of the way.)

"I like to build things," I manage to pluck from nowhere, since Ms. Voss is clearly expecting an answer. "For fun. I built my desk out of an old sewing machine I found at an antique shop," I say, and then, thankfully, I gain some traction. "I'm not, like, *great* at welding? The desk was my first real project that wasn't building a box or something really straightforward. Oh, and sometimes I help my brother with his car. I'm not into cars myself, but it's interesting."

I pause, but since Ms. Voss is apparently still waiting for me to arrive at some grand conclusion, I keep going. "I also had a knife phase for a while," I say, before realizing she's going to send me to some kind of school psychologist or something if I stop there. "Not like I was *into* knives," I hurry to explain, "I just liked making them. My dad has a woodshop and a home forge. He's a contractor—a hobbyist, he calls himself—so I just use his stuff. Or I used to, anyway, before he—"

I stop. As much as I don't want to talk about my future, I *definitely* don't want to talk about my parents' divorce.

"Sorry," I say, blinking. "What was the question?"

For some completely unguessable reason, Ms. Voss smiles at me.

"Your catapult," she says. "It's brilliant."

Ummmmm, *what?*

"Oh. I, um. Wasn't expecting that—"

"I can't give you an A, considering there was supposed to be a written report consisting of slightly more than a scribbled diagram," she tells me with something I swear is a smirk, "but since your catapult has the best power-to-weight ratio, I can give you a—"

She stops to consider it, humming to herself. "C."

"What?"

The word leaves my mouth with way more panic than I intended.

"Sorry," I amend quickly, "I didn't mean to…it's just…"

She waits, arms folded.

"I don't mean to be rude," I say in something my mother would definitely call my rude voice. "I just think that considering my catapult outperformed everyone else's, I should get a little higher than a—" God, it sickens me just to consider it. "C."

"There is another option," Ms. Voss says, and my pulse, which has quickened considerably at the thought of telling my mother I got a C on an assignment, doesn't exactly find relief. I don't really have time for another project, and if I'm going to have to write a paper or something—

"I want to move you," says Ms. Voss, cutting off my frantic spiral. "Into one of the other Physics classes. The AP Physics class, specifically."

I freeze. "What?"

"I'll have to bring it up with Mr. MacIntosh," she adds, "but I also want you to try out for the robotics team."

"You're joking." I have a feeling I'm gaping at her. "Robotics? Is that supposed to be some kind of punishment?"

"Absolutely not. This," she says, holding up my little deck of tape, "is ingenious. It's so clever I would have thought you cheated if I didn't know perfectly well you put it together this morning."

This afternoon, but that's irrelevant. "Ms. Voss," I plead with her, "I'm really sorry I forgot about the assignment, but—"

"Look." She turns stony for a moment. I'd heard she was strict, but I hadn't seen it for myself until now. At the transformation, I nearly swallow my tongue.

"Isabel, you're bright," she admonishes me. "*Too* bright. You'll waste it just getting by in my class when I know you have the potential to really shine somewhere else. Have you considered applying to programs in mechanical engineering?"

My mind goes white with industrial lighting, shiny lab coats. "Engineering?"

"You'd get to build things," she tells me. "Anything you wanted. You could build it."

Nonsensical mathematical formulas flash before my eyes. The thought of it makes me suddenly overcome with hives.

"I just...I'm not really a math and science kind of girl, you know?"

"That's not a thing," she says, and nobody—*nobody*, certainly not a teacher—has ever been so dismissive with me before. "You obviously have a talent for creating things, Isabel. There's no such thing as a mind for one subject or another. You have a mind that *works*, and works well. So use it."

"But—"

"I'm going to recommend you for immediate transfer to Mr. MacIntosh's AP Physics class," she says. "I know for a fact he keeps his numbers small. There will be room for you."

I can't believe this is happening. I'm not my brother Gabe; I get good grades, sure, because my mom would kill me if I didn't, but I don't run around chasing them.

"But, Ms. Voss—"

"The world is not very helpful to a smart girl," says Ms. Voss. "More often it will try to force you inside a box. But I urge you not to listen." She glances down at my catapult, and because I'm moderately speechless and can't figure out where to direct my confusion, so do I. "If I'm pushing you into something that you have no passion for, Isabel, then tell me so. But if you're only hesitating because you have doubts in your abilities, then let me ask you, sincerely, to take a risk."

She looks up at me, and I feel oddly shaken, still staring at the little stolen deck of tape.

"Can you do it?" Ms. Voss asks me.

"I," I attempt, and immediately fumble. "Well, I'm...it's—"

"Can you do it?" she repeats. "I don't mean will you," she adds. "I mean *can* you."

Oh god, oh no. Oh no—

"Yes," I say, like an idiot. "Yeah, I can do it."

"Wonderful." Her smile warms with satisfaction before she clears her throat, pleased. "I would truly hate to have to give you a C," she remarks.

"Oh," I say with a frown, "that was real?"

Ms. Voss gives me a look that reminds me of my mother. "Yes, Isabel. You do have to actually *do* the assignment, which you technically did not."

"Right," I concede, wincing. "And, um. As for...*robotics*—"

"Yes, you'll want to set aside some time for that this week." Oh great! Just what I wanted; more schoolwork. I already spent most of last night trying to ignore the makeup brush challenge that my friends "forgot" to include me in. ("We just assumed u were busy, but we should totally hang out on thursday!!" they said, as if I could actually get away with going to Van Nuys on a school night.)

"The team will expect to see a schematic of some kind," Ms. Voss continues, "which I hope you'll spend a bit more time on than you did your catapult. Tryouts are Friday afternoon."

"Cool," I say glumly.

Ms. Voss rests a hand on my shoulder in sympathy, which is ironic, since this is completely her doing. "I'll help you with anything you need," she assures me. "If you don't like it, that's perfectly fine, you tried. But if you *do* like it..."

She trails off and shrugs, directing me back to her classroom.

"If you do, then we can both be satisfied knowing I was right," she says, so I roll my eyes, giving in to my anarchist teen impulses and groaning loudly as we step inside.

TEO

Dash: is it just me or is this really easy
Teo: it's easy
Dash: ok, sure
Dash: but is mac like
Dash: testing us?
Dash: or like
Dash: what
Teo: how would mac be testing us
Dash: idk it's just a question
Dash: nvm
Teo: no i'm serious
Teo: i'd really like to hear your answer
Teo: tbh i'm desperate to hear it
Dash: ok here's what i'm thinking
Teo: ok great here we go
Dash: so say mac is like...recruiting for a secret society
Teo: good so far
Dash: and this is one of those situations where we're supposed to know something's up
Dash: like, these are not the droids we're looking for
Dash: that sort of thing
Teo: totally
Dash: and then there's probably a secret code?

Dash: in here somewhere
Teo: like in the assignment?
Dash: ya
Teo: cool cool so what's the code?
Dash: idk
Dash: that's as far as i got
Teo: ok well you didn't quite stick the landing but it was close

"Teo!"

I look up when my mother calls me from somewhere else in the house; probably the gym downstairs. Her figure is very important to her, which is something she tells me far more frequently than I'd like. "My looks are my job," as she puts it, so needless to say, I'm very familiar (too familiar?) with the rigorous workouts and ten-step skincare routine that *Self* magazine would consider "hot" and "exclusive." Admittedly, it does boggle the mind.

Dash: ok but i think i'm onto something tho
Teo: keep working on it
Teo: brb

I jog down the stairs and skid across the hall to find my mom using one of those weird mirrors where a personal trainer coaches her through her reflection. Real time metrics, streaming, the works. Augmented reality is a real trip, man. The Peloton bike is in here, too, somewhere. Probably behind the Pilates reformer.

"Teo," she says, panting. "Are you all packed for tomorrow?"

"Mom, I told you, I can't go tomorrow."

"What? But you love Vail."

"It's not Vail, it's Denver, and it's just another one of Dad's conventions." My father, also named Mateo Luna, founded one of the most successful software companies in recent history, so he speaks at a lot of industry conventions. With all the coders who try to pitch their apps to him all day, even his coffee breaks are like high-stakes *Shark Tank*.

"I have a thing on Friday," I remind my mother. "Can't miss it."

"What, a game? Already?"

"That's next week. Friday's robotics tryouts."

"The nerd thing? You're still doing that?"

"*Mom*." She's joking, but also, she somehow doesn't think of what my father does as a nerd thing, which is kind of hilarious. Sure, the apps he makes now are popular with influencers and celebrities, but he started out writing code, like me.

"What?" she says, flinging back her dampened ponytail. "Nerds are hot now, sweetie—"

"Mom, I truly can't have this conversation again," I groan, and she winks, enjoying her opportunity to heckle me, as always.

"Can't you take the weekend?" she asks, toweling off her neck.

"The weekend, yeah, but not Friday." It's *tryouts*. I know my mom tries, but she's sort of fundamentally incapable of understanding that I basically *am* the robotics team. I've been there since freshman year and look, not to be an asshole about it, but basically everyone on the team who's any good only showed up because I recruited them. The others—Kai, Emmett, Dash, even Justin, who's at least solidly competent at welding to make up for his other personality flaws—are here because every year that I've been involved, Essex Academy Robotics has been the team to beat. Last year we even won Nationals. So it's not like this is the cool thing to do at any school but ours.

"Well, I can hardly leave you here alone, sweetie. I think the guidebook says something about that." My mom likes to joke about a parenting guidebook that doesn't exist, which is basically just code for conventional parenting. (I love my mom, but the finer details of motherhood do tend to escape her.)

"I'll be fine," I assure her. "I'm staying back to do *robotics try-outs*. Are you really worried I'm going to have some kind of rager?"

"Are the kids still having ragers?" she comments thoughtfully. "Surely they'll have moved on to something more interesting by now."

"Nobody's having a rager," I remind her. "That's what I'm saying. No ragers."

"Teo." A wagging finger. "Are you being smart with me?"

"With you, Mom? Never."

She sighs, then brushes a bit of sweat from her brow.

"You know I adore you," she says, looking grave.

"Yes, I know."

"Probably too much."

"Yes."

"And we both know you're lying." Easily distracted though she may be, careless she most definitely is not. For purposes of efficiency, we've developed a system where if I'm going to get up to shenanigans, I honor her preconditions: one, keep it in the house where security is tight and chances of loss of limb are minimized, and two, don't watch any of her shows without her. That's actually an unrelated rule, but it is effectively ingrained in my head.

"I'm offering you plausible deniability," I remind her. "Isn't it better if we just...play along?"

She slides me a look of affectionate warning.

"And Dad said it was fine if I flew out on Saturday," I add, which is true. While my relationship with my dad isn't quite so... progressive, I suppose, he has more reason than my mom to consider robotics tryouts a matter of critical importance. Even at his level of success—a point where most other CEOs would have floated off to their private islands or succumbed to their inevitable golf addiction—Mateo Luna still selects his own tech teams by hand; even the outsourced ones and short-term consultants. Put simply, zealous oversight is in my blood. (As is corporate lingo; he often asks me to "circle back" on our previous discussions and he never texts or calls me, he pings me. Synergy!)

"Ah, well then," Mom says. That's enough to reassure her, as I suspected it would be. After all, my dad is the strict one. "But Grandma's going to check in on you, okay?"

"Okay." That's not a problem. My mom's mom, who lives in Beverly Hills, generally enjoys three things in life: fine dining, sharing her opinion, and post-Lagerfeld Chanel. She, like my mother, is really more culturally Jewish ("Jew-*ish*," as my mom likes to say) than strictly beholden to the Good Book; if anything, she'd be insulted if I didn't make an effort to mark my status among my peers, purely as a matter of social obligation. My abuela, on the other hand, lives in Miami and enjoys home-cooking, sharing her opinion, and a healthy dose of Catholic guilt. Potentially this explains why my mother and I are dancing around a subject that I'd never get away with even trying with my dad.

"Well, all right then," Mom says, reaching out to pat my cheek. "You run off to your little nerd convention, and I'll meet you at the Vail airport first thing."

"Denver."

"Hm?"

"Denver, Mom, not Vail."

"Yes, yes." She looks distracted for a moment, then smiles at me unexpectedly, like a sudden burst of light. "How did I end up with such a smart kid, huh?" she demands with a chuckle, tousling my hair. "Handsome, too."

"Gross," I groan, and she gives me a nudge.

"Do your homework," she calls after me. "That's in the guidebook."

"Yeah, that tracks," I say, doubling back to let her kiss my cheek before she yells for Siri to start her 2000s alt-pop workout mix.

"Thai for dinner?" she adds over the opening chords to "Teenagers."

"Sounds good," I shout back, taking the stairs two at a time and letting the door shut behind me. There's about eight new messages on my phone from Dash continuing his conspiracy theory, plus something from Kai fretting about Neelam's design.

Ugh, Neelam. It's not like she's bad at what she does or anything, but I already know what it takes to win. I've been to Nationals three times to her two. I type something generic to Kai about not worrying, though of course he will, and then I return to my window with Dash.

Teo: ya so all of this sounds legit
Teo: also, party friday night at my house after tryouts?
Dash: niiiiiiice
Dash: i'm in

three

PRESSURE

Bel

Thursday arrives resplendent with chirping birds and the bloom of impending calamity. A paranormal force hits snooze on my alarm (definitely not me, definitely a ghost) and then a belligerent pair of my brother Luke's shoes—abandoned by the door in typical negligent fashion, as per the laws and customs of our shoeless household—sends my big toe directly into my mother's beloved curio of Porcelain Things We Never Use. Naturally I respond with a shriek of something profane—which Luke does not hear, because while *I* am flirting dangerously with tardiness, *he* is not even awake. I'll be shocked if he gets out of bed before I get home from school—though if he does it will only be to clutter up my Netflix profile, so it's kind of lose-lose either way.

Things do not improve. By late morning, thirty or so of my classmates have joined the Greek chorus of my suffering, snickering in harmony as I receive an official Essex Academy summons to Ms. Voss's classroom just before lunch.

"All right, so." Ms. Voss slides a sheet of paper across her desk to me, cheerfully oblivious to Jamie's wild motions from our usual meeting spot in the hallway outside. The classroom door shuts and then it's just me, the perils of mortality, and Ms. Voss.

"I got a response from Mr. MacIntosh last night about tomorrow's robotics tryouts. It looks like you'll just have to download this software," Ms. Voss says, tapping an unpolished fingernail beside one of the instructions, "and then design and run a simulation of an egg drop. Do you know what that is?"

"Um, I think so? Yeah," I say, squirming a little in my chair. I've never been very good at anything with software or computers, and I have no idea what an egg drop involves aside from, you know, dropping eggs. Still, I'm worried if I tell her that she'll try to explain it to me, and I'd rather figure it out on my own. Always best to look stupid in private, in my opinion.

Ms. Voss gives me a scrutinizing glance like she knows I'm lying, but thankfully she continues.

"What's important is that you try," she says simply. "You have the right instincts, Isabel. You have the interest. Learning the skills can only be a good thing." She pauses, eyeing me again, and says, "Have you been working on your college applications?"

Since yesterday? Haha, *nope.* I spent most of yesterday arguing with Luke about whether he ate my yogurt (which he ABSOLUTELY DID) until I fell asleep over the book I was supposed to be reading for English.

"Of course," I lie cheerfully.

"Given any more thought to engineering?"

"Yeah, kinda." As in, I've thought a lot about how I'll never live it down with my old friends if I join this school's robotics team. Or any team, or club. Or basically if I do anything on purpose, which isn't even to address the issue of robotics. ("Umm, this is *LA*," Sabrina once said to Cristina when she wanted to try out for the spring musical. "You can just get discovered or start a vlog or whatever without having to embarrass yourself in front of the *whole school.*")

"Well, think of this as an opportunity to try it out. See if you like it." Ms. Voss gives me a small smile. "You never know unless you try, right?"

"Totally," I say, which even I know makes me sound like an idiot.

I know Ms. Voss is probably right, but I can't shake my looming sense of dread about all of this. It's not like I hate trying new things, but knowing I'll have an audience for whether I succeed or fail is making me deeply uncomfortable. I've always found it easier to keep to things I already know I'm good at.

Robotics is...definitely not one of those things.

Of my two brothers, only one could be considered conventionally successful. Luke looked very promising at first, given his model grin and his pitching arm and the string of broken hearts parading through our kitchen on what seemed to be a weekly basis, but my second brother, Gabe, is my mother's favorite. You wouldn't think so by looking at his highly scrawny, too-tall frame, but as far as qualifications go for Favorite Son, Gabriel Maier's packing the big guns. While Luke is currently living at home and "taking a sabbatical" for the semester after his ACL tear (meaning: he's currently on academic probation from Cal State Fullerton baseball), Gabe is a sophomore at Dartmouth. He's a double major in computer science and pre-med, and it's *an Ivy*. Need I say more? Sure, it's not that hard to be a big fish in our pond—Luke in particular likes to jokingly call us "dumb Asian" or "jungle Asian" because we're half Filipino, which my mother loathes—but even so. You can't deny that those are favorite son credentials by any culture's standards. Gabe's the embodiment of my mother's dream—and sure, maybe he only took to books because he was laughed off the field during his first T-ball season (by Luke, obviously). Regardless, Gabe's always been the brains, Luke's the jock, and I'm...

The girl, I guess. And girls aren't usually into robots.

But then again, if I don't make the team I won't have to worry about it, right?

At that very timely realization, a wave of relief washes over me. I mean, let's be real, there's absolutely no way anyone else is going to want me on this team. I have zero understanding of CAD or whatever this software is. I don't even *want* to be there. And again, I'm a girl.

So yeah, there's no possible way I'm going to get in. But at least no one could say I didn't try, right? Like, specifically Ms. Voss can't say that.

"Thanks," I tell her, suddenly cheerful.

She smiles back at me. "Of course, Isabel."

Ugh, still hate *that*, but at least the window of danger has officially passed. I turn to leave, giving Jamie an apologetic glance through the window.

Just as I'm about to push the door open, Ms. Voss calls out to me again. "Sorry, one more thing—"

I brace myself, turning back to face her. "Yes?"

"Do you hate being called Isabel?" Ms. Voss asks me very seriously.

"Oh. Um." I blink, surprised, because I was not previously aware that other people could see how much I die inside anytime someone calls me by my full name. "Well, yeah, kinda. I prefer Bel."

Ms. Voss gives me a little shake of her head, like my mom does when she wants me to sit up straighter.

"Open with that when you start in AP Physics tomorrow," Ms. Voss tells me. "Take up your own space, Bel. Don't let other people tread over it."

She turns her attention back to the papers on her desk and I push the door open, pantomiming a slow decline as if I've just been poured out of the classroom.

"God, you're so dramatic," says Jamie with a laugh. "What was that?"

"Indentured servitude," I say, and Jamie rolls her eyes, hauling me to the quad for lunch.

"Still better than totally failing Voss's class, isn't it?"

"*Is* it?" I counter doubtfully, but Jamie's too scandalized at the thought of failing to treat that as anything but a cry for help. "Oh my *god*, Jamie, I'm joking, seriously—"

"Lora's in robotics," she reminds me, recovering from her moment of panic about my future. Lora's one of Jamie's best friends, though I have thus far only spoken to Lora alone once: when we went to the bathroom with Jamie and had to wait together in line. "If all else fails, you can hang with her. And tomorrow we'll be in the same Physics class," Jamie adds, completely lighting up at the thought of it.

"True," I acknowledge. "Super not looking forward to it, but at least you'll be there."

"It's really not so bad," Jamie assures me. "And you're better at math than I am."

I roll my eyes. "That's an ill-founded rumor."

"Is it, though? Oh, sorry, Teo, didn't see you—"

Jamie bumps into Teo Luna while she perp-walks me to lunch, though he only glances up from his distraction. He's back in his usual button-down today, which presumably he picked because that shade of Capitalism Sage makes his tan glow. He looks at me like he's confused that I still exist, so naturally I give him a military salute before Jamie nudges me forward again.

"Well, *that* was super cool of you," she mutters sarcastically, elbowing me in the ribs. "What's your deal with Teo?"

"What deal? No deal," I say, because unlike the gaggle of underclassmen whispering from a distance, *I'm* not the one staring at him. "I don't even know him."

"Apparently he's having a party tomorrow night." Jamie fusses with her hair self-consciously, like she's suddenly remembered she has it. My earliest impression of this school was Jamie—who was hyper-enthusiastic about me from the start, despite me being not even *close* to awake enough for her whole vibe—looking fresh out of a J.Crew catalogue in her pleated midi-skirt and box-cut cardigan. It was all very East Coast prep except for her natural hair, which she ties back from her face with a seemingly unending assortment of eclectic scarves she gets as gifts from her mother. I remember thinking we'd get along because her taste in scarves matched my taste in everything else.

"Teo Luna is the party-having type of guy?" I ask skeptically. "I assumed that high school archetype was a myth at this school."

"No, it's not like a *party* party. Just some people from the soccer team and robotics and maybe a few other cool people, I don't know. But we're going, so get on board," Jamie says, using her Future Entrepreneurs of America voice. "He lives up on Mulholland with all the other secluded celebrities."

While I would hardly call Teo Luna a secluded celebrity, living in the Hills would explain why he's so popular. "I guess, if you want to." Not like I have anything better to do; the thought of wandering aimlessly around Target with my other friends kind of loses its appeal when I have to drive through rush-hour traffic to get there.

"His house is *huge*, Bel. Huge. I heard he has a moat."

"Uh, okay?"

"Plus it's totally architecturally significant."

Honestly, she is ridiculous. "I'm not sure that's a reason to go to a party, but—"

"Ohmygosh hi," says Lora, beaming when we walk up to the table where she's sitting. "Saved you guys seats."

"I was just telling Bel about Teo's party," says Jamie, huffing into the seat beside one of the other girls and pointedly giving me a look to suggest I sit by Lora. I comply, because clearly she's on a mission. "You're going too, right, Lo?" Jamie adds.

Lora nods. "Don't worry, it's totally low-key," she assures me, flashing me a sunny smile. She's blonde and blue-eyed and perky as hell, which is both endearing and a total mystery to me. "And anyway, you should get to know everyone on the team. I'm so excited you're trying out for robotics!"

I give Jamie a glare of *why did you tell her* and Jamie gives me a forced smile of *omg Bel it's not a big deal STOP* and Lora, still waiting for my response, doesn't falter for an instant until I turn to her with the answer I'm pretty sure she's expecting.

"Totally!" I say, and internally cringe, because I'm two for two today on terrible uses of "totally."

For the record, it's not that I don't like Lora or I don't like Ms. Voss or I don't like Teo Luna, who I don't even know. I just feel like everybody here already has everything figured out. Even doe-eyed, golden Lora is secretly cutthroat; she's on the robotics team as their business and social media manager, and she plans to go to USC for public relations—not *hopes*, like a normal person, but *plans*.

Everyone at this school has plans, and then they want *me* to have plans, and I'm just so overwhelmed by their good intentions that I constantly feel the need to lie down for a solid five minutes before trying again.

"Don't worry," Lora says, reaching over to give my forearm a quick squeeze. "It's really intimidating at first, but robotics is a family. We're really close, and it's honestly super fun. Just trust me, it's not as scary as it seems."

"I'll take your word for it," I assure her, opening my lunch with a groan to find that Luke stole my yogurt again.

TEO

"If I have to work with Akim again on the new fifteen-pound bot I will scream," mutters Kai, glaring down at whatever his mom packed him for lunch today.

"What is that, kimchi?" asks Emmett, glancing across the table.

"Yeah, I don't know," says Kai moodily, shoving the plastic container away. "I'll just get a burrito or something. You coming?"

"No way, man. Give me that," says Dash, immediately reaching over for Kai's lunch. "Your mom's kimchi is the shit."

I hold up my hands to steer clear as Kai tosses the container to Dash. When Kai rises to his feet, grunting for Emmett to come with him, our other friend Jake kicks my foot.

"*Ouch*, Jesus—"

"Please tell me you're not planning to talk about robotics our whole lunch period," Jake pleads, and Andrew manages a nod of agreement despite being nose-deep in his enormous Yeti water bottle. "If you start up this early, I swear, I'll never make it to Nationals. I'll just spontaneously burst into flames."

"It's Kai, not me," I remind them. "You know he freaks out about everything."

"He's high-strung," adds Dash, who currently has a mouthful of kimchi. "Can't help it."

"Let's talk about your party instead," suggests Jake, and I roll my eyes, though Andrew's finally surfaced from his gallon of hydration. (He's a state champion swimmer. I don't know if these things are necessarily related, but there you go.)

"It's hardly worth a discussion," I say, because this isn't some weird high school movie where shit gets broken or people have sex in my parents' bed. For one thing, my dad has insane security where most of the house can be locked down with just my fingerprint, and for another, I don't go to school with total morons. I'm mostly obligated to throw these things so people can satisfy their curiosity about how a celebrity tech CEO lives. If I didn't, I'd be a widely resented snob, like the kid whose dad won an Oscar or something. (I don't know, I don't care about movies.)

"Is Elisa coming?" asks Andrew optimistically. "I heard she's single again."

"Good luck with that," Jake mutters to him with a laugh. "According to Kate, she's been dropping hints about Luna for weeks."

"Look, whatever," I say, which is meant to indicate the obvious: that I don't really have the time or energy to speculate about what Elisa Fraticelli wants from me. She wouldn't be the first person to decide I'm a lucrative investment. "I just figured we'd have something to celebrate tomorrow, assuming robotics tryouts go well," I say. And by "go well," what I mean is that we don't take anyone new and I get to hang out with the exact same people I always hang out with.

"Tryouts?" echoes Kai, reappearing over my shoulder with a growl. "Don't get me started—"

"That," Jake points out with a pursed glance at me, "was completely your fault."

I throw up my hands in concession. "Look, I didn't mean to bring it up, okay? The point is we can go to my house right after. And weren't you getting lunch?" I remind Kai, who shrugs.

"Line's too long," he says, falling back into his seat. "But seriously, about tryouts—"

"Ah, good timing, I was just about to throw myself into the ocean," says Jake when his girlfriend Kate waves to him across the quad. He rises to his feet, calling "Byeeeeee!" over his shoulder while Andrew stares longingly after him.

"Bye," says Dash, who has now finished the kimchi. He slides the empty container back to Kai, adding, "We're not talking about tryouts. It makes you look like that lady yelling at that cat."

"What?" demands Kai, even though Dash is right—he looks exactly like the meme of that Real Housewife (not my proudest pop-culture reference, but my mom loves a Bravo binge). "But we need to, though, seriously. What the hell is an egg drop going to tell us about whether or not someone can build a bot?"

"Kai," Emmett sighs, "for the millionth time, it's about assessing basic skills—"

My Apple Watch vibrates on my wrist, and I look down.

"Look, you guys settle this one between you. I've got to go," I say, dismissing my calendar nudge.

"Go where?" asks Dash, who usually knows what I'm doing at every single moment of the day.

"Elsewhere," I say.

"Can I come?" asks Andrew hopefully.

"No," I say, throwing my backpack over my shoulder. "Okay, later," I call with a parting nod, and then deliberately head toward the library before veering off to the administrative offices once I'm out of sight.

For the record, it's not like meeting with my counselor is usually a big deal, but this particular meeting has some weird undertones. The only times I ever have to go to the school offices are to fill out permission slips and accept awards, so this is something I'd rather keep to myself.

"Teo, hi," says my counselor when I knock on his doorframe. "Have a seat."

"Hey, Mr. Pereira," I say, setting my backpack at my feet. "Listen, if this is about my applications—"

"It's not," says Pereira, "but why don't we start with that? How are your apps coming?"

"They're done," I say, and Pereira looks surprised.

"All of them?"

"Well, there were only, like, five besides MIT," I say. "And it wasn't really that difficult for me to write an essay about how I've wanted to go there for my entire life."

The others—Stanford, Caltech, Michigan, Berkeley, and Carnegie Mellon—are basically fallbacks by comparison.

"Ah," says Pereira, as if I've unpacked something deeply revelatory about my development as a human being. "And how's soccer?"

"Good." Most of us play sports in addition to doing robotics.

Dash, believe it or not, is on the football team. "I'm senior captain this year."

"Congratulations! I'm sure your parents are very proud."

"They are, yeah." My mom definitely is, though she'd probably prefer it if I were a quarterback or something. Her interests and mine find very little overlap.

"And robotics is going well?"

"Yeah, team's looking strong for this year."

"Great. And everything at home?"

I blink. "Sorry, what?"

"Everything's good at home? With your parents, family...?"

"It's just my parents, and everything's fine," I say, a little defensive despite my best efforts. "My mom and dad aren't divorced or fighting or anything. They're great."

"I wasn't suggesting they weren't," Pereira assures me. "I just wanted to ask in case there was something you wanted to talk about."

Okay, I knew it. There's definitely something weird about this.

"What would I want to talk about?" I ask bluntly.

Pereira gives me a once-over before leaning forward. "Look, Teo, I don't want to make you feel like you're on the spot, but some of your teachers seem to think you might have overbooked yourself this semester. You're captain of varsity soccer and robotics, you've got a full schedule of AP classes with very few breaks—"

"It was Morgan, wasn't it?" I ask tightly.

"Mr. Morgan," Pereira corrects me.

"*Mr.* Morgan," I say, not especially politely. "It was just an essay."

"There is no 'just' anything when it comes to essays, Teo. Words have a great deal of power," Pereira says, sliding a copy of my AP English Lit paper across the desk to me. "Yours are no exception."

This whole thing is ridiculous. "He wanted us to write about mythology. I was just doing what he asked."

Pereira picks up the essay, which I'm not touching, and reads aloud, "Atlas carrying the weight of the heavens on his shoulders as punishment for leading the Titans against the gods is, in many ways, similar to any leader asked to bear the consequences of personal responsibility—"

"I wasn't saying that *I* was Atlas," I cut in, frustrated. "I was just...the assignment was to pick a myth and explore its themes—"

"And you chose Atlas," Pereira said, setting the essay down to look at me.

"I thought it was interesting. Atlas is a scientist, and—"

"And so are you."

"Yes," I say, annoyed, "though I'm not credited with the invention of astronomy. And anyway, I just thought it was interesting that this dude who liked math and the stars got saddled with carrying everything—"

"Saddled with it," echoes Pereira. "Interesting choice of words."

I stifle a groan in frustration. I honestly, truly hate literature.

"I'm fine," I say, picking up the essay. "And I got an A on the assignment."

"Yes, I know," says Pereira. "It's an excellent paper."

"Thanks. Sorry, I have to, you know. Soccer," I offer ambiguously, gesturing to the door. "School and stuff—"

"Teo," Pereira sighs. "You do know you're just a kid, right?"

There's nothing I hate more than being told I'm just a kid.

"Yeah, thanks," I say, and turn to walk out of the office, crumpling the essay in my hands.

four

DROP

TEO

Everyone groans when I shove open the door to the classroom.

"Oh, whatever," I say, rolling my eyes. "Like you guys have anywhere better to be."

"It's Friday after four p.m. and we're still in school," Akim points out irritably. "Literally anywhere would be better than here."

"Look, I told you I had—never mind, doesn't matter." I barely had time to shower after soccer practice, which was a doozy; suicide sprints, agility drills, basically everything you'd assume people would do if they were clinically unhinged, which maybe I am. I have extra responsibilities as both captain and offensive midfielder (Kai, who plays wingback, was able to duck out early to make it to the classroom on time while our offense ran a few extra drills), so everyone else in the room is clearly annoyed they've had to sit around waiting for me.

"Are all the applicants here?" I ask, glancing at the time. I'm only seven minutes late, which you'd think was the end of the world by the looks on their faces.

"You didn't see them in the hallway?" asks Neelam, using the special voice she reserves for when she thinks someone's being an idiot. Usually me.

"I was in a hurry." This is clearly a losing battle. "Look, whatever, just bring them in."

I throw myself into a seat in the front row beside Dash, who's scrolling through Instagram looking at food accounts. I nudge him and he startles like I've woken him from a coma.

"You ready for this?" I ask him.

"Hm? Oh, yeah, sure."

A handful of people enter the classroom door, a few of whom I recognize. Lora's already connected the laptop to the projector and is thankfully corralling some of the more lost-looking freshmen to pull up their Essex accounts.

"Hi, everyone!" Lora says, smiling so brightly that several of the candidates visibly relax. (This is why she's our business manager.) "Okay, so if you could all just—oh, Bel, hi!" she half squeals as someone hurries in late, looking flustered.

"Yeah, um. Hi, Lora," says the New Girl, who I learned today is, in fact, called Bel. She made a big show of it in AP Physics when Mac called her Isabel. *Yeah, sorry, Mr. MacIntosh? I prefer Bel*, she said, and then quickly, *like, as in bel canto, not Belle the princess.* I had no idea what she was talking about, but Mac responded with a pun, like he usually does. I noticed that Bel didn't laugh.

She's wearing her usual weird jewelry—this one is a necklace made of carved wooden beads—which makes a clatter when she sits down. Her hair isn't tied back with those bungee cords that all the girls (and my mom) seem to be wearing these days. Instead, there's a ballpoint pen sticking out of it.

"Did you want to pull up your email or anything?" asks Lora, looking over the head of a freshman who's apparently incapable of remembering his own password. (He's out.)

"Ummmmmm, no?" says Bel, clearing her throat. "Not...not at the moment."

Weird answer. I frown, and Dash leans toward me.

"This girl is everywhere today," he comments in an un-Dash-like voice.

I shrug, and Lora gets started.

The assignment is way more basic than anything we'd actually have to build for the team, but since there's so many applicants to get through, this is the easiest way to tell who actually knows what they're doing at first glance. The simulation is simple: the software is pre-programmed (by me) to apply the same amount of force to each drop, and the construction as designed by the applicant will either break the egg (eggs are obviously super fragile) or not. "Break" or "not break" is a really easy way to tell whether someone can build something, and then we can determine additional points of finesse from there.

If there is any finesse to be found, of course, which I really doubt there is.

Lora introduces me as the team lead and then reads off a list of names in alphabetical order, starting with a freshman whose last name is Abbasi. His egg doesn't break, but it's suspended in a cube of some kind that doesn't look like it could hold up to more pressure. That could be precision, if he used the fewest materials in order to survive only the exact height of the drop, or it could be mediocre design. Given that we didn't set any limitations on how it could be built, I'm not convinced it's the former. Either way, I don't think he's necessary to the team.

I sneak a glimpse at Bel, because she seems to be paying the most attention to the projection of the egg drop. At first I think she's squinting, but then I realize she's frowning. She noisily takes out a page from her notebook and starts sketching, which causes a few people's heads to briefly turn.

The next two eggs break. The third, a weird teepee design, crushes on impact, though the egg itself is fine. Bel has completely stopped paying attention at this point, and now so has Dash, because he's staring at Bel's piece of paper. Another egg gets dropped and I don't even notice.

By the time we're about seven more egg drops in, basically nobody is paying attention. Everyone's busy with whatever the hell Bel's doing at her desk, so finally I rise to my feet in annoyance, walking over to where she's sitting.

"Hey, can I see this?" I ask, and Bel looks up.

Jesus, she has huge eyes. They're big and brown and she's wearing a little bit of glitter eyeliner, I think—you can't have a mother like mine and not understand in some basic way how cosmetics work—but also, I can see the tiny dusting of freckles around her eyes, like distant constellations.

She looks like she's forgotten I was even here, which is...interesting. Most of the time people are looking at me like they're hoping *I* haven't forgotten about *them*.

"Oh, well I'm not—" She breaks off when I slide the paper around anyway, glancing down at where it sits on her desk. "Done," she finishes in an irritated voice.

"Well, you're distracting everyone," I inform her, though once I take a closer look at what she's drawn, I immediately stop listening to whatever her defense happens to be.

Okay, so I said egg drops are pretty basic, right? There's not a lot of ways to make them interesting, but Bel's drawing is...good. No, it's more than good, it's *cool*. She basically designed a spaceship on the spot, where the egg is nestled in the center of a tightly constructed triangle and then encased in some kind of futuristic rocket. She's taken the time to draw a front and a side view, and from the top view, I can see she's deliberately created a pinwheel pattern with small wings.

In terms of the physics, if she dropped this it would rapidly spin, converting translational energy into rotational energy. In simple terms: it would fall slower and hit the ground with less force. Even if the rocket itself weren't enough to protect the egg, the effort to break the fall by allowing it to spin would almost certainly do the trick.

Also, she drew the egg like it's a golden cartoon egg. It's glowing and shaded to show its depth, which makes this drawing way more interesting than anything else I've seen today.

"Lora," I say, popping my head up and walking away with the drawing as Bel half-heartedly reaches after me, like she wants to snatch it back to make more changes. "Yeah, hang on," I say to Bel, and then I turn to Lora, who looks absolutely *bonkers* confused. "Can you pull up my creator files in the drafting software? Just start a new project."

"Hm? Yeah, sure, Teo—"

She taps it a couple times and then hands me the laptop. I take it from her and sit down with Bel's drawing, building the dimensions into the software to run a new simulation.

"Oh, so um, Teo," says Lora in her trying-to-be-helpful voice, "we have a few other applicants that need to test their egg drop, so—"

"Yeah, just a sec." I finish programming Bel's drawing into the computer program and hit go on the simulation. There's a smattering of whispers as the others look at what I've done, and then we watch as Bel's rocket does exactly what the physics suggests it should do: it slows down and coasts just before it lands tilted on its side, the egg perfectly unharmed.

"Yeah, everyone else can leave," I say, looking up. "Bel, right?"

She blinks at me. "What?"

"That's your name, isn't it?"

"No, I—sorry, I mean yes, but..." She trails off. "I was just—"

"I said you guys could go," I say impatiently to the others, who are all crowding me kind of annoyingly to look closer at Bel's drawing. "Thanks, we'll email you if we need anything."

"You can't just make a unilateral decision, Luna," snaps—who else?—Neelam. "She didn't even do the assignment. Did you?" Neelam demands, rounding on Bel, who blinks again.

"Well, I was…I mean, I just found out about tryouts yesterday—"

"And Luna just ran the entire simulation in less than five minutes," says Neelam curtly, who even I know is being especially rude to Bel. "We pick a straightforward project for a reason. And Luna," she says, turning aggressively to me, "she's a senior—right, you're a senior? Yeah, she's a senior," Neelam continues, hardly waiting for Bel's answer before continuing, "and it doesn't make sense. Next year we'll all be gone. We need to talk about the implications for the good of the team."

"Okay, here's the talk," I say, gesturing for Lora to turn the lights back on. "Her egg drop is the best one. It's creative, it's well-designed, it's complex, and it works. Any chance you know how to work with metal?" I ask Bel. That part is relatively easy to learn, but I have a feeling she already has some idea how to make things work. After a lifetime of expensive engineering camps and three years of competitive robotics, I've noticed that people who can design like this usually have a concept of how to put it into practice.

"Oh, yeah, mostly," she says half-heartedly.

"It's a yes or no question," I say.

She gives me a look of annoyance. "Fine, then yeah, I do."

I knew it. "See?" I say to Neelam, who folds her arms over her chest. "We need someone with practical skills."

"Luna, you're obviously not considering—"

"Look, I've made my decision. If you really want, we can pick up one of the freshmen to shadow us during the year. Um, you," I say, pointing to the freshman who had the most structurally secure egg drop.

"Teo? So sorry," Lora interrupts me gently, "but there's only enough in the budget for one new member, so—"

"Oh, my bad," I tell the freshman. "You'll get 'em next year."

"*Luna*," huffs Neelam, but before she can continue, I've already turned to the rest of the room.

"Look, let's just settle this democratically," I suggest to them, because this is the perfect solution. We get the new member Mac insisted on and boom, she already knows how to design. As an added plus, it's not like she's weird-looking or smells bad. Not that I care, but she's pretty if you can get past the initial oddness. "Everyone in favor of Bel joining the team?"

I glance pointedly at Dash, who's miraculously paying attention. "Yep," he says.

"I'm with Teo," says Emmett.

"Me too," says Kai.

One by one, everyone raises their hands in my favor. Lora, who's still standing by the light switch, gives Neelam an apologetic glance, but then she smiles at Bel.

"I definitely vote for Bel," says Lora, looking pleased.

"So it's settled," I tell Neelam. "Bel, uh. Last name?"

I get the feeling all of this moved way too fast for her, because she looks totally dazed.

"Maier," she manages to say.

"Bel Maier." I rise to my feet, holding out a hand, and she hesitantly takes it. "Welcome to robotics," I say, and I know it sounds kind of formal, but even I can hear the pride in my voice when I say it. This is the most important thing in my life, and I picked her. I *chose* her. I want her to know that means something.

But I'm pretty sure she doesn't, because the look on her face makes it seem like she wants to crawl into a hole and die.

"Oh yeah, cool, thanks," she says, and releases my hand to force a smile, looking like she's going to be sick.

Bel

Jamie: omg bel i just heard from lora
Jamie: that's amazing, i'm so excited for you!!! you must've really impressed teo

Jamie: which is like, very hard to do, so congrats
Jamie: so now you're definitely on board with the party, right??

I wonder if there's a word in Tagalog for "whoops, I accidentally succeeded when I had every intention to fail"? There's one for when something's so cute you want to bite it (*gigil*, one of four total words I know), so I can only assume it's more adept than English when it comes to matters of human frailty.

Bel: ugh
Bel: fine
Jamie: !!!!!!! ok GREAT
Jamie: just tell your mom you're sleeping over at my house and i'll pick you up in an hour
Jamie: WHAT A GOOD DAY

I love the girl, but she's just way too much right now. I take a few calming breaths and wander down to our apartment complex's garage to find the only person recognizable from my old life, who also happens to have no interest in anything I do.

My brother.

"Hey," I say to Luke, who's working on his car. He's only ever doing that these days or playing some sort of video game where he kills people in a fake world war, which I guess is probably worse, even if his car's destroying the ozone layer. (Like, is anyone monitoring the violence content on those games? I'm supremely worried about what this is doing to his already very questionable brain.)

"Yo," he says unironically, and then, "What are you wearing?"

"This?" I look down at the outfit I wore to school today. It's one of my favorite skirts, something I found at a thrift store, and I've always felt very Romantic in it—with a capital *R*—because of the swishing. My mom says it makes me look "provincial" or "taga bukid," which means absolutely nothing to me. "It's a skirt, Luke."

"It looks like something Tita Carmen would wear," he says, which is extremely rude. Tita Carmen would throw it over her sofa, maybe, but she would not *wear* it. That would require panache, which I've spent my entire life cultivating.

"What do you think people wear to parties here?" I ask, feigning sincerity, because I would *love* to know what my brother thinks is fashionable. He glances up from whatever he's wiring, which I have to guess is some new addition to his stereo system.

"Slutty clothes?" he says, and then adds, "Can you grab the adaptor harness?"

"Can you please not be so heteronormative?" I counter with a roll of my eyes, and then, after picking up the piece he's looking for, "Do you need me to plug it into the output converter?"

"What?"

"*Slut* is super offensive."

"No, I meant the other thing."

"Oh, the output converter."

"Yeah, grab that. And also, I said slut-*ty*," he says emphatically. "It's different."

"Still gross." I reach over to where he's wrangling the excess wires. "You need an antenna adaptor for this."

"Yeah, it's over there." He points with his chin, a thing my mom hates, and I reach for the little convertor while he plugs in the radio's wiring harness.

Luke and I don't always get along, but it's been weirdly okay having him around lately. For one thing, my mom doesn't have time to yell at me for swearing or forgetting to clean up after myself when she's busy nagging Luke to stop being lazy and go back to school. (Also, he's messier than I am.)

For another, more complicated thing, I can't always reconcile the way my life looks now with how it used to look. Sometimes I wake up and have to remember that the last year of my life even happened, which sucks, or I go to bed feeling sad for no reason at all, which really sucks. I don't want to talk about it because either people don't get it, or, if they do, then they just wind up feeling sorry for me, which makes me feel even worse.

It's nice to have someone I don't have to explain anything to, even if the person in question keeps eating my snacks.

"So, I got onto the robotics team," I offer experimentally, because I don't really know how I feel about it yet and for some reason, Luke's an easy litmus test.

(And again, there's no one else to tell.)

"What?" Luke says.

"Robotics," I repeat.

"Be careful with robots," he replies without looking up from his car, which is older than both of us combined. "I heard there were these two robots that some software company designed," he says, "and within five minutes they started speaking this secret language and the whole thing had to be shut down before they conspired to terrorize the earth."

"Um, okay, there's a lot to unpack there," I say. He's definitely been playing too many video games since he took the semester off. "But I'm thinking I don't have to give the robots brains or anything? Just, like, arms and stuff, I guess."

"So just building stuff?"

"Yeah?"

He wipes his forehead on his sleeve. "You like that, right?" he tells me with a shrug. "You've been bugging me while I worked with Dad since you were, like, ten."

"Maybe." That's definitely true, but what else was I supposed to do? Our mom's a nurse who works long shifts, and there's only so much macramé to be done in a day before you run out of plants that need holders. "I've never built anything on my own, though."

"Isn't it a team?"

A team of Teo Luna and his minions, from what I saw today. "I . . . guess so? But—"

"I mean it sounds kind of lame? But Gabe does way weirder stuff, so whatever," Luke says, which appears to be his conclusive opinion on the matter.

"True," I say, and sigh. "Okay, well, I'm going to a party, I guess. Don't tell Mom."

"She's working late," Luke says, starting the car to test the new speaker. Immediately the bass gets so loud that I can hardly hear what he says next, which I think is something like: "If you get home by ten I doubt she'll notice."

"I was thinking I'd stay at my friend Jamie's?" I shout over the sound of Kid Cudi.

"Whatever," says Luke.

Okay, conversation over, I guess. It's way too loud in here and one of our neighbors is bound to complain.

"Just don't get sloppy," Luke yells after me. "Or do. Whatever."

"Super good advice, Luke, thanks," I yell back, deciding to put on my bird jeans when I get back to our unit.

About a year ago, I wanted this really cool pair of jeans that had two delicate little sparrows stitched onto the front of them, but my mom insisted they were too expensive. *Anyone could make those*, she said in her usual don't-waste-my-time kind of way, so since I figured I was as good as the "anyone" in this scenario, I begged my dad to take me to a craft store after he got home from work.

I ended up buying loads of other stuff there besides bird patches. Dad taught me how to use a tool to put on these little bronze circles called grommets, so I took an old pair of jeans and ripped up the sides, fastened the grommets on either side of the torn seams, and then laced them back together with some velvet ribbon. Now I have a pair of jeans with birds *and* velvet for like, fifteen dollars, which I can tell you right now is *not* what the jeans in the store cost. Plus I had a great day with my dad, which I don't get a lot of anymore.

Or any of.

"Oh my god, *great* jeans," exclaims Jamie when I step into her car.

"Oh, these? Just something I had lying around," I say. You know, like a liar. Truthfully, I think these jeans are just about the coolest thing I own, so even though my T-shirt is just a basic crop top that's a couple of years old, I feel great. "You look awesome."

"Thanks." She beams. She's wearing black skinnies and a button-down that she tied at the front, but like always, I'm especially in love with the scarf she's using as a hairband. This one has little rivulets of sequins in it—I'm a fool for shiny things.

"So, good day?" Jamie asks me, turning on the radio.

"I mean, I'm glad I'm in AP Physics with you, at least." I lean my head back with a sigh when the song switches to something upbeat and catchy. I like to think I have eccentric tastes in most things, but I like Taylor Swift, too. I'm human, after all.

Jamie adjusts her necklace with a smile, waiting the exact right amount of time before pulling into the bike lane to turn at the light. ("Super not interested in getting pulled over," she once said in a dark voice, which I obviously didn't argue with. There's a reason she wants to be a lawyer.)

"Mac's great, right?" she comments idly.

"Oh, um. I guess?" I say, because actually, I didn't think "Mac" was very great at all. He seemed really desperate, in my opinion. Also, what kind of adult goes by Mac? "It's not like Ms. Voss was bad or anything. I liked her."

"Well, she obviously likes you," Jamie says. "You're like, her pet project."

I make a face. "Maybe she just wanted me out of her class."

"Oh, shut up." Jamie's humming along with the song, too excited to deal with me second-guessing myself, and after the chorus she turns to me with a broad grin. "Oh my god, we're going to Teo Luna's partyyyy!" she half shouts, half sings, and it's easy to be enthusiastic when she's sitting right there, the portrait of complete adolescent bliss.

By the time we make it up the winding canyon road to Teo's private gate—"He texted me the code to get in," says Jamie smugly, poking me to pull it up on her phone—I kind of get why this is such a big deal, because his house comes into view from afar like a freaking palace. I see the house through my dad's contractor eyes, admiring the landscaping and the very hip, ultra-modern design, but even from the (very steep!!) driveway we can spot the figures sipping from red cups on what appears to be a roof deck.

"Whoa," I say, getting out of the passenger seat. There's a few other cars in the drive—mostly new Jettas and Civics, like Jamie's car—but nothing looks nearly fancy enough for this house.

"Yeah, his dad's some sort of genius," Jamie says, pausing beside me to look up at the house. "And his mom used to be a supermodel. I think she's an influencer now, like Gwyneth Paltrow."

"Doesn't Gwyneth have an Oscar?" (My mom loves her.)

"Does she?" asks Jamie, shrugging. "I thought she just Gooped."

"It's before your time," I say solemnly, and Jamie laughs, dragging me into the house.

I'm not really sure what I'm expecting to find when she opens the door, because truthfully, I still don't know what to make of Teo Luna. On the one hand, he's essentially the cult leader for a squad of worshipful dorks, and watching him in AP Physics today gave me the impression that maybe he knows it. He's clearly Mac's favorite student, and he's definitely not dumb, but he's pretty entitled—which I guess he *would* be, wouldn't he? With a house like this and parents like that. That being said, he's also sort of...quiet.

Except when he's bullying his way into roping me onto the team, that is, which leaves me back where I started.

I didn't know what to say at the time, and I guess I still don't.

It was kind of cool to have Teo be so sure that I was the right fit, but it was also really hard to overlook the way he cornered the girl, Neelam, who's supposed to be his teammate. He interrupted her at every possible turn, and he didn't even ask me whether I wanted to be on the team or not.

I get the feeling Teo Luna isn't used to asking other people what they think in general.

Speak of the devil. "Oh, hey," Teo says, materializing when Jamie and I follow the chorus of voices from the house's enormous entryway (my dad would *die*) to the back patio, which overlooks a distant view of the ocean. Other people appear to be drinking beer from a keg they've set up in the backyard, but Teo's got one of those Pellegrino bottles in his hand.

"Glad you could come, Howard," he tells Jamie, playing the role of effortless host, and then he turns to me. "Hey," he says. "Can I get you to look at something?"

"Me?" I can feel Jamie absolutely *buzzing* beside me with curiosity, though I'm afraid if I look at her I'll start laughing. "Uh, sure?"

"Great. Want a drink?" he asks, walking into the kitchen without waiting to see if I'll follow. I shrug at Jamie, who mouths *O-M-G* just as Lora dashes over to her, and then I turn with a sigh, hurrying a little to catch up with Teo.

"No, I'm...good. I think."

"You think?"

Jamie's not the only one feeling some type of way about me being alone with Teo, but if he notices anything about the way people's eyes are following us (mostly me, and mostly skeptical), he doesn't acknowledge it. Instead, he pauses with his hand on the fridge, apparently waiting for me to change my mind. "I've got beer, White Claw, soda—"

"Any Diet Coke?" I ask.

"Um, *yeah*," he says in something of a playful voice, and for the first time, I feel like maybe he really is just trying to be nice. "My mom's all about her DC. We've also got Diet Dew, Diet Dr Pepper, zero sugar Red Bull—"

"Whoa, um. Diet Dr Pepper, then, I guess," I say, and he nods, pulling one out of the fridge and tossing it to me. "So luxurious," I comment, tapping the top of the can before opening it. "Nobody ever has Diet Dr Pepper just sitting around."

"You know diet sodas are really bad for you," he says with a shrug, which I think is an attempt at…humility? Or he's teasing me. Hard to tell with the way he's looking at me. (It's very intense, like he's focused on me and nothing else, which is oddly not terrible.)

"Yeah, but it's a party," I joke in reply, taking a pointed sip. "If you come to the den of vice, do as the serpents do."

He frowns. "Is that a quote from something?"

"No." Oops—forgot that I have to reserve my weirdness until people know me better. "Sorry, what did you want to show me?"

Teo starts traversing his castle again, gesturing for me to follow after he holds up a finger to a touch screen on the wall. "Just have to grab it from Dash. Hey, have you seen Dash?" he shouts to a couple of dudes playing video games. (I'm sure I don't need to tell you, but the living room. Is. *Huge*. The TV is the size of like, my entire apartment.)

"Roof," say the two dudebros in unison.

"Figures. Come on," Teo says to me before taking the stairs two at a time, so I guess I have no choice but to chase him. Behind me, though, I hear the two dudebros exchange a muttered conversation:

"Must be a diversity thing."

"Well, you know what Teo says about optics."

Ah. So I guess I wasn't the only one to notice I was the only girl at today's tryouts.

Eventually we emerge onto the roof deck I saw from the driveway, where I recognize a few faces from AP Physics. They give me a look of scrutiny before returning to their conversations, and

Teo pulls aside the guy that must be Dash. He's taller than Teo, darker-skinned and slightly less messy-haired, but he still looks and dresses similarly, like maybe they have the same vision board on Pinterest. Dash has a faraway look on his face and a loud, easy laugh, which Teo interrupts by dragging him over to me.

"Hey, you still have the schematic saved on your iPad, right?"

"Yeah, it's right, uh…HEY, WHERE'S MY IPAD?" bellows Dash, startling me. Teo looks used to it.

"Yo," says a kid in my Civics class, handing the iPad to Dash from where it's sitting on a high-top table.

"Oh cool," says Dash happily, like he didn't just explosively make demands on Teo's behalf. "Here," he says, handing it to Teo, and then he looks at me. "Hi."

"Hi," I manage, smiling because Dash reminds me of a baby Great Dane, but then Teo's nudging me.

"Okay, so here's the deal: there's task robots and combat robots. Task bots are for the underclassmen with less experience—don't worry about them." Terrifying to think I'm considered *experienced*, but okay. "Combat robots do exactly what it sounds like: they have weapons and they battle. There's a fifteen-pound bot and a 120-pound bot, though it costs way too much to build a new 120-pounder so we're just going to work with what we have. Thankfully last year we only lost one round, so the damage was minimal." He glances at me for evidence of comprehension, then seems to decide my silence is irrelevant. "The fifteen-pound bot is the one we're building from scratch."

"Okay," I manage. He's very much in his comfort zone, which makes me acutely aware of both my supreme *dis*comfort and how close to me he's standing. The sunset is gorgeous from this high up in the hills, distractingly so, but he seems used to it, like it's background noise. A breeze feathers his hair until he pushes it back, raking his fingers through it and shading his eyes.

"Anyway, here's what we have right now in terms of future

builds," he says, and oh, duh, of course, I've been on the robotics team for a grand total of five seconds, so naturally we're going to continue discussing robots. *Here*. At a party. "Just wanted you to have an idea what we're working with for the year. We're pretty sure St. Michael's is going to use the same bot they used last year, so— Oh, sorry, that's our main rival," Teo explains, naming what's probably an all-boys Catholic school without looking up, "and anyway, last year it was basically just a solid metal box with a really low center of gravity. It was super cumbersome, though, and really slow."

I glance over the sketch of the bot that Teo clearly designed. "Is this a claw?"

"Yeah, to come over the top and down, like that—"

He demonstrates, grabbing at something below like one of those vending machine claws.

"So anyway, you get points for aggressive driving and strategy, where we usually do well, but the judges are really weird sometimes about design. It was the only area we didn't win last year."

I'm not really listening, because something's bugging me about the rendering in front of me. "What's this at the bottom?" I ask Teo, pointing. "Spinning blades? Like a helicopter?"

"Yeah. Well, ideally it d—"

"It's not going to work."

The voice behind me—which prompts me to turn, though nobody else notices—belongs to Neelam, the girl who argued with Teo at robotics tryouts today, who's broken off from the small group she was chatting with in order to (apparently) listen to my conversation with Teo. She's actually in a couple of my classes, though we haven't interacted. Even today wasn't really an interaction, and at this particular moment, she's still not looking at me.

"The weight distribution is off, Luna," Neelam says, "and the circuit board—"

"Will be fine," says Teo impatiently. "We can get it perfect and I told you, some things are just better. She uses spaces," he mutters to me in an aside, which is of course meaningless to me, though it's kind of hilarious that he thinks of me as some sort of co-conspirator. He's still standing close to me, which I think pisses Neelam off even more.

"Look, you don't have to listen to me about programming, but at least don't waste our time with bad design," Neelam tells Teo flatly. "Personally, *I* do not want to spend the next three months of our lives trying to get something impractical to work before you finally admit it's unnecessary."

"It's not *unnecessary*," Teo retorts, plainly annoyed. "We obviously have to have a weapon, and last year—"

"Last year we got lucky. *This* year—"

"Um, hi, sorry," I interrupt, and Dash, who hasn't said anything aside from nodding along with Teo, looks up at me, prompting me to continue.

"So um, Neelam's right—these dimensions aren't going to work," I say, zooming in on the spinning blades. "Not because it can't be *made* to work," I add quickly, because Teo's eyes immediately narrow at the prospect of me criticizing his idea, "but the um…what's the word? The, like, you know," I say uncomfortably, trying to think of what my dad's said about this sort of thing before. "The force or whatever for this to do any damage is just going rip the blades off completely, and then you'll have no weapon."

"It's called torque," says Neelam.

"Yeah, that," I say, a little embarrassed by the way she's making me sound like an idiot just because I can't think of the word right now. "And anyway, it seems like Neelam's only trying to explain that to you, so maybe if you just heard her out—"

"I don't need you to defend me," Neelam snaps at me before glaring at Teo. "And I told you she wasn't experienced enough."

Then she walks away and I blink, totally taken aback. I thought I was being nice, wasn't I? God, people at this school are *so weird*.

"Look," I exhale, turning toward Teo and trying to brush it off, "it's just—"

"I really disagree," he tells me, not looking up from the screen. He does some kind of software wizardry and conjures up a simulation of the claw in action, followed by the spinning blades. "See? There shouldn't be any issue with speed or weight, and when you use it to attack another bot—"

"Yeah, but I think you're forgetting to factor in the, like, probability of impact. I mean, when both bots are in motion the factors are different, right? Like, what if that blade does anything that's not at a direct angle." I touch the screen and immediately feel bad that I've gotten my fingerprints on it, but whatever. "Have it hit at anything other than a straight-on impact—like, if something hits the edge of the blade, instead of taking the full intended damage? It'll just break off."

But instead of running the simulation like I suggested, Teo stares at the screen.

"You said you have trouble with design, right?" I remind him, trying to sound positive.

After about a hundred years, Teo finally looks up at me.

"Yeah, well, it's a long process," he says, his voice sounding different. "And look, Neelam's right that you're going to have to learn how to talk about this sort of thing," he adds, stepping away. "You're probably going to have to do interviews at Nationals to defend our design. It's not like we can let Justin do it."

He and Dash snort like this is some kind of obvious hilarity, but I'm a lot less concerned with being on the outside of their inside jokes than I am about the other things he just said. Like, for example, is he honestly going to critique *me* right now when all I did was tell him why it wasn't going to work? We're at a party, for god's sake. I thought we were just coming here to see who got drunk and jumped into the swimming pool of Teo Luna's museum of a house.

"Look," I attempt diplomatically, "I really didn't mean to insult you—"

"I'm not insulted." He snaps the cover shut on the iPad and hands it to Dash just as Jamie and Lora come up behind me.

"What are we talking about?" asks Jamie, who's sipping White Claw through an eco-friendly metal straw that I know for a fact she carries in her purse.

"Nothing. Sorry, I gotta go. I forgot Andrew's waiting for me to sub in downstairs," says Teo, not really looking at Jamie or me. "Dash?"

Dash has been almost completely silent through this whole thing, but he nods when Teo summons him.

I'm feeling a little exasperated (and more than a little annoyed) when the two of them turn to leave, so I pivot after them. "If the other bot has such a—" What did he call it? "A low center of gravity," I recall, "then why even bother drilling into it? Just, like—" I make a motion with my hands, flipping an imaginary pancake. "It's not like it'll be able to turn itself back over any faster than you could do further damage, right?"

Teo stops and doesn't say anything. I'm not sure whether that's because I haven't explained it well—which, fair, I haven't—or if it's something harsher than that, like irritation. Or maybe active dislike.

"That's actually hilarious," says Dash, and Teo glances at him, rolling his eyes.

"Yeah, we'll talk Monday," Teo says. "Or, you know, later. Have fun," he adds over his shoulder, and with that, I'm pretty sure his very brief obsession with me is over.

"Yikes," whispers Jamie, staring after Teo and Dash as they mutter to each other down the corridor. "What'd you do, kill his dog?"

I grimace. "Insulted his manhood, I think."

"Oof," says Lora, patting my shoulder. "Well, don't worry, he'll come around. Teo likes people who can keep up with him."

"Keep up with," I grumble, "or *agree* with?"

Lora gives me one of those slanted looks of sympathy. Jamie, meanwhile, contributes a lofty snort of derision. "We all know the male ego is notoriously fragile. Even the cute ones are a lost cause," she points out with a lamenting sip, reminding us that she does not *like* boys. (She's just unfortunately attracted to them.)

"It's fine," I assure them, since both Lora and Jamie seem to be scrutinizing me for trauma. "It's not my first day of Masculinity 101. My brothers are the same way." In their own niche little worlds of sports and math, but still. "I'll figure it out."

"Of course you will," Lora says firmly. So firmly that for about half a second, I can almost believe it's not a big deal.

But what I don't want to admit to Lora and Jamie is that I'm definitely feeling stung. Teo brushing me off was humiliating and dismissive; Neelam calling me out in front of everyone was mortifying and rude. I wasn't even sure I was qualified for robotics to begin with, so now that I'm second-guessing (and third- and fourth- and fiftieth-guessing) myself, it feels... Well, not to completely fail at words, but, like, *bad*. Would it have killed Neelam to take my side when Teo was clearly being a jerk to me? I took hers. Does she just...hate me?

By the way she's standing with her own friends and ignoring me completely, I'm guessing so.

Which really sucks, because if that's the case, then this thing I didn't even want to do to begin with is going to make for a very, very long year.

five

TOOLS

Bel

It's pretty clear after the first couple of twice-weekly robotics meetings that even though Teo unilaterally decided to put me on the team, he either regrets that decision now or still needs to cool off from me telling him his bot isn't going to work. He doesn't explain anything he's doing—he only lets Dash or one of his other friends talk to him while he's fiddling with the robotics software or the circuit boards—and he really, really understated how much Mac, the teacher that I assumed would do most of the explaining, actually helps the team. Mac mostly flits in and out to check whether someone needs something or to make enthusiastic noises about Teo's designs, but it's pretty clear that the robotics team *is* Teo Luna.

So basically that means the whole room hates me. I can feel it in the way they suddenly tense up and start muttering to one another when I come over to ask questions, or the way they exchange doubtful glances when I offer to help. It's like they have one of those BOYZ RULE clubhouse signs hanging on the door and I stupidly failed to see it when I was being glorified at tryouts.

I try to help Neelam, who seems to have focused on the task-oriented robots because it's the one thing Teo doesn't micro-manage (they're beneath him), but she still thinks I'm an idiot or something.

It doesn't help that she's the same way in class. Lora and Jamie seem relieved that I've shown up to round out their lab group containing the only four girls in AP Physics, but not Neelam. *She* seems to think I'm just here to cozy up to Teo, which is beyond annoying. If I were here for him, wouldn't I have noticed my efforts weren't working and bailed on the whole thing by now? However inept she thinks I am at physics, *that* would be spectacularly dumber.

"Hey, do you want help with those?" I attempt while Neelam looks over her portion of the calculations we need for our lab. We split the work four ways, but I think I inadvertently got the easiest fourth.

"Why," she says without looking up, "do you not think I can do them?"

"What? No," I say, taken aback. "I just thought..."

I trail off, because to be honest, I'm not 100 percent sure how I've insulted her.

"I was just trying to help," I mutter to Neelam, who glares at me.

Ironically, Ravi chooses that moment to make an identical offer to Lora from the lab table to our left. "I can look over those if you want," he says, and Lora gratefully exhales, handing him her page of answers.

"Thanks. I'm not sure if the numbers are right, though," she says with a wince. "I couldn't really see the board."

We have the lab table farthest away, which is inconvenient for more than just Lora. Mac seems to spend most of his time checking in with the front group, aka Teo, because their lab table is closest to Mac's desk. Coincidentally or not, Teo's lab results are usually better, because he—or more likely, Dash or Kai or Emmett—only has to look confused for half a second before Mac's on his feet to answer their questions. In the back half of the room, we have to rely on ourselves. It's like the Wild West, but with extremely low stakes and no dysentery (that I know of).

"See?" I say to Neelam, gesturing to Ravi. Lora didn't throw a fit about his offer to help.

Instead, Neelam's hand tenses around her pencil. "Do you think anyone has ever asked Ravi if *he* needs his numbers checked?" she hisses to me. "Or Teo?"

"I have literally no idea," I grumble, stung, though even when I say it, I know I'm lying.

There's no way anyone in this class has ever done anything but trust implicitly that everything Teo Luna does is correct. I notice later that Ravi doesn't ask for Lora's help, either, which makes me feel even worse. I already can't let go of how embarrassing it was to get shut down by Teo at his party, and now? I have no idea where to put all these awful feelings, which only seem to be piling higher in my chest until I can barely find room to breathe.

I make a point not to say much in robotics that day, which isn't that hard to do. Lora's my only friend and she's the business manager, not one of the engineers, so it's easy to avoid the design or software stuff while I'm sitting next to her. Neelam's already made it clear that I don't have the vocabulary to talk about this sort of thing and I don't have the energy to fight with Teo like she does, so mostly I just do whatever I'm asked until we break for the day.

It hits me later, hard: none of the boys think I can build anything. They never say so out loud, but I can tell they don't think I know what any of the equipment is called when they ask me to hand it to them. Emmett even asks me if I want help with the dynamics lab for class—which seems like a perfectly nice offer, but it's not like I didn't sit through the exact same lecture he did. At first I tell myself it's because the others sometimes need more help, or because Mac doesn't seem to like me, but after a while, I have to force myself to admit it isn't that.

I know what it is. They'll never say it—maybe they don't even realize they're doing it—but Emmett and the others look at me and automatically assume I must be struggling with the material because I'm a girl, which makes me feel even worse about screwing it up with Neelam *yet again*.

Honestly? Physics is easy.

What's hard is feeling like I want to be invisible all the time.

Jamie: how'd it go??? any better???
Bel: nobody seemed actively repulsed by me today
Jamie: !! improvement??
Bel: it was more of an extreme unspoken dislike
Jamie: ☹ oh come on
Bel: okay fine maybe they don't hate me
Bel: but i can tell teo is starting to regret his decision to put me on the team
Jamie: they ALL voted you onto the team, b
Jamie: it wasn't some freak accident
Bel: no, it was teo
Bel: and his band of merry men
Jamie: well, you know i love taking shots at men
Bel: it's true, you do
Jamie: i rly rly do
Jamie: but the point is they didn't hesitate to pick you, right?
Jamie: so they're not total idiots
Bel: are you kidding? putting me on this team is the dumbest thing they
    could have done
Bel: i know literally nothing

"Hey," Luke says, barging into my room while Jamie's text bubble pops up again with some floating dots. "Wanna do something?"

"With you? No," I say, not looking up from my screen.

Jamie: chin up, buttercup
Jamie: you just have to show them that you're brilliant and creative and
    clever as heck!!
Bel: oof
Bel: yeah i'll get right on that

62

"Seriously," Luke says. "Please?"

He never says please, so naturally I'm suspicious. "Why?"

"Can't tell you. Car."

We're not the closest siblings ever, but even I understand that Luke's car is a safe space. No, more than that—a *sacred* space. He drove me to school for a couple of years when he first got his license and those were the only talks we've ever had that were anything of substance, so for him to call "car" right now is basically the equivalent of Jamie sending me an SOS text.

"All right," I sigh. I'm supposed to be working on college applications anyway, which of course I'd rather not do. It's a homework assignment from my counselor, who doesn't seem to understand that "I don't know where I want to go to school" and "I don't know what I want to study" are not exactly brilliant foundations for a stellar admissions essay.

In the car Luke is quiet for a bit, instructing me to find a playlist on his phone before connecting it to the *very* mismatched audio system that we both know is extremely new compared to the rest of the car. He pulls out of the garage and takes the usual right, then chooses the left that'll wind us aimlessly through residential streets.

Then, finally, he says, "So, about Dad."

Oh boy, here we go. Just the person I've been trying not to think about for the past six months. I stare out at the endless collection of apartment buildings we pass, wishing I'd thought to negotiate some kind of dessert as a reward for this mysterious car confession.

"Yeah?" Maybe I can talk him into those taro buns we used to have to hide from Gabe.

"Dad found me a job for the fall. Or maybe longer." Luke taps the steering wheel along to some Pusha T diss track he loves. (I don't understand the origins of most rap feuds, but they strike me as mildly poetic? It's all very distantly Shakespearean to me; blood wars and betrayal and stuff...which is totally beside the point.)

"Wait," I say, frowning. "You've seen him? Dad?"

Luke shifts in the driver's seat. "Yeah. Well—"

He clears his throat.

"So, you're not eighteen yet," Luke says slowly, "but I'm twenty-one."

"Yeah, and...?"

"And..." He's clearly very uncomfortable. Not that I like where this is going, but I wish he'd get there sooner. "So look, Dad's got plenty of room, and if I'm going to be working for him—"

"You're going to be working for *him*?" I interrupt, because he didn't exactly specify that.

"—if I'm going to be working for him," Luke repeats, "it's just easier."

"But Mom," I start to protest, and then trail off.

Suddenly I'm not hungry anymore.

"I know." Luke stares out over the dash, contemplating the red light in front of us. "But honestly, Ibb"—he's the only one who calls me that, Ibb as in Ibb-el, his baby name for me, which sucks to hear right now, when he's maybe-probably leaving me behind—"Mom wants me to be something I'm not."

I grimace. "More like Gabe, you mean."

"Yeah. Well, yeah, basically." He brings a hand up to his mouth and I think again about how much he looks like our dad.

I don't really look like either of our parents.

"So you're moving out?" I glance down at my hands. It's not like Luke and I hang out or talk more than a few words at a time, but the idea of coming home without him playing video games or working on his car in our complex's garage suddenly hits me so hard I can't breathe. What am I going to do now when I'm supposed to be writing college essays and Mom's not home? It was different when Luke went away to college; I was relieved back then, probably because I knew he'd be back. But now I'm not so sure.

"I have to talk to Mom about it. But yeah, I think so." He turns to look at me. "Are you cool?"

"Am I *cool*, Luke? No, I'm not cool." I had no idea I could ever feel this lonely just because my annoying older brother was moving out of the apartment he was never supposed to live in in the first place. "I mean, obviously I hate that I never get to see Dad anymore, and now—"

I exhale, not sure what to say now that I'm forced to think about the one thing I've been trying not to fixate on, which is the fact that my dad and my mom are two separate entities now. The divorce has been gross and messy and it made my dad yell and my mom cry, which made them both seem like strangers to me.

"You know what Dad did," I say. No one will come out and say it, but I know the separation was my dad's fault, which is hard. It's really, really hard to recognize someone as the villain in someone else's life when you're pretty sure you love them both.

Luke's mouth tightens. "I know."

"And you're fine with that?"

"Of course not. But under the circumstances—"

"What *possible* circumstances?" I demand, because as far as I know, Mom hasn't changed her tune, and Dad certainly didn't *un*-screw things up.

"I mean—" Luke shifts uncomfortably, one hand tight at the top of the wheel. "Are we supposed to be pissed at him forever? Like…Dad's canceled, the end?"

The thought batters me. "No, but—"

I swallow, unable to finish the sentence.

"Does it really matter whether we don't speak to him for six months or six years?" Luke asks me. "At some point, we have to get over this and move on."

"But Mom," I remind him, faltering.

Luke slides me a grimace.

"But Dad," he says.

Neither of us knows what to say from there.

Even though I know my dad broke my mom's heart—and even though I *know* he should have fought harder to keep us from

65

leaving—there are still plenty of times that I want to see him more than anyone else on earth. It's this weird situation where loyalty to my mom keeps me from picking up the phone, but then loyalty to my dad burns a hole in my chest. I am who I am because of him. Where am I supposed to put all the stuff about me that I used to think of as his now that he's gone?

It was easy for Gabe to leave Dad behind. It was even easy for Luke, Dad's sidekick, to move out with us when Mom did, because we were all on the same team—or so I thought, though clearly Luke has some lingering reservations.

"You could visit whenever," Luke offers when the light changes.

Yeah, right. Sure.

"It's just that he doesn't try to force me into anything, you know?" Luke continues, still not acknowledging that this is obviously the least cool thing I've ever heard in my life. "Mom wants me to be a CPA or a doctor or something and, like, I just can't. Why is it such a crime that I don't like school? I just want to build stuff and be outside."

Of course Dad would tell Luke that he doesn't have to be anything. They were always two peas in a pod, I grumble internally—but then I try to remind myself that I'm being unfair.

I know Luke misses Dad more than anyone. I know Luke's just trying to do what he thinks is best. I know he reminds our mom of our dad, who she's angry with, and that makes things harder for both of them. I know this isn't about me.

But is it ever going to be?

I close my eyes and breathe out, trying to understand. I know I'm more upset about the circumstances of Luke leaving than I am about his absence. If he were just going back to school, would I be mad? Of course not. But this…

As a last-ditch effort, I consider that it'll be nice to have a fridge full of yogurt again.

"If it's what you want, Luke, then I'm happy for you," I say, because it seems like maybe the worst thing I could do right now is cry or get upset. Worse, I don't even think it would work if I did. He looks relieved, and then he starts humming along to the song, and I can tell he feels better—that he's choosing to believe the words I'm saying, even if we both know I don't.

Taking up your own space is honestly really hard to do. I wish Ms. Voss had taught me how before she switched me into AP Physics.

TEO

"Focus, Luna!"

Sweat drips into my eyes and all I can think is *ouch*. My legs are burning and so are my lungs. It's hot out here, well over a hundred degrees in this infernal part of the Valley, so I can see the heat rising off the turf and feel it drying out my throat. I hate these afternoon scrimmages.

Focus.

The midfielder I couldn't catch (a sophomore who probably didn't stay up half the night working on bot schematics) takes the ball up to the goal and thankfully misses his shot, but my half-second delay works to my advantage. I'm right there when it bounces off the edge of the post. I turn to aim it safely up the field, bracing myself for a hard run despite having almost nothing left in the tank, when Marcus Ferrar, our resident foul magnet, charges into me headfirst. I don't drop levels in time and end up taking the impact hard in the sternum, my breath temporarily knocked out of me.

"It's a scrimmage, Ferrar, not Sparta!" Coach yells.

I wish we could just break this tie with a penalty kick. I'm good under pressure. Not a lot of people can carry the whole game on their backs, but I can. When it's just me and the thing I really want, the whole world goes quiet.

Unfortunately, it's just going to be a free kick. I get the ball upfield to where Kai's waiting and then he's off and running, Coach yelling at me to get moving. Like I don't know that.

Focus.

In the end I do manage to score, though my legs are cramping so hard I think they're going to collapse under me.

"Hey," says Marcus, chasing me down after practice. "You good?"

"Me? I'm fine," I tell him. "How's your head?"

"Been worse." He grins at me. "You coming? We're getting Chipotle."

The thought of a burrito almost makes my stomach growl on command. "Nah, gotta get back for robotics," I say, and Marcus shrugs.

"Your loss," he calls to me, jogging backward.

Yeah, yeah. As good as it sounds, I'd much rather have a second national robotics title and a spot at MIT than a burrito.

I make my way across campus, expecting to have to use the key Mac gave me to the robotics lab for when I stay after school. The lab is full of expensive equipment—one circuit board alone is at least ten thousand dollars—but he's seen me work often enough to know I can be trusted with it.

To my surprise, though, he's still here.

"Look, Bel, you're doing fine with the AP Physics material," Mac says, and I keep out of sight, pausing in the little no-man's-land between the Physics classroom and the robotics lab. "But robotics is a team sport. If you want to be successful here, you have to learn to be a team player."

I wait for Bel's response, but she doesn't say anything. At least, nothing I can hear.

"I'm not trying to single you out," Mac says. "I had to have the same talk with Neelam when she started. You have to learn that everyone else on the team wants you to succeed."

"Okay." Her voice is flat and dull, the same way it was when I first told her she was my pick for the team. "Yeah, I understand."

"Good! Excellent," says Mac, and I make a show of jangling my keys, letting them know I'm there. "Luna, is that you?" yells Mac, and I shut the door behind me loudly, making it sound like I just arrived.

"Yeah, just got done with practice," I shout back.

Mac materializes around the corner. "Bel's in here finishing a lab," he says, gesturing over his shoulder. "But I'm heading out in about fifteen."

"I can lock up if you want," I assure him. "I'm not using any of the big stuff."

Mac shrugs. "You know the rules: no fire, no heavy weights, no sharp edges—"

"Software only," I tell him, hand over heart. "Scout's honor."

"Luna, I already know you were never a scout," Mac sighs, feigning exasperation, but he chuckles when he walks into his classroom.

I plug in my noise-canceling Bose headphones and start up the design software, testing some of the changes I've been sketching before Neelam tries to argue with me tomorrow. I get a text from Dash almost immediately, something about the dessert nachos he just invented, but I ignore it.

Then someone taps me on the shoulder and I jump.

"Jesus, sorry, hi," says Bel, taking a step back after I round on her. Before I can hit pause on the Skrillex I exclusively play while coding, I faintly hear her saying something like, "...some sort of extreme focus disease?"

I slide the headphones fully from my ears. "What?"

"Never mind," she mutters. Today she has purple glitter sweeping out from her eyelids and a pair of mismatched earrings; one's a dangling crescent moon, the other's a tiny sword, like a dagger. "I just finished my lab. Mac wanted me to tell you when I was leaving."

"Okay," I say, and turn to put my headphones back on, but Bel doesn't move. "Is there something else?" I ask her.

She's saying nothing, looking at my computer screen, and I sigh loudly. "What?"

She hesitates for at least thirty seconds before saying, "I don't think that would make for a very strong weld."

"What?"

"My dad had to do something like this once. Any pressure and this'll come apart." She points to the part of my design she's talking about. "Looks cool, though," she says, and then turns away.

I have every intention to let her go, but something in me feels an urgent need to keep her there.

"What would you do?" I ask her, and she freezes in place.

"Ummm. I mean, I'd have to think about it."

She turns over her shoulder to look at my screen again, and I think she's lying. I think she knows *exactly* what she'd do instead, but she clearly doesn't plan to share those ideas with me. Suddenly, I wish I'd let her leave.

This is the thing about her that's making me regret my decision to pick her for the team. It's not like she's not smart, but she's not *saying* anything. It makes me feel like she's got some secret internal monologue about how she hates my ideas, but as far as I can tell she's not willing to actually come up with any of her own.

"Mac's right, you know," I say. "This is a team."

She slides me an irritated look. "You're gonna lecture me now, too?"

"It's not like it came out of nowhere."

Her mouth stiffens.

"He's a good teacher," I tell her. "If you need help, all you have to do is ask."

"Is that what you think?"

Her tone is unexpectedly harsh, and I blink. "What?"

She stares at me. "Have you ever had to ask Mac for anything?"

"What?"

"No, you haven't," she answers herself. "And yeah, maybe that's because you're smarter or more gifted, or maybe not. Maybe he decided right away that he wasn't going to let you fall behind. Either way, you don't notice, do you? That you have things easier. That you don't have to ask for anything, it just comes to you."

That feels like an unfair thing to say, though I'm a little bit frustrated once I realize I can't think of anything to directly refute her point.

"If you're struggling with the material, or if you can't keep up in robotics—"

"I'm not struggling," she snaps.

"Okay, whatever, I was just—"

"It's a weak weld," she tells me, suddenly storming up to the screen. "You can't just shove two separate pieces together like that and expect them to hold. If you want something to be strong, it has to come from a strong foundation."

"Okay, fine," I say, because clearly she just wants to argue with me. "You saw me working with this design last week. Why didn't you say something then?"

"Why, so you could shut me down the way you shut down Neelam? So Mac can lecture me about being a team player?" She scoffs. "No thanks. You've already made it clear my input isn't wanted."

"What are you—" I stop, realizing she must be talking about the suggestion she made to the bot design at my party, if you can call an ambivalent pantomime a suggestion. "Okay, first of all, I'm not sure that counts as *input*—"

"Oh, come on," she mutters, fidgeting with her sword earring. "You knew what I meant!"

I did, though I don't feel like rehashing it now.

"We're not shutting anyone down, we're just—" There's no point having this conversation. She clearly won't listen to me. "Look, just design something basic tonight and then we'll call for a vote tomorrow," I tell her. "If you think I'm the problem, then let's see what everyone else thinks."

Her expression goes stiff again. "Whatever, fine," she says.

I take that as a yes and turn away.

If I were any less annoyed, I'd make a point to notice how different she looks now from how she looked a minute ago. That was the same as how she looked while she was drawing, which I haven't seen again at any point since the day she joined the team. While she was yelling at me her cheeks were flushed and her eyes were wide and she was like, actually *alive*, which is the version of her I find way more interesting than this one. Even if I'm not exactly thrilled with anything she's saying.

I pick up my headphones to put them back on when Bel suddenly blurts out, "It's really ridiculous that you're being such a dick to me just because I saw problems with your bot. I thought that was what you wanted me to do. Otherwise, why even bother adding someone to the team? Were you just looking for someone new to say yes to you all the time? Because trust me, you don't need it."

Luckily I have my headphones on, so even though I heard everything she said, I can pretend I didn't. I wait until I know for sure she's gone before I take them off again, stewing in something I think is frustration.

Or maybe guilt.

The truth is she's right. I *have* been kind of a dick to her, and it *is* because she saw problems with my design (*sees* them, apparently, since even if it wasn't very coherent, there's no denying she's now called me out twice), but it's not about her, not really. It's just hard to see flaws in something you worked so hard on. It makes me question myself, which I'm not used to doing.

Because she's right. Everyone says yes to me. Me included.

I start to get a headache, probably from staring so long at a screen, so I shut down the program and lock up the lab, walking out to my car. There's only a handful left in the parking lot and I stifle a yawn, suddenly exhausted.

I like being busy. I like being in charge. I like that people trust me with things—with the winning goal, with the keys to the robotics lab—so yeah, it's kind of driving me crazy that Bel doesn't. I feel like she thinks I'm just some smug asshole, and I'm not. Or I don't think I am.

At the very least, I try not to be. (Don't I?)

But then I drive to my gated house and up my long driveway to the suitcase I still haven't unpacked from meeting my parents in Denver, and I think oh, maybe she just can't see me through all of this. Or maybe I haven't actually bothered to show her.

"How was soccer?" asks my dad when I walk into the living room from the foyer. I'm not used to seeing him on the couch, so his presence there startles me for a second. He's always a bit formal, like he's posing for an invisible *Forbes* interview, and everything about him looks purposefully curated, from the gray at his temples (*GQ* called him "the silver fox of Silicon Beach" last year) to the rolled cuff of his sleeves.

"It was good," I say dismissively. Against the backdrop of my mother's sparse Nordic tastes, he's much too distinguished for small talk about what I did at practice today. "Where's Mom?"

"Out with friends for the evening. Did you win?" he asks, glancing down when his phone buzzes once, then twice.

There's no point explaining it was just a scrimmage; that would take longer than this conversation will even be. He'll have a call to take or an email to send any second now. "Yes."

He looks up again, nodding. "Good. And school?"

"Fine."

His phone buzzes again. "Just fine?"

I shrug. "Got an A on my AP Gov paper."

"What about Physics?" he says, frowning at his screen.

"Like Mac would ever give me less than an A," I reply without thinking, before suddenly remembering the look on Bel's face.

Have you ever had to ask Mac for anything?

It's something Neelam would have said to me. Though, if Neelam had said it, I would have ignored her.

So you could shut me down the same way you always shut down Neelam?

Damn. I hate this. She's right, and that's on me.

"What's wrong?" asks my dad, gesturing to my expression. "Something not going well in school? I told you, if you want us to get you a tutor—"

I blink away Bel's look of wide-eyed disappointment and shake my head. "I don't need a tutor, Dad. I have a 4.3. I'm fine."

"Harvard doesn't usually settle for 'fine,' Teo."

"I'm—" I cut myself off before reminding him (again) that I'm not applying to Harvard. I don't know what it is about parents wanting their kids to go to Harvard, but for a guy who went to state school on a scholarship, my dad is not immune. "I'm not having problems in school, Dad, I promise. I've got As in every class." Assuming I manage to get through the book we're reading in English: Dante's "Inferno."

(Which is really quite appropriate, given how hellish things have been.)

"Well, it's only the start of October," says my dad. "I would hope you haven't fallen behind yet."

I nod, unsurprised. According to TechCrunch, my father is notorious in the industry for his "ruthless efficiency," a vestigial quality from his early experience as the rare person of color in his white-dominated program. Mateo Luna doesn't accept mistakes because he can't afford to make them, and all that work fighting his way up from the bottom means he doesn't have much patience for people who don't pull their own weight.

I turn to the stairs, ready to put on sweats and decompress, when my dad calls after me again.

"You know I just want to prepare you, right?" he says. "You're going to have it different than I did, kiddo. You're Mateo Luna's son. People expect things from you."

"I know, Dad."

"Which means things will be easier, but also harder."

"I know."

"You can't just coast on your name."

"I won't."

He scrutinizes me for a minute, then nods. "Hungry?"

Oh, yeah. Nearly forgot. "Yeah, actually."

"Your mother left some of last night's Thai in the fridge for you," he says, rising to his feet. "I have to take a call with a potential investor in Osaka. Ping me if you need anything," he adds, clapping me on the shoulder and strolling down the hall to his home office.

I watch him go and then head to the fridge, reconsidering my plans while I throw some drunken noodles in the microwave.

I was going to maybe try to get to bed early tonight, but instead I think I'll get back to the "Inferno." My dad's right—I don't want to screw anything up this early in the year, and people expect big things from me.

Me most of all.

six

SECRETS

Bel

At first I didn't plan on seeing Luke or Dad for a long time. Mom's clearly very upset about Luke moving—they fought for *hours* until he finally stormed out—and the last thing I want to do is give her something else to stress about.

But then Teo Luna decided to be difficult and I needed some tools my mom doesn't have, soooo...I'm going to need *someone's* help designing a weapon for the team vote tomorrow. Even if it's just Teo being Teo, I do not intend to prove myself inept again.

One thing they'll never tell you about your parents separating is how weird it is to pull into your driveway and knock on your own front door. Or what used to be my front door, anyway, until my mom decided that a shiny new town and an exorbitant new tuition were a better environment for me, the last of her still-at-home children. ("Could be worse," Jamie said when I first told her why I had transferred. "She could have enrolled you in, like, a school for mimes," she pointed out, which, believe it or not, was not that helpful.)

"Bel," says my dad when he opens the door, looking surprised. He's got an easy laugh, a big smile; the dimples I got from him are visible right away, and his shock at seeing me here melts quickly to warmth. "I didn't know you were coming."

I fiddle with my keys. "Should I have called first?"

"What? No, sweetheart, I just meant...never mind." So now you see where I get my habit of not finishing my sentences. "Come on in," he says, taking a step back. He's wearing his usual jeans and a faded T-shirt; a red one he's had since I was a kid. I can practically smell my childhood in the threads of it—a mix of sawdust and my mom's gardenia fabric softener.

Only then I remember that my mom doesn't do his laundry anymore.

"Actually, is Luke home?" I ask, unsure about stepping inside the house. It seems less disloyal if I stay out here—or at least generally not *in there*, where I'd become complicit in whatever my father does without my mother. "I just needed to use some of his tools in the shed."

"He's not," my dad says slowly, "but I can help you. If you want."

He looks optimistic, and I feel terrible. I should just leave, right? I should go.

(But it's this or...no, it's just this. I already spent half an hour trying to figure out the design software at home and it just doesn't make any sense to me, so...)

"Okay," I say. "Yeah, okay. Thanks."

"So what are we working on?" Dad asks me, shutting the front door behind him. Maybe he figured out that I don't want to walk through the house, because instead we pass through the side yard to reach the shed in the back.

"It's...a school project," I say, not really wanting to get into the fact that I did the least Bel Maier thing ever and agreed to join the robotics team. He'd probably put his hand on my forehead and ask if I'm feeling okay, which is a fatherly thing I can't deal with right now. "I need to build something that can, like, go under something? And then flip it over?"

"For school, really? Jesus," Dad says, shaking his head. "They're really serious about that STEM curriculum now, huh?"

"Yeah, looks like it," I say, as if I, too, can't believe how wild academia has gotten.

"How long do you have to work on it?"

"Oh, well...it's kind of due tomorrow."

Dad arches a brow. "Bel."

Oh god, he's onto me. "Hm?"

"Procrastination much?"

"Oh. Yeah." I force a laugh in relief, since leaving things to the last minute is definitely a more Bel explanation than the truth. (See also: catapults.) "Well, I thought I already had everything, but..."

"No worries, no point getting upset now. Though I hope I have the components you need." He flips on the lights in the shed, tugging open one of the massive metal drawers. "Are you thinking hydraulics?"

"Actually," I begin, and because this is my dad, I just go ahead and tell him what I wasn't sure how to say to Teo Luna. "I'm thinking we could attach an electrical sensor to make it work. Like a motion sensor from a garage door or something. So when something gets close, it'll just automatically slide under and then, you know. Flip."

Dad cocks his head to the side, nodding. "Could work. Hang on, let's see what we have here."

Hydraulics aren't as complicated as they sound. Actually, nothing is really that complicated once you break it down to its fundamental pieces, but hydraulics specifically sound a lot more complex than they actually are.

Basically, hydraulic systems push fluid (usually oil) through valves to a cylinder, and that pressure determines whatever you want your mechanism to do. Push down on one aspect and then, because the fluid only has one direction to go, it will push down on something else.

Most people's fathers probably do not have compression cylinders lying around, but mine is not most fathers. "Make sure there's no air bubbles," he tells me. He's had me "bleed" things before, which means making sure there's no air in the hydraulic fluid of a car or a bike brake. If there's air bubbles in the oil, then the pressure gets used up on compressing the air bubbles, not on accomplishing whatever it is you want the hydraulic system to do.

"Pretty complex for science homework," my dad comments, watching me sketch out what I'm thinking for the design. Instead of questioning me, though, he says, "Better get to work."

At some point Luke shows up, making surprised noises for a second before disappearing with Dad's wallet and then reappearing with a pizza. He chews noisily and talks with his mouth full, mumbling about the proper PSI to make the hydraulics function until his phone rings and he slips out again.

"How's this?" I ask Dad, showing him where I attached a piston rod to the inside of the cylinder barrel.

"Looks good," says Dad, handing me the valve he's put together based on the sketch I drew up. "So your plan is to push into the cylinder to extend the piston?"

"Yes. And then change the direction to retract it." I sort of pantomime what I mean. "So if I had an electrical sensor—"

"Ah," he says with a nod, "it would change the directional valve on its own, okay—"

But when Luke comes back, Dad and I can both feel the way the energy in the room goes sour.

"She needs to go home," Luke says, not looking at me.

"I can't," I tell him impatiently. "I'm still working on—"

"Ibb. Now," Luke says.

Dad turns to me sharply. "Did you not tell your mother you were coming here? Bel, it's after midnight. She must be worried sick."

I wince, having forgotten about things like time and curfews and my phone.

"Yeah, well, she's not worried anymore," Luke says tightly. "Now she's just pissed."

Great. And I'm not even done.

"Well, fine," I say. "I'll just…finish this another time."

"Isn't it due tomorrow?" my dad says, at the exact same time Luke asks me, "Is this for that robotics club you were talking about?"

"Wait, robotics club?" my dad echoes. "Since when do you talk about a robotics club? Or *any* club?"

"No, I'm not...Look, Mom's waiting for me," I say, gathering up the hydraulic pump and the pieces I still have to put together. "Sorry, I'll explain another time."

On my drive home I think a lot about why I didn't just explain to my dad that this was something I was doing for...well, for fun, basically. I think because he might have asked questions, or because he might have thought that I'm like Luke—that I'd rather spend my time with him than Mom. I don't really want him to think that. It was easier to let him believe it was some kind of scholastic emergency.

When I come home I expect to get yelled at, but my mom doesn't even speak to me.

Well, not exactly. She says three words.

"Go to bed."

Then she walks into her room and closes the door on me. It's a classic case of parental disappointment and I feel terrible, but at the same time, I'm glad she didn't ask me to explain myself. I feel like every day I get less and less interested in explaining anything to anyone.

I think working on my hydraulic pump today was the first time in weeks—possibly months—that I haven't felt like some enormous, invisible weight was slowly crushing my chest.

Luke: r u dead
Bel: no
Luke: bummer

I roll my eyes.

Bel: i hope you're not eating pizza for dinner every night in your bachelor pad
Luke: it's bulking season
Bel: gross

He sends me a GIF of some veiny dude flexing.

Bel: i repeat, GROSS
Luke: it's ur bachelor pad too
Luke: u can get swoll w me and dad anytime

I think he's trying to be nice, but currently it just makes me feel weirdly depressed and left out.

Though I bet my mom felt that way too when she figured out where I was tonight.

Bel: i love you mom
Bel: i'm sorry i didn't tell you where i was going
Bel: please don't be mad at me

I wait for a few seconds, wondering if she's already asleep.

Mom: I love you hija
Mom: but if you ever do this again I'm commandeering your car keys and shrinking your favorite sweatshirt in the wash
Bel: harsh but fair
Mom: go to sleep
Bel: ok
Bel: night mom

The next day Jamie accosts me the moment I get to school.

"There's a pop quiz in AP Physics," she says, looking wildly distressed. "Lora was doing something for robotics this morning and she saw exam sheets on Mac's desk."

"Presumptuous much?" I say, but the more I think about it, the more it does seem likely we'd have a quiz. We've just finished a unit and Mac didn't tell us what lab we're starting next, so it's probably an opportune time for us to be evaluated on our questionable abilities.

Kinda wish I'd gone to bed when my mom told me to.

(I didn't. Hydraulic pump, etc.)

"I'm *screwed*," Jamie says, her tie-dye hair band much too cheerful for such a doomsday proclamation. "I was up all night working on my mock trial argument. And Mac *barely* gives us points on anything, so if I don't get an A on this—"

"You'll spontaneously combust?" I guess.

"—then I won't get an A in the class and then I'll lose my shot at valedictorian and then I won't get into Stanford and I won't get into law school and then I'll just DIE," she wails, so I grab her arm with a roll of my eyes.

"All right, we can study at lunch," I tell her. "I'll help you, I promise, and I'm sure Lora will be fine with studying a little extra—"

I get momentarily distracted as Teo Luna walks by with Dash, who's animatedly discussing something with a broad sweep of his hands. Dash waves to Jamie and me, interrupting himself mid-sentence while Teo glances up.

For a second I think Teo's going to say something to me, and my words get caught up in a knot somewhere near my throat. But then he just brushes his hair out of his eyes and half smiles at something Dash says, nodding in our direction once before walking away.

"—so it's fine," I finish unconvincingly, not that it matters. Jamie's already pulling out her calculator and figuring out the *exact* minimum number of points she needs to score on this exam in order to maintain her insane GPA.

For the record, it's not like I don't worry about my grades. I do, obviously, but it's hard to be obsessed with them when I'm not even sure they matter in the long run. I mean, does whatever I do in life really require me to have gotten an A in Civics? Assuming I even *figure out* what I want to do in life, which is already way more trouble to consider than it's worth.

Luckily I do understand projectile motion, which is what the quiz (if it exists) is actually about. Sure, Teo may think that I'm struggling, but actually the truth is quite simple. Mac favors the boys—inadvertently, I think, and in small ways, like giving them the best lab table or checking in with them more often, or pulling Kai aside to tell him he can do better when Lora, who got the same grade, didn't get a pep talk after class and therefore didn't improve when Kai did. Yesterday, I thought if I tried talking to Mac about our lab after class, I could make him see it wasn't a matter of the four of us being less capable. Instead, I just made him defensive, probably because he already thinks I don't care about contributing to the team.

Knowing Teo clearly overheard Mac's little lecture yesterday is embarrassing, but worse, it's frustrating. I feel like everything I do just reinforces Teo's belief that I don't know what I'm doing—which he clearly *does* believe, given the way he brushed me off when I pointed out all this to him in the robotics lab. Even more unfairly, the more Teo suspects I can't be trusted to do things right, the more Mac seems to believe it.

Sometimes I think *I'm* starting to believe it a little bit, too.

I think that feeling of frustration stays with me throughout the day, because after school (and after the pop quiz, which really wasn't worth the panic), I stop by Ms. Voss's classroom.

"Oh, Bel," she says, looking up from something very gross that I assume was for her Bio class. "I've been meaning to check in with you."

"Saved you the time," I tell her, and reach into my backpack for my hydraulic pump. "So, I got onto the robotics team—"

"I knew you would," she says, almost smugly.

"—and I just wanted to show this to you. For no real reason, I guess," I mumble, suddenly feeling silly, but Ms. Voss shakes her head.

"Show me," she says.

Amazing how two small words can really be the right ones sometimes.

"Okay, so the air from the compressor goes here to pressurize the system," I say, showing her the directional piece that determines where the air goes. "I'm assuming there's one I can use in the robotics lab—but anyway, then it goes into the cylinder and moves this piece. And then when it goes the other way, the piston goes back in."

"Bel, this is really good work." She looks over the pump, nodding to herself. "So what are you thinking the pump will do?"

"Well, ideally I'll be able to hook it up to something electrical, like a motion sensor, and then anytime an opposing bot gets close, it will automatically slide out"—I demonstrate with the pump—"and then the hydraulic pump will allow it to go under the other bot and flip it."

"That's very creative, Bel. What did Mr. MacIntosh say?"

"Oh, I haven't shown him yet," I admit, and her brow furrows.

"You built this on your own?"

"Well, my dad and brother helped a lot," I say. "I just sketched it out once my dad gave me the parts."

"You designed it, Bel. You didn't 'just' anything." Ms. Voss hands the pump back to me. "I'm sure the rest of the team will be really excited to see what you're capable of."

"I hope so." I tuck the pump back into my bag. "So anyway, I just wanted to tell you that, you know." I clear my throat, suddenly uncomfortable. "I had fun building it."

Her smile broadens knowingly. "And?"

"And . . . what?"

"And have you thought any more about your major? Electrical, mechanical, and civil engineering could all involve things of this nature," she says, pointing to where the pump is sitting in my backpack.

"Oh. I mean, yeah," I say. "Okay."

She purses her lips. "That's not an answer, Bel."

"Well, I'm not going to base the rest of my life on one little hydraulic pump," I tell her, accidentally allowing myself to slip into a slightly sulky tone. "I don't even know what the rest of the team is going to say about it."

I brace myself for further argument, but she only shrugs.

"Fair enough," says Ms. Voss. "But it's still worth thinking about, don't you think? You really took a lot of initiative here. You went above and beyond a basic schematic. It's something you built, Bel, and you're allowed to be proud of that."

For a second, I think it might be possible to believe her. I even think that maybe she's right.

"Thanks, Ms. Voss," I say, suddenly feeling like it would be stupid not to listen to what she's telling me. What reason does she have to lie? It's not like my success in life gets her a bonus or anything. She gets paid the same whether I go to Harvard or fall into the Grand Canyon over spring break. "I'll think about my college apps."

But unfortunately, my sense of accomplishment doesn't even last the afternoon.

TEO

I thought Bel was going to run a schematic in the software. It was what I *told* her to do, but instead she pulls a hydraulic pump out of her backpack, attaches it to a compression valve, and essentially builds a portion of a task robot right in front of us.

"So, yeah," she says, directing the air from the compression valve to release the piston rod. "And then it would, you know. Flip."

For someone who's just built something legitimately complex, she can barely summon the enthusiasm to form full sentences.

"You're talking about using a sensor to operate...a pneumatic arm?" I ask.

She blinks at me.

"Yes," she says, unconvincingly.

"As in it works with air under pressure," I clarify, because it seems like maybe she doesn't know what *pneumatic* means.

"Yeah." This time she's much more emphatic, so she definitely didn't know what it meant until I told her.

"Oh. Well. Okay." I feel like I should be having a much better reaction to this, seeing as she figured out the complexity of something I've been trying to design myself. This clearly saves me a lot of time and effort. "Thanks."

At this point I'm 100 percent sure Bel is much smarter than she pretends not to be. Or, I don't know—it's not like she's *acting*, but there's definitely some mechanism catching incorrectly in terms of her participation on this team. I saw her going over some of the projectile motion stuff from class with Jamie and Lora, so clearly she understands the concepts well. She can draw them out; I've seen her sketches. So what's the problem?

Before I can come to any sort of conclusion, Neelam cuts in.

"So are you just showing off?"

"What?" Bel turns, giving Neelam a wounded deer sort of look.

"Teo said we were voting on the design. You just...built it?" Neelam asks. "Without consulting anyone on the team?"

"Well, I thought it would be easier t—"

"Easier for who? For you?"

This is very typical Neelam behavior, FYI. She's probably thinking the same thing I am, but *unlike* me she goes straight for the jugular, which isn't exactly How to Win Friends and Influence People 101.

The rest of us are used to it. Bel, for obvious reasons, isn't.

"What's the point of designing a schematic if I can just build it myself?" Bel snaps, and two of the sophomores on the team exchange a loaded glance. "I don't see you coming up with any ideas."

Neelam's eyes narrow. "I have plenty of ideas. You never asked."

"At what point was I supposed to *ask*? Teo's drawing wasn't going to work, so I just—"

"Hey, hey, ladies, let's take a step back and calm down," says Mac, interrupting from across the room. He's typically working at his desk while we have our robotics meetings, but the conflict between Bel and Neelam seems to have drawn him out of his usual solitude.

"We're not *not calm*," says Bel. "Emmett and Kai argue all the time. So do Dash and Teo. We're just talking."

"Okay, well, let's just try to get along, okay?" says Mac. "Talk this out like adults."

Mac's eyes slide to mine and he gives me an expression like, *Women, am I right?*

I suddenly really hate that I'm the one he chose to situate at the other end of this glance.

"Bel," I say quickly. "It's really cool. And I like the motion sensor idea. But since it's not completely finished, you can still design a full schematic, right? We can vote on it next week. That way Neelam can submit one, too," I say, turning to her.

"Great idea, Teo, thank you," says Mac, but both Bel and Neelam give me a look like they wish I'd get swallowed up by the floor, so I don't think I did this right.

After practice I end up jogging after Bel, who's practically racing to her car.

"Hey," I call after her, but she ignores me. "Hey, Bel, come on, I ran like a thousand suicide sprints today—"

"*What?*" she bursts out when she rounds on me, which startles us both.

"Sorry, I just—"

"Sorry," she says immediately, and glances down. She's wearing a pair of Doc Martens that look like disco balls and knee-high socks with cartoon pugs on them, and suddenly I can't think about anything other than the pugs.

"Cool socks," I say.

"Yeah, well." She tugs at her hair. "They're stupid and I love them."

"Yeah they are." I kind of can't fight a laugh, and she looks up with a roll of her eyes.

"Can I help you with something?"

"I just...I get the feeling—" I stop. "Don't get mad."

She arches a brow. "No promises."

"Yeah, okay, well...I don't think you know how to use the software," I say flatly. "I'm guessing that's why you didn't do it for tryouts and why you didn't do it again for the hydraulic schematics." She opens her mouth to argue, but I quickly say, "I'm not judging you, I get it. It's tedious and it takes practice. But I can help you, if you want."

"Why?"

I should probably be relieved that she's actually speaking coherently, but from the time I've spent watching her (that sounds bad, but...you know what, forget it), I've noticed she only has two modes: super aggressive or super passive. "Because I want this team to work," I say. "Because I want us to win."

"And you think I'm hurting the team?"

"No, I just—"

"You don't like my attitude? I'm not a team player? So just cut me loose, then." Her mouth tightens.

"No, Bel, listen to me—"

"If I'm not good enough for your precious little robotics team—"

"Bel, just stop for a *second*," I growl, but by then the rest of the team has started filtering out to the parking lot behind us. She and I can both feel their eyes on us, so Bel unlocks her car with a grimace, pulling open the passenger door.

"Get in," she says.

"What? I have a car, it's over th—"

"Get in," she repeats. "The car's a safe space."

"Bel, if this is, like, an abduction—"

"It's a safe space," she says firmly. "No judgment."

Okay, whatever. "Fine."

I slide into the passenger seat and she walks around to the driver's side, yanking open the door and sitting down. She drives an old Subaru, which is kind of cute. It's an outdoorsy car, but I really can't imagine those glitter Doc Martens working well in the wilderness.

"Talk," she says.

I get the feeling that she won't interrupt me now that we're in the car, but I also sense she doesn't want to hear anything that sounds like something Mac or Neelam have already said to her. She puts her hands on the steering wheel and I face straight ahead too, like we're just driving somewhere.

"Sometimes it's really hard," I tell her, deciding to just be honest, which I almost never am. Not that I'm a liar; it's just that usually people don't want to hear this sort of thing from me.

But she said no judgment, so I decide to believe her.

"School's a lot," I exhale. "Soccer's a lot. Trying to make time for volunteering and a social life and having a job and still getting good grades...it's a lot. Trying all the time—trying not to screw up—just makes me feel so tired. There's all this pressure to plan for a future, you know? And like, *what* future?" I say, suddenly agitated. "The earth's basically falling apart. Politics are stupid. Plus, I don't know, racism? I feel like I'm so conscious of what I have to live up to, but also, what happens if I disappoint everyone? Like, I get it, I come from money and that makes me lucky, but it also makes me feel really guilty. And yeah, I'm a guy and there's all this feminism and stuff and it's just like..."

Okay, I'm rambling. She doesn't say anything.

"I like to build robots," I manage to say, which is the point I was actually trying to make. "It makes me happy. It matters to me. The only time I really like who I am is when I'm trying to make something work."

Silence.

"I really do think you're smart and creative, Bel. But I also think you don't know as much as other people on the team. Which isn't your fault," I add quickly, "but it's a *team*, so of course I'm going to check in with you. It doesn't have to mean I don't think you're good enough. It just means I want you to be good at this, because you're on my team. Because we're teammates."

For a long time I stare at my hands, wondering if I made any sense. But when I sneak a glance at Bel, she's already looking at me, the light from the parking lot spilling over half her face and illuminating the way her hair falls over her shoulder.

"That was a super weird rant," she comments blandly. "Did you say you feel stressed because of racism?"

"I mean, yeah, aren't you?" I say. "And I think climate change is actually really damaging to our generation's collective psyche."

She raises a hand to her mouth and for a second I think she's crying, but then I realize she's laughing.

"Oh my *god*," she says. "Oh my god. Oh. My. Godddd."

"Okay, stop," I grumble. "It's not funny—"

"Ohhhhh myyyyy goddddd—"

"Look, I saw you helping Jamie today," I tell her, twisting around in the front seat to face her.

"You did?" She seems suspicious, which is absurd. It's not like I was stalking her in the middle of the *quad*, where people typically *eat lunch*. If I happened to notice her explaining how projectiles work, it's fully coincidental.

"Yes, I did," I confirm, "and you're really good at this, Bel. You're in the right place, trust me. You're more than good enough. You just have to figure a few more things out, and then we can really do something great. I promise."

Bel twists her hair around her finger and looks away from me for a second.

"Can you just…not tell Neelam?" she says, wincing, and my suspicions are instantly confirmed: I'm not the only one making her doubt herself, though I guess I haven't been very sympathetic up until now. "I'm not, like, afraid of her or anything," Bel adds hastily, probably catching the look on my face. "I'd just really rather not let anyone know I need help. Okay?" She gives me a sincere, imploring look.

"Hey, I get it," I assure her. "Neelam's not my biggest fan, either. I wouldn't trust her with my weaknesses. She'd go full Ides of March on me."

"You think she'd stab you on the floor of the Roman Senate?"

If anyone could, it's Neelam. Which is basically a compliment, by the way. "I think it's definitely best I don't find out."

Bel sighs out the remainder of a laugh and shakes her head.

"I tried," she finally confesses, looking guilty. "I tried to do it with the software, but I'm just…I don't get it."

"It's not very intuitive," I admit. "Even my dad says the user experience leaves something to be desired."

"I just feel really lost," Bel says wistfully.

"Well, you aren't," I tell her. "You have the ideas. Clearly you know how to put them into practice. You just have to put another tool in your toolbox."

"And are you a tool?" she asks me, arching a brow.

"I'm *the* tool," I correct her.

She cracks a smile, and for a second I feel like there's some atmospheric shift happening between us. Just a small tremor, like a 3.0. I get a wild idea in my head about how this car smells like girl and Bel probably smells like that, too, and if I leaned forward just a little bit, just a couple of inches, then maybe I could find out.

But then Dash knocks on the window and the aftershocks settle, both of us jumping upright.

"Hey," he says, yelling at me through the car window. "Can I get a ride?"

"Sorry, he's a child," I tell Bel, opening the door for Dash to immediately poke his head inside.

"Hiya," he says to Bel.

"Hi," she says.

There's a long, awkward pause.

"Okay, bye," I cut in, shoving Dash's head out of the car and climbing out. "So, um—?"

"Gimme your phone," Bel says, remembering our agreement and reaching across the seat. "You can text me when you get home."

"Oh yeah, okay, great." She types her number in and hands it back to me. "See you."

"Bye." She gives Dash a little flutter of her fingers and starts the car, pulling away.

"So what was that?" asks Dash. "Was it, like...? You know."

He makes a moony, romantic face at me and I shove him away, groaning.

"I just offered to help her with something, that's all."

"That's all?"

"That's *all*."

"You're sure?"

"I'm sure."

"You're *sure*?"

"Dash, am I a ghost? You know I can't get involved with her," I remind him, climbing into the driver's seat of my BMW hybrid. "We're working together."

"So?"

"So, what if things went wrong? It'd be a super long year."

"But you like her?"

"Dash, what did I just say?" I roll my eyes and hit the push start. "We're barely even friends. At best we're, like, colleagues."

"Okay," he says cheerfully. "Just checking." He buckles himself in and arranges all my air-conditioning vents, angling them at himself. (Needless to say, Dash runs hot.)

"Where's your car?" I ask him.

"My sister drove it home from school."

"Are you unaware that your house is in the opposite direction from mine? You could have gone home with Kai. Or Emmett."

"Yeah, I know," Dash says with a laugh. "But I guess I just love inconveniencing you."

Vampire Weekend starts playing automatically and I toss him my phone, the screen with Bel's phone number still pulled up. Wherever she moved here from, it wasn't far. She has the same area code as the rest of us.

"Put on something good," I tell Dash. "*Not* Pitbull."

So of course Dash puts on Pitbull, leaving me to pull out of the parking lot with a groan.

seven

EXPERIMENTS

TEO

For someone who supposedly has so much going on, you're, like, eternally available," says Bel, setting down her bag and pulling up a chair next to the laptop I'm using to run the CAD program. "Aren't you on the soccer team?"

"Are you hacking my private calendar or something?"

She slides a dubious glance in my direction. "Did you think it was some kind of huge secret? Because there's a bag with a soccer ball right there. Basic deduction suggests it's yours."

"Advanced deduction," I correct her. "AP Deduction. Don't sell yourself short."

She rolls her eyes. "Are you going to answer the question?"

No, of course not, because I actually *am* very busy and being here means I basically had to sprint out of the locker room after practice, plus I'll probably have to stay up late to finish my paper for AP Lit. But I'm definitely not going to tell her that.

"Would you prefer it if I didn't help you? Because no offense, but you're not exactly a CAD wizard."

She doesn't look offended. Honestly, she barely looks fazed. "I won the vote on component designs last week, didn't I? Even Neelam didn't have anything to say about it."

"Only because I basically did that schematic for you."

"Yeah, well, that's called 'productive delegation,' as Jamie would say. Micromanagement isn't my style." She slides one leg over the other, peering over my shoulder at the bot I left pulled up on the screen. "What's this?"

"Just something I was thinking about for a fifteen-pound bot." It's nothing; just the last thing I was working on the last time I signed in.

"I thought we agreed on our final design already?"

"Oh, it's not for Regionals or anything. Just a thing I was playing with." I move to click out of the window but she pauses me, resting a hand on my arm.

"Wait. Show me."

I clear my throat, trying not to glance at where she set her hand. "Yeah, okay."

I click a corner of the bot and drag it around for her to view it from different angles. "I took your motion sensor idea and used it for a flipper, but I carved out the center of the bot so that less of the flipper extends out." I point to the claw-like structure. "It does the same thing yours was designed to do, but instead of being an extension of the bot that sits at the base, it pops up from where it's attached at the top." I hit play on the simulation and she hums to herself in acknowledgment.

"It's like a toaster," she says.

"Yeah, kinda, I guess."

"That would require a higher PSI than I accounted for, I think."

"Yeah, but that's doable. With this shape the design is lighter."

"Would you use aluminum?"

We go back and forth for a bit on the design before I remember that we're supposed to be talking about the software.

"Get up, we're switching. You run it."

"Ugh," she groans, but swaps seats with me, the smell of her rose shampoo briefly wafting in front of my face. "Should I start a new project?"

"Yeah, sure. Let's do...a submarine."

"A submarine, seriously?"

"Why not?"

She rests her chin on her hand and glares at me. "You're just torturing me, aren't you?"

"Yes. Definitely."

Just like I'm not going to tell her that I should really be writing an essay right now, I'm *also* not going to bring up how the most interesting thing that happens to me from day to day is my personal game of guessing her outfit. (I never get it. I mean really, my imagination is not this rich.) While she signs into her account, I take stock of a pair of jeans with birds on them, dirty white Vans, and a vintage-looking T-shirt that says YOSEMITE on it. I, meanwhile, am wearing a plain Henley with black jeans, which suddenly makes me feel very conventional.

"You've worn those before," I recall out loud.

"Hm?" She's busy opening a new window in the program.

"Those jeans. You've worn them before, to that party at my house." I remember thinking it was a relatively normal look for her until she turned and I spotted the birds, which were a surprise.

Actually, her entire presence there was a surprise. I had expected to find the whole night kind of boring, which it eventually was.

"Oh, yeah," she says absently. "The day I challenged your masculinity, you mean?"

"I wouldn't say *challenged*."

She grins over her shoulder at me. "I would."

"Okay, I feel like you think the worst of me," I remark with a groan.

"Who says I think anything of you?"

"Ouch, Bel-as-in-bel-canto." I pause. "What does that even mean, anyway?"

"What, bel canto?"

"Yeah."

"It's an opera thing," she says. "It means 'beautiful song,' though there's no real metric for how to use it. It's not specific like an aria or an overture."

"Oh." I already looked it up the first time she said it, but I still have no idea what she's talking about. Mentally, I add *aria* and *overture* to my list of things to understand at some unknown future time. "Are you into opera or something?"

"Sometimes," she says with a shrug. "I don't really like to close the door on anything. There's something interesting about most things, I think."

"Even robots?"

She smiles faintly at the computer screen. "Even robots."

I'd be lying if I said I didn't enjoy these secret software tutorials. Luckily they're secret, so nobody asks. It's just that Bel keeps surprising me, either because she learns things really quickly or because she asks interesting questions that make me think. Maybe it's just because she's new and therefore automatically more interesting, but lately, even hanging out with my friends is stressful. They always want to know what I'm doing for robotics or if I can help them with college apps or if I've thought about how we're going to beat our rivals or when I'm having a party again.

With Bel, I never really know what she's going to say next.

"Wouldn't it be weird if all software was just, like, a genie cursed to a new form?" Bel says suddenly. "I mean, you tell me this is all code, but I don't know if I believe you. It feels distinctly genie-esque."

"Nope." I fight a smile. "Just a whole bunch of binary, zeroes and ones."

"Yeah...sorry, but a genie makes way more sense to me than this just being a random assortment of numbers." She shakes her head. "I'm not buying it."

"Sounds like one of Dash's conspiracy theories." Dash almost exclusively wants to talk about weird stuff like that, or whether I think there are aliens (definitely yes, at least microorganisms). That, or food. "But even if you're right, they obviously changed the rules. We get way more than three wishes."

"Yeah we do. Poor genie." Bel rubs the side of the computer sympathetically. "I'd set us both free if I could," she sighs to it, giving me a look like I'm the one who cursed them into this.

"Oh, come on. Better to learn it now," I remind her. "You'll need it in college, and I doubt you'll have such a talented benefactor when you're in some freshman engineering program."

"Mm. I guess."

It's a fairly half-hearted answer, which makes me suspicious. Before I can push her on it, though, she's asking about something else.

"How do I add thrusters again?"

"That was a good call today on the vertical spinner," I tell Bel the next time we see each other in the robotics lab, which isn't until the following Tuesday.

I thought I'd be able to get out of going with my mom to Palm Springs for the weekend, but evidently she felt I was stressed and needed some kind of aura cleansing while my dad was in Chicago for a tech conference. Mostly I stayed in the hotel and did homework while my mom got a hot stone massage, but it wasn't terrible. I always prefer spending time with her if I have to go somewhere with one of my parents. She doesn't introduce me to her colleagues as "my son Teo, very bright, though I'm sure you must hear that all the time" or "I've told you about my son Teo, haven't I? Very promising with the right direction," nor does she make me sit through long conversations about VC funding.

"Well, *some* of us have to work," Bel jokes, or at least I hope she's joking. I know she watched my Instagram story where I checked into the Parker, which I suddenly wish she hadn't seen. "How was your weekend, by the way?"

"Enlightening. According to a tarot card reader, my future looks good."

"Promising?"

"Oh, very promising. With the right direction."

She rolls her eyes, but this time I can tell it's not at me. "Sometimes I think I'd rather be forty and wondering where my life went instead of seventeen and relentlessly hounded about my future," she says. "I can't wait for my life of quiet desperation so I can finally meditate on all the ways I wasted my precious youth."

"I think you might already be forty and desperate?" I joke.

"Well, you would know," she says perfunctorily, which makes me stop for a second.

"What?"

"Hm? I didn't mean to insult you. I just meant you're, like, very serious."

"What? How?"

She looks up. "Well, you're definitely, like…a very serious dude," she says, which isn't any clearer.

"What? No I'm not." I'm distinctly aware this is the third time I've said *what*, which makes me suddenly irritated.

"Okay, sure," she says, sounding bored with me, which only makes it worse.

"Because I don't own any eccentric bird jeans, you mean?" Today she's wearing a sundress that's kind of an ugly color, like rust or copper. It's certainly nothing I would choose, though it looks sort of nice on her. Like a sunset.

"First of all, those jeans are not *eccentric*," she corrects me, "they're zesty. Second of all, no, that's not what I meant, but I can see you're in a weird mood, so let's just work."

She pulls up a new project and says, "Should I do a task robot? Akim asked me to do a torque reaction and I *sort of* get it, but also I don't—"

"Do you think I'm like...human cargo pants or something?" I ask her.

She frowns at me. "What?"

Okay good, so at least the tables have turned. Or are turning. Whatever.

"You're acting like you're more interesting than I am or something," I say. "Or, like, I'm boring. Or I don't know." I do know. I know exactly.

It's a matter of bird jeans and pride.

"Okay, fine, let's do this." She turns to face me and her hair, which is in a messy braid, falls over her shoulder. "I think you're very intense," she says without any particular inflection. "When you're alone with me you seem fine, and Dash always says you're the funniest person he knows—"

"Dash says this *always*? Since when?"

"—but you just, like, steamroll people," Bel continues. "Like today with Lora."

I think back to what she could possibly be talking about. "You mean when I talked to her about the website?"

"Oh, did you talk *to* her? Because from my perspective you talked *at* her," Bel says, slightly obnoxiously. "You know she spent a whole week on that new interface, right?"

"I was just telling her that if we want to maximize profits from the fundraiser, then the contact page needed to be more prominent—"

"You know, everyone's willing to make excuses for you," Bel says, cutting me off. "Lora said the same thing when I pointed it out to her, that you 'just' want things to be this or that. But you get that this is high school robotics and not NASA, right?" She stares at me for a full, uninterrupted pause before saying, "I feel like someone should tell you that."

"Okay." Whereas I feel a little bit like she just punched me. "Fine. I'm sorry. I was trying to make the team better, but if you think it's hurting morale, I'll fix it."

"You don't have to—" She exhales deeply, like I'm exhausting her, so I turn toward the screen, suddenly wishing I'd just gone home straight after practice.

"No, it's fine. Akim's only talking about torque reactions because he still wants an axe on the—"

"Teo, can you listen to me?" Bel folds her arms over her chest. "I'm not done."

"Sorry, did I steamroll you?" I ask bitterly, and it's meant to be a joke, but I think it's obvious to both of us that it isn't one.

"Teo, you don't need to *fix* anything. I'm not asking you to change. I'm explaining that I think you're a very serious person because you take everything very seriously."

"So I should take nothing seriously instead?"

"No. Forget it." She turns away.

I know I should let it go, but I can't. "Since when do you and Dash talk about me?" bubbles out of my mouth.

"We have Stats together. It just came up."

"How?"

"What is this, the Spanish Inquisition?"

I bristle. "Am I trying to purify Spain, no. Am I asking a question, yes."

"Okay, so are we going to fight, then?" Bel says, turning to me. "Is that what you want? Okay, let's fight."

"I—" I stop. "What the hell does that mean?"

"It means that obviously I upset you and now you have all this weird energy that you need to get out, so let's fight. We can do it like this, or we can do it like that," she says, pointing to the computer. "Pick your poison."

"We're not fighting."

"Fine, I'll choose. You design a fifteen-pound bot over there," she says, pointing to the spare laptop, "and I'll do one here. Then you can upload yours and we'll run a simulation. K?"

"You don't know how to do that yet."

"Well, no time like the present, right?" She shifts her chair, angling it away from me so she can face the computer. "Go," she says, which sounds a lot like *Go away*, which makes me even angrier.

"Fine." I reach over and pick up the laptop.

Since Akim and axes are on the mind, I design something that's basically a reverse guillotine: a long-arm weapon that comes up over the back and slices down. The process of putting it together distracts me a bit, especially because at the last second I decide to change my specifications slightly and make the axe go in both directions. I have no idea what sort of thing Bel will design, obviously, because I never do. I never have any idea what she's thinking or how she comes up with ideas or what she really meant when she said I'm a "serious dude," and I don't know why she's talking to Dash or why Dash never said anything to me about them being in Stats together, and I don't know why her opinion of me is suddenly so important.

"Done?" she asks.

No, not really. I'm a tinkerer by nature. I could spend hours on this bot, changing and reworking things until it's perfect, which nothing ever is.

"Yeah, you're done," she says, walking over and snatching the laptop from my hands.

"Wait, Bel, it's not—"

She pauses, looking at the screen, and then looks back up at me.

"Wow, you are just..." Her mouth tightens. "You just suck *so much*."

My stomach lurches. "I told you it wasn't finished—"

"No, stop, I'm—I meant it's really good." She winces. "Sorry, my brother is...He always tells me I suck when what he means is 'that thing you did is really cool,' so apparently I'm the one with toxic masculinity. You're fine."

She turns away and uploads my design. By the time I bring myself to rise to my feet and join her again, she's already pulled it up next to hers.

Hers is a thwackbot, a bot that spins like a top, with a side weapon that gains momentum as the bot itself speeds up. Super effective, though difficult to control once in motion.

"You'd need really sophisticated electronics to make that work," I say dully.

"Yeah, but this is fake, isn't it? We're not actually building them."

She hits play on the simulated combat and mine lands a few good hits, preventing hers from spinning fast enough to damage mine.

"Nice," I say, relieved. "I win."

"You got lucky. Best of three," she says, and hits play again.

This time, hers slams into mine and practically shreds it open. "Again."

Mine wins again, and she frowns.

"Best of five," she suggests.

"Sore loser," I tell her.

"Yeah, I know," she agrees, and hits play.

After five, she's won.

"Seven," I say. "That last one was stupid."

"Sore loser," she says.

"Absolutely," I confirm, and reach over, running it again.

By the time we're up to thirteen her phone buzzes, and she turns it over with a groan.

"God." She types something hastily in reply, then shakes her head. "Can't believe I'm going to let you win."

I ignore the little dip of disappointment in my chest. "*Let* me win? You lost, fair and square—"

"Ugh, I did *not*—"

"Who was it?" I ask, gesturing to her phone.

"My mom. She's home earlier than I thought. She's an ER nurse," she explains.

"Oh, that's cool. And you have a brother?"

"Yeah, two of them, I'm the youngest. One of them's the absolute worst, and the other is…substantially worse, actually." She pauses absently, then looks at me. "I'd ask you about your siblings, but I know you don't have any."

"You always talk about me like you already know everything there is to know," I say, and it's only when the sentence leaves my mouth that I realize that *that* is why I'm so angry.

Because she's acting like she knows me, and I feel like that's not fair. I've been enjoying getting to know her, but apparently to her I'm nothing new. I'm just some guy that people talk about, and what other people say seems to be plenty of information for her. She sees Palm Springs on my Instagram and she sees my house and she watches me talk to Lora without knowing that Lora was practically my sister when we were kids and our moms are best friends and yeah, maybe things are different now, but I don't always soften the things I say with Lora because she knows me.

So to Bel Maier, I'm this entitled rich guy who plays soccer and has no siblings and she and my best friend talk behind my back about how I'm too *serious*.

Which is when I realize that I'm not angry. I'm hurt.

"Yeah, I'm...just noticing that I guess I've been sort of a dick, too," Bel says.

She picks up her backpack slowly, kind of mechanically.

"Thanks for today," she says, and she's chewing her lip. "I really do appreciate it."

"It's fine. It's not a problem."

"I just...I have to get home or my mom will, like, ground me forever, so—"

"I get it. See you in class."

She nods and turns away. After she's gone, I'm not quite ready to go home yet, so I hit play one more time on the simulation.

"Wait, Teo—"

I turn over my shoulder to see her standing in the doorway of the Physics classroom, cheeks flushed bright like she ran.

"I forgot to tell you that serious isn't a bad thing," she says, a little breathless. "Not a lot of people take things seriously. And it's especially not bad with you, because you take people seriously. You take *me* seriously. I'm not a joke to you and that's...that's cool. It's really cool and I appreciate it, I do. And you take Lora seriously and the website does work better now because of it. And you take your work seriously and that's way better than someone who just doesn't care, so..."

She trails off.

"What's the score now?" she asks, pointing to the screen, and I look at the outcome of our last round of simulated combat.

"We're tied," I say, because it's been an even number of simulations. "Should I hit play again?"

"No, let's leave it. Yeah, just leave it. We can do it again some other time." She gives me one of her bizarre half salutes. "On the morrow, then."

She's honestly so weird. "On the morrow," I echo with a roll of my eyes.

But when she's gone, I suddenly feel like a weight's been lifted. Like maybe she does know me a little bit, or at least she's willing to try and see.

Bel

You said you were going to be home twenty minutes ago, Isabel," says my mother when I arrive home, though before I can respond to that, she's already moved on. "I made your favorite," she calls over her shoulder, disappearing into the kitchen, where I can smell the tamarind for the sinigang, a sour soup. This is not actually my favorite food; lasagna is, but because my mother always says, quote, "anyone can make that," I never actually get to have it. (Don't get me wrong—sinigang is definitely good. I enjoy the tartness, which I like to think contributes to the sophistication of my palette in some way. But yeah, lasagna.)

I still haven't quite adjusted to the fact that coming home feels different now, or that all the reflexes I've developed since we moved here have been rendered totally pointless. I don't need muscle memory anymore to keep me from tripping over Luke's shoes where he kicked them off by the door. I used to just slip unnoticeably into the preexisting static when I came home, but now I feel like I'm constantly disrupting something. Like I should enter the apartment on tiptoe, just in case the atmosphere shatters when I arrive.

Which sounds bad. And truthfully, it's not ideal? I'm used to Luke being the one getting yelled at or Gabe having most of everyone's attention, so me being the only kid here is like falling into some bizarro rabbit hole where I'm the favorite but also the biggest problem.

"How was your day?" my mom yells from the kitchen. She's wearing her DARTMOUTH MOM sweatshirt again, which I swear she never takes off. She also drinks from a Dartmouth water bottle and has a Dartmouth key chain, plus a Dartmouth sticker on her car. (The CSU Fullerton one below it is peeling slightly.)

"It was good," I call back, glancing down when my phone buzzes.

Jamie: hellloooooooo do you have those notes
Bel: sorry sorry yes i just got home, hang on

"Good, that's it?" my mom asks.
"What?" I shout back.

Jamie: wait, just now??
Jamie: one of these days you're going to have to tell me why you're always at school so late

Jamie: you're not failing are you?????
Jamie: omg if you are i'm going to feel like the WORST transfer buddy ever
Bel: . . . do you still think of yourself as just my transfer buddy
Bel: because I feel like we have progressed in some ways
Bel: one or two
Jamie: let's not get hung up on the technicalities
Jamie: is everything okay??

I pause for a second, because given everything I've just said about my home life, you'd think my answer would be no. Weirdly, though, it isn't.

I start typing back to Jamie, but then my mom interrupts again.

"Bel, are you coming?"

"Be right there!" I call, walking blindly into my room to drop off my school bag. "Just have to send something to Jamie."

"Don't let the food get cold, Isabel!"

If Luke were here, this would not be an issue; instead it'd be more like "Lucas, I asked you to put your things away" or "Lucas, you come here while I'm talking to you," which is background noise I'm really starting to miss.

I shake the thought away, sitting down to email Jamie my notes.

"I know, Mom, one second!" I say, and then hesitate.

Bel: want to know the truth?
Jamie: no i'm comfortable with lies
Jamie: OBVIOUSLY THAT'S A JOKE TELL ME IMMEDIATELY

Okay, it's ridiculous, I know, but . . . I *do* kind of want to tell someone what I've been up to after school. I can feel it bubbling up, always the next closest thing to the surface, perpetually on the tip of my tongue. Getting it out of my system feels important, if only so that I don't accidentally blurt it out in some random and horrifying way.

Bel: ok but it's not a big deal
Jamie: I WILL BE THE JUDGE OF THAT
Bel: ok well
Bel: teo's been helping me after school with some of the robotics software

I wait for her response, chewing my lip and wondering if I've messed up. If anyone is going to make way too big deal of this, it's Jamie, who already thinks Teo's interest in me is somehow intriguing. Which it isn't.

(I'm pretty sure it's not.)

Jamie: like . . . alone? or are you in some kind of software for dummies course that he's teaching for volunteer credits
Bel: ok first of all, thank you for that vote of confidence
Jamie: i'm JUST CHECKING
Jamie: and tbh I would totally sign up if he were
Bel: of course you would
Bel: but secondly no, it's just us

She starts typing immediately, so I wait.

I mean, okay, before she gets into it, let's just pause to look at this logically. Exhibit A: Jamie, unlike me, is fully under Teo's bizarre spell, so her instincts are obviously suspect. I am a realist, and therefore I cannot be swayed by stupid hair or extremely intense eye contact.

(I think.)

(I hope.)

Exhibit B: Jamie, unlike me, has been convinced that there's something between Teo and me ever since he pulled me aside at his party—which, as everyone knows, ended with him bailing almost immediately, so if she thinks something's there, she's *objectively* wrong.

Given all of this, it's clearly very stupid for me to mention it to her, and I have no doubt I will regret it forthwith. But what could I possibly say to someone else? I mean…Teo Luna? AP Physics? Robotics?? It's like my old friends and I don't even speak the same language anymore, so—

Jamie: **OMG**

I exhale, relieved she's so predictable.

Jamie: **OMGOMGOMG**
Bel: **jamie**
Bel: **this is way too much**
Jamie: **OOOOOOMMMMMGGGGGG**

I'm smiling. (Don't tell anyone.)

Jamie: **OMG THIS IS EXACTLY HOW PEOPLE FALL IN LOVE**
Bel: **uhhhh stop**
Bel: **we're friends**
Jamie: **FRIENDS WHO SPEND SECRET HOURS CLOISTERED IN THE ROBOTICS LAB**
Bel: **you watch too many hallmark movies**
Bel: **tell your mom she needs to stop enabling you and intervene**
Jamie: **SECRET!! ROBOTICS!! TUTORING!!**
Jamie: **this is a CLASSIC trope**
Bel: **this is not a classic trope**
Bel: **nobody has ever, in the history of time, fallen in love in a robotics lab**
Bel: **the lighting is horrible**
Bel: **robots are not sexy**
Bel: **and it's really not like that**
Jamie: **not YET but INEVITABLY**
Bel: **no**
Bel: **stop**

Jamie: omg i hate you so much and also i ship it so hard
Bel: he literally hated me, like, last month
Jamie: even better!!
Jamie: enemies to lovers
Jamie: the perfect ship
Bel: we're just friends
Bel: less than that
Bel: we're academic colleagues
Jamie: enemies to academic colleagues to lovers
Bel: stop saying that
Jamie: i mean i would die of jealousy but also
Jamie: of joy
Jamie: CAN YOU IMAGINE DATING TEO LUNA

I definitely can't. And actually it's best if I don't, because then I'll start to let myself get distracted.

Because I know I said he has stupid hair. I know I said he dresses like a rich kid and does stuff like stay in nice hotels over the weekend while I sit around and binge Netflix while eating rice pudding out of a cup. I know that for all intents and purposes this would never happen, because we're really different and he's not my type and he'd probably be a huge headache to actually go out with.

But I swear there must be something in the water, because his hair looks so soft and when he's designing something he gets this kind of squinty, concentrate-y look on his face and he smells like clean laundry and summer and I hate it. I hate all of it.

Bel: it's really, really not like that

What I mean is: I really, really need to believe it's not like that.

Bel: today we spent like two hours fighting with robots
Jamie: so?? he loves robots

Jamie: everyone knows this

Bel: yeah exactly, he loves ROBOTS

Bel: i'm just there

Bel: a human girl

Bel: with almost no electrical parts

Jamie: AGAIN, FOR NOW

Jamie: wait sorry

Jamie: not about the parts thing

Bel: no you're right i can totally get a microchip any day now

Jamie: omg SHUT UP YOU'RE THE WORST

Jamie: you're too sensible and i hate it

Bel: well, at least that we can agree on

I swear her to secrecy because obviously the only thing worse than the rest of the team knowing I need help would be the rest of the team thinking that I, like literally all of the girls at our school and probably some of the boys, have a crush on Teo Luna.

My phone buzzes in my hand and I groan, thinking it's Jamie again, but it isn't. Well, it's Jamie, and also there's a random Sesame Street GIF from Dash, but there's something else, too.

Teo: just wanted to tell you that i won best of a thousand

Bel: stop

Teo: actually your bot just kind of . . . rolled over and quit? weird i know

Teo: something about the failures of your management style

Teo: sorry, you know how robots are

Teo: i don't make the rules

It's not a crush.

Bel: ummm i'm going to need witnesses

Bel: sworn statements

Bel: psychological evaluations

Bel: unaltered footage

Teo: what do you think this is, a true crime podcast

Bel: is my robot's pain and suffering a JOKE to you??

Teo: uh oh she's lawyering up

Bel: ladies and gentlemen of the jury, what you will see here is a man consumed by his own tyrannical aims

Bel: innocent robots strewn in his path

Bel: his intelligence may be artificial but his thirst for power is real

Teo: objection

Bel: to what?

Teo: the scope

Bel: of...?

Teo: this questioning

Jamie's name pops up again.

Jamie: you know i'm kidding right

Jamie: i actually think it's really cool if you and teo are friends

Jamie: and anyway we can talk about something else

Bel: like your sister's dj career?

Jamie: omg do not

Jamie: are things going better with your family??

"Bel," my mom shouts at that exact moment, "are you coming or what?"

Oops.

My realities collide for a moment: the one where I stayed after school with Teo bumps right into the one where I've accidentally sat here for ten minutes avoiding my next meal, and for a second, I have to think about what I'm going to say to Jamie.

The truth is that lately, I find I have to brace myself for sitting down to dinner with my mom. Not because I don't like spending time with my mom, but because so many conversation topics are off-limits.

Dad? That's a no. I can't bring myself to answer his messages.

Luke? Definite no. My mom gets teary if she even comes across a sock he forgot.

Gabe? My mom can talk about him all night, but I definitely can't.

School? Things are fine, but that conversation always leads to questions about my college apps, which I still haven't finished.

So mostly that leaves us with the weather.

I reply to Jamie—**yeah, everything's fine, brb dinner!**—and then I glance at Teo's last message, slipping seamlessly into my other world.

Teo: you're dangerous, bel canto

I know he calls me that to tease me about the way I corrected Mac on my first day in AP Physics, but now that I know he knows what it means and still calls me that anyway, it doesn't bother me. It doesn't bother me at all.

(Not a crush, not a crush, not a crush.)

eight

FRIENDS

TEO

Hey," I say, glancing over Bel's shoulder while she works on the circuit board for our 120-pound bot, which we're currently calling Puccini. Bel always deadpans things like "Puccini is currently in utero," as if we're literally giving birth to him. This, like many things she says, is totally ridiculous. "How's he doing?"

"Baby boy is healthy and developing well," says Bel. I elbow her in feigned annoyance and she nudges me back, which might be an enjoyable moment until Neelam interrupts.

"Are you two done?" she says tightly.

"Were you waiting for something?" asks Bel.

"Yeah, some peace and quiet," Neelam mutters.

Bel and I exchange a look.

"I need a break anyway," Bel says, setting down the pliers. "Want to show me what you and Dash are doing with the task robots?"

I beckon her over to the corner where Dash is currently popping balloons. "Sure."

Neelam glares at both of us as we slip away, and Bel releases a heavy sigh like she's been holding her breath for the last half hour.

"She *hates* me," she mutters.

"She hates everyone."

"Yeah, but like, *especially* me."

Neelam does seem to be particularly annoyed around Bel, but admitting it feels like stepping into way more complicated territory. "Ignore her. She's just jealous."

"What could she possibly be jealous of?"

A lot of things. "I don't know. Your zesty footwear."

Today Bel's wearing pink rain boots. In her defense it *is* raining, but only in the way it ever rains in Los Angeles, aka not very hard.

"These," she says, "are practical. Practically Marxist."

"In terms of what, the equitable division of labor? Try again, Bel Canto."

"Ugh, I meant they're proletarian. Whatever." She makes a face at me. "Someone did well on that AP Gov exam, I take it."

"Always," I say. She elbows me sharply in the ribs and I give her a shove, lightly.

"What's going on over here?" she says, rain boots squeaking as she kneels down beside Dash. "These look like a bunch of dead balloons."

"Correct," Dash confirms, adding theatrically, "These men were slain in battle."

"A moment of peace for their immortal souls," Bel says, holding one hand over her chest.

"You guys are so weird," I mutter, and even though no work needs to be done here, I hop on top of the desk beside Dash's.

"Hey, do you guys want tickets to homecoming?" asks Lora, suddenly appearing with breathless enthusiasm behind me. "Jamie needed my help selling them," she adds in apology, because Lora is perfectly aware that the majority of the people in this room haven't even considered the prospect of attending a school dance, nor are most of them capable of human interaction.

"Is it really time for homecoming already?" asks Kai, overhearing from where he's just finished shaping an aluminum sheet. "I thought it was after the SATs."

"Mm, it is, the week after. Didn't you take yours last spring?" Lora asks him.

"Yeah, but I can do better on the writing portion," he says in a defensive, very Kai sort of way.

"I'm not sure any engineering programs are going to care what you got on the writing section of the SATs," I tell him.

Bel's not saying anything, which reminds me that she's always sort of cagey about college applications. I want to ask her what her deal is—maybe she didn't do well on the SATs or something?—but it never seems like the right time.

"And anyway," I say, quickly changing the subject before Kai can go into any further detail about his many exam-related neuroses, "this year is flying by."

"Good," says Dash firmly. "I'm desperate for Thanksgiving."

"We all need a break," Lora agrees, thinking Dash means he's excited to have a week away from school, like a normal person.

"Unfortunately, Dash means *actual* Thanksgiving," I remind her. "Despite being firmly anti-colonialism—"

"I'm Team Indigenous Peoples," Dash confirms to Bel, who smiles in a way I can only describe as helplessly fond. (Of Dash, that is, not Eurocentrism and/or imperialism.)

"—as are we all," I rush to add. "Obviously. But still—"

"Considering the alternative is Team Grand Theft Genocide, this is very reassuring," Bel agrees in the wry tone I sometimes get out of her, to which Dash opens his mouth, probably to make her smile again.

"—I'm pretty sure Dash finagles a way to come to every single one of our houses to eat the leftovers," I finish loudly, only realizing that I've directed this to Bel instead of Lora, the person who actually brought it up, after the error has already been committed. "Including mine," I add, straining for some semblance of chill, "which isn't even home-cooked."

"My parents don't do stuffing!" Dash insists. "It's offensive."

"Mine don't either," says Bel. "My mom says it's just bread."

"It's *bread* that's been baked *again*," Dash informs her, aghast. "It's essentially the perfect food."

"Okay, well, before we get into this again, is anyone going to buy tickets?" Lora says, waving them around. "It's for the student council budget, you know. If you guys want to have a nice prom—"

Everyone groans.

"Okay, let me rephrase: if you want to go to Disneyland for grad night—"

That, on the other hand, gets a much more enthusiastic response.

"It's not like I was ever getting out of going anyway," mutters Kai, gesturing to Lora. "I'll take one for me and Sarah—"

"Yeah, put me down for two as well," adds Dash, and I blink.

"Two?" I echo, because this is news to me. "Who are you going with?"

"Oh, I don't know. Whoever, I guess. I assumed we were all going. Do you want to go with me?" Dash asks Bel, who looks up from where she's been playing with one of the emaciated balloon skins.

For a second, my heart stops. I mean sure, it certainly doesn't sound like anything more than a friendly invitation—and honestly, it's *Dash*—but...

If she says yes, what exactly is she saying yes to?

"Oh," Bel says, and clears her throat. "When is it again?"

"The last weekend before Thanksgiving break," says Lora.

"Oh, cool," says Bel, and glances at Dash, who's giving her one of his easy Dash smiles. "So I mean sure, yeah. Yeah," she says, smiling back at him. "I'd like that."

Oh.

Okay.

"What about you, Teo?" Lora asks, turning to me.

I hadn't actually thought about it.

Not much, anyway.

Not *that* much.

"Sorry, Lora, I can't," I tell her. "I'm out of town that weekend. My dad has some kind of pitch fest in Salt Lake he wants me to go to."

"Oh, that's cool," says Lora energetically. "I heard they're calling Salt Lake City the 'Silicon Slopes' or something."

"Yeah, they are. I'll still buy a ticket, though," I tell her. "Donation or whatever."

"Awesome, thanks, Teo," she says happily. "Bel, Jamie and I thought maybe we could have a sleepover at my house after, if you want to join."

"Oh, that sounds fun," says Bel.

I notice that she hasn't looked at me yet.

"We can sneak you in if you want," Lora adds to Dash. "My parents super don't care."

"My mom would definitely kill me with her bare hands," says Dash. "But who knows, it might be worth it. I probably have it coming anyway."

Was I supposed to know he was going to ask her? He never mentioned it. Is this a big deal? Probably not. Am I overthinking it?

Yes, definitely.

(Also, I should stop asking myself pointless questions and do something useful.)

"Okay, well, I'm gonna get back to work on Puccini," I say, rising to my feet and making an exaggerated show of checking my watch. "Bel, do you mind if I finish the circuitry you were working on?"

"My baby robot is your baby robot," she says, but instead of being funny this time, it just feels kind of weird.

I sit down with the circuit board and start to dive in, thinking it'll relax me to put pieces together, but of course Neelam is there, which is the opposite of relaxing.

"So can we be done with this now?" she asks without looking up from the part she's been welding.

"Done with what?"

She glares at me.

"The last thing this team needs is some angsty teen romance," she says. "Get it together, Luna."

Then she puts the visor on her helmet back down and I suddenly realize that whatever Dash's intentions were, he did me a favor. Much as I hate to agree with Neelam, it's probably best if I just nip this thing with Bel in the bud before anything gets out of hand.

Bel

I've never been one for school dances, so in a lot of ways going with Dash is my ideal scenario. He asked me in front of everyone the same way he'd ask to eat Emmett's leftovers, so there's nothing for anyone to talk about. I know he's not going to expect me to get a full hair-and-face appointment like the girls at my old school used to do, and anyway, I'm pretty sure he's color-blind. He makes me laugh and I make him laugh and we have fun together, so it's really nothing.

Though part of me thinks it wouldn't be nothing if Teo had asked me.

Luckily it's a chance to hang out with Lora and Jamie, who've agreed we're all doing our hair and makeup together in what Jamie's calling a "pre-bacchanalian summit" between our coven of senior girls. Lora's going with Ravi, Jamie's going with a bunch of girls from mock trial, and I just told Dash to meet me here whenever he feels like it, which I assume he's going to do with a bucket of McNuggets in hand.

"I invited Neelam, too, but she already had plans," says Lora, who's experimenting on her wrist with a bunch of metallic eye shadows. "Do you think this color works with my dress?"

"Oh, I love that," I say, glancing over. I was worried she was going to do something basic like match her eyeshadow to her dress, but instead she picked a plum color that's going to look great against the green. "You have a really good palette, Lo."

Lora beams over at me, and Jamie, who's trying to remove one of those weird hanging strap things from her dress, finally finds a pair of scissors and returns to the conversation.

"So, what's going on with you and Teo?" Jamie asks me, which is exactly the question I was hoping to not have to answer. "I thought he would've asked you to homecoming."

Yeah. Me too.

"I keep telling you, James. We're just friends."

"I think he likes you," teases Lora.

"Well, obviously not," I say with a long-suffering sigh, "or why would Dash have asked me, hm? Riddle me that."

"Maybe it's like how Catherine the Great had her ladies-in-waiting test out her lovers in advance," says Jamie, and I make a face.

"First of all, I'm pretty sure that was about testing for diseases," I say.

Jamie shrugs. "She was a smart lady."

"And second of all, can we *please* not talk about this? Bechdel test," I remind Jamie, who groans.

"Adolescence is about sexual awakening," she says, which is quite a claim for someone who, quote, "isn't interested in dating until she's thirty or makes partner at her firm," whichever comes first. "Can't we be secure in our womanhood while *also* talking about the fact that you and Teo would look stupid cute together?"

"I think that's just the curse of heteronormativity," I say.

Lora, for whatever reason, giggles.

"Well, we can talk about school if you want, but I think my brain might melt," groans Jamie. "I mean, I already consulted my vision board this morning." She does it every morning; something about putting out into the universe what she hopes to get back. "How are the robots?" she asks me.

"We're in great shape for Regionals," I tell her, and Lora nods approvingly, being the person who wrote the script we used when we called to thank our donors for sending us to our first round of competition for the year. "We're just using updated versions of last year's bots, so I really had very little to do with it."

"Not true," Lora says firmly. "You fixed that weight distribution problem, and the new vertical spinner is—"

"Okay fine, I'm a genius," I say. "Neelam and I argued for thirty minutes yesterday over whether my only real design contribution is even necessary, but I am single-handedly responsible for all of our future success. Happy now?"

Lora holds her eye shadow–covered wrist up to my face.

"I think this color for you, and yes," she says smugly, "I am."

It's actually really nice to spend time around girls again, even if these ones happen to be foolishly and impractically supportive. Not that I couldn't call my old friends if I really wanted some gossip and a makeover, but there's something about the warmth of Jamie and Lora's idle chatter that makes me feel like this is different. Like maybe I've been lonely for longer than I thought.

"I'm glad you're here, Bel," says Jamie, startling me into catching her eye in the mirror. "Do you ever get the feeling like you know someone from a past life and you're sort of half recognizing them?"

"Aw, James, are you saying we're soul mates or something?"

"No," she says. "Actually, I was going to say it feels like I've never met you before."

"Oh." I make a face, and Lora bursts out laughing.

"No, no, it's a good thing," Jamie rushes to assure me. "Like...
you're new, you know? You're this new color I didn't know existed
and now I see it everywhere and I'm like, thank god I can see it now.
Such a bummer if I never did."

It strikes me as the nicest thing anyone's ever said to me, so
instead of answering, I pull Jamie in with one hand, tucking the
other around Lora.

"Thanks for letting me in," I tell them, looking at us in the
mirror. Jamie's hair is absolutely everywhere and Lora has splotches
of experimental color all over her arms and I've got a zit the Mars
Rover can probably see from space, but I think we look really pretty.

Just then, the doorbell rings.

"I really hope that's Dash with chicken nuggets," Lora says,
and it's great, right? That my date is so fun and easy that we're all
looking forward to seeing him, with or without makeup. I probably
wouldn't feel so relaxed if it were Teo at the door, but the knowledge
that it definitely isn't—that Teo's in Utah and I'm definitely not going
to see him at all tonight—feels slightly off-color.

Sometimes when Teo's around me I feel like there's this golden,
shining thing between us. Or like maybe *I'm* the shining thing, and
the rays of myself radiate further and wider and they stretch out so
far that, for once, I'm not contained to the shapes of my usual worries
and fears. For once, I get to feel vast and unstoppable and...bright.

But he's not here, so I shake myself of the realization, deciding
I should probably start doing my hair if I want to be done in time
for pictures.

It's not Dash at the door, which means we end up getting majorly
sidetracked by what I can only call a YouTube spiral. Jamie's brilliant, but I'm starting to doubt her ability to tell time. By the time
the others get here, my skin is still dewy with Urban Decay setting
spray. (Thank god for concealer—definitely not trying to leave evidence of that zit behind for future historians to ponder.)

Dash arrives wearing a very retro getup, suspenders and all. He even slicked his black hair to the side, like he's a swing dancer at a very swanky nightclub or an extra in *The Great Gatsby*.

"You look absolutely ravishing," I say, offering him a polite golf clap in appreciation, and he bows.

"My lady," he replies, giving me one of his especially goofy grins. "You look *divine*."

I'm wearing strappy sandals and a belted dress with a Grecian design, so to say I look vaguely like I'm cosplaying as Athena is a perfectly fair assessment. "Good sir, is that wordplay I hear?" I ask, fanning myself in a theatrical swoon.

"Indubitably," Dash confirms, offering me his arm. "Shall we?"

"So you guys are like the same person, huh?" notes Kai, who's here with his girlfriend Sarah, a junior.

"It's like looking in a mirror," Dash declares in a terrible British accent, and for the rest of the night nearly all of our dance moves involve us miming the other's motions, much to the dismay of everyone we know.

It probably won't surprise anyone that school dances are a sight to behold at Essex Academy. According to Jamie, the homecoming committee is made up of the daughter of a sorority board of directors, the daughter of an interior decorator to "the stars," and someone distantly related to a Coppola. I barely know what any of that means, but believe me, it shows: our big gymnasium's been completely transformed, from the string lighting overhead to the papier-mâché recreations of old lamp posts (you know, the ones everyone takes pictures with outside of LACMA) to the Avenue of the Stars posters that litter the walls, some more artfully than others. It's all very *La La Land*, which is a movie I once had to explain to my mother. ("The story was always about their *dreams*," I told her while she cried over lost love.)

The dance is much more fun than I expected, minus my rich internal fantasies. Every now and then I accidentally picture Teo popping up unexpectedly—Teo rounding a corner I'm about to turn, Teo magically materializing somewhere in the center of the dance floor, Teo jogging over to tell me that his flight was canceled, should we work on Puccini instead?—but it's easy to brush away, and anyway, it's...fun. Did I say that already?

Whatever. The point is I'm having a good time.

Eventually I get very winded from trying to keep up with Dash's running man, so when Jamie yells something about needing to go to the bathroom, I'm quick to offer my services as a necessary female companion. She loops her sweaty arm through mine and, as to be expected, there's a line—though it's difficult to tell who's in it, because half the girls are just there to fix their makeup or talk about their breakups.

"He's a dick," says Jamie to a freshman girl who's sobbing over a boy. "And a woman needs a man like a fish needs a bicycle."

"And you look really pretty," I add, because even if Jamie's too intellectual to make this about serving looks, it's still important to build each other up. Intersectional feminism and all that, which makes me think of Teo again, which I immediately shove away. "And the best revenge is living your best life, right?"

The girl nods tearfully, agreeing to return to the dance with her friends, and Jamie and I exchange a benevolent glance (we, the older and wiser, have clearly done good work) until it's Jamie's turn to use a stall.

She slips inside it and I spot something from outside. Another episode of female distress, by the looks of it, but this time I recognize the distressee.

It's Neelam.

Someone emerges from a stall, rendering it my turn, but I was mostly here to get a break from the hormonal smog of our school gymnasium. "I'll be outside," I call to Jamie, letting the person behind me take my spot as I make my way out of the bathroom.

As I get closer I realize that Neelam's friend Mari, who's in my Civics class, is speaking loudly and aggressively.

"—enough, okay? It's not my fault that you *refuse* to have fun—"

"I'm not refusing," Neelam says flatly. "This just isn't fun. What am I supposed to enjoy about this? Should I take it as a compliment that some guy wants to rub himself on me in the dark?"

"Ugh, come on, it's not like that—and why can't you just be *nice*? He's cute, he's funny, he wants to dance with you—"

"So what? Just because he's Mason's friend doesn't mean I have to hang out with him. You having a boyfriend doesn't mean I need one, too."

"Okay, but can't you just pretend for like, five seconds?"

"Pretend to be what? More *likable*?"

"God—you just don't have to be such a bitch all the time, Neelam!"

With that, Mari storms off, and even though I know it's none of my business, I can't help feeling like the expression on Neelam's face is more hurt than angry. I wait a few seconds, then slip around the corner.

"Hey," I say.

Neelam is standing with her back to the gym wall, her arms folded over her chest.

"What?" she snaps at me.

"Nothing, I just—"

She glares at me. "It's really rude to eavesdrop."

"Okay, it really doesn't count as eavesdropping when everyone can hear it, but sure," I say. "I get it, I just—"

"Do you? No, actually you don't." Neelam gives me another blistering look. "I bet people don't have to tell you to smile, do they? Nobody ever tells you to look like you're having fun."

I hesitate. "I mean, I wouldn't say—"

"Anyone who thinks life peaks in high school or that this is the best time of our lives is just kidding themselves." Neelam slides me a look like maybe I'm one of those people. "No matter what Mari or anyone says, I don't *owe* it to anyone to smile and act like I'm happy when I'm not. And I know you think you're being nice," she says in a distinctly mean voice. "I know you think you're a *nice person*, Bel, and maybe that's true, but what you really are is someone who has it easy. You walked into robotics without doing any of the work, and now you think that because Teo Luna listens to you, that means you *deserve* to be listened to? Good luck with that."

She turns away from me and I know I should just let her go, but I can't. I don't know what to say, exactly, because yeah, she was really mean and she obviously hates me and I don't really know what to do about that, but mostly it just seems unfair to not say *something*.

"I'm trying," is the only thing that comes out of my mouth. "It wasn't like I wanted to steal robotics from you. I didn't even *want* to do it, but—"

I can tell by the look on her face that I said the wrong thing.

"Life is just something that happens to you, isn't it?" Neelam snaps. "You never actually do anything. Want anything. It's pathetic." She glares at me. "Teo Luna may be an asshole, but at least he knows what he wants."

I swallow. "He's not an asshole."

Neelam rolls her eyes. "Sure. He's hot, so he can't be an asshole, that's how that works—"

"*You're* an asshole," I say without thinking, because there's tears pricking at my eyes. I think they're tears of frustration, not pain, but either way it's mortifying. I'd rather get swallowed up by the earth right now than let Neelam see me cry.

Neelam gives me an angry, bitter smile in response that I know means we will never, ever be friends.

"Yeah," she says.

Then she turns and leaves.

I'm still standing alone wondering why I feel like I've been hit by a truck when someone taps me on the shoulder, and I jump.

"Hey," says Dash, giving me a look that says he probably heard everything.

"Oh, sorry. Hi," I say, glancing at my toes. Jamie painted my nails pink for me this morning while she told me a funny story about her sister, but it doesn't make me feel any better at the moment.

"You okay?" Dash says.

"Yeah. Yeah, I'm fine." I'm super *not* fine, but I can't admit that to anyone right now. "I mean she's right, anyway. It was none of my business."

He shuffles his feet on the pavement. "I don't think she was right."

"Well." I force a laugh. "Hopefully not about everything."

There's a pause, and Dash tilts his head toward the gym.

"Wanna come back inside?" he says.

"Sure, in a minute."

"Want me to get Jamie?"

"No, that's...no, it's okay, Dash." I try to smile at him, because I really *am* grateful that he's doing his best to make me feel better. "I'm glad you're here."

He nods, though he's still not smiling. I'm not sure why.

"I guess I should tell you that it's okay if you like Teo," he says.

I blink. "What?"

"I mean—" He gives me a coltish shrug. "It's *Teo*. He's, like, my favorite person in the world. So I wouldn't be surprised if you thought so, too."

"Oh...um." I guess I've been trying to convince myself that there was no possibility Dash might want me to have...certain other feelings.

Like, say, for him.

"Dash," I say carefully, unsure how to approach the situation, "it's not…it's not like that. With Teo." And it isn't. I've said that to Jamie a million times, because nothing has ever led me to believe that Teo and I might be anything more than friends. "But, um—"

This is hard.

I really, honestly wish that I felt something for Dash, who's funny and caring and easy to be myself with. I wish I could say that my heart banged around in my chest when I knew I was going to see him, or that being close to him made me want to move a little closer every time. I also wish there were classes like AP Not Hurting People When You Say You Don't Like Them Like That or Honors Preserving Your Friendships, because the last thing I want to do is cause any damage to someone who matters to me, and who I really like.

But in the moment that I'm doing all this wishing, I know there's a difference between wanting something and feeling it for real. There might not be anything going on with anyone else, but that doesn't mean there isn't someone in my life who makes me feel something slightly…more.

To my surprise, though, Dash chooses that exact moment to give me his usual happy smile.

"We're friends," he assures me. "It's not like that's a worse scenario or anything. I like being your friend. I want to be friends."

Okay, I know I said it would be mortifying, but I think I might have to cry a little.

Luckily Dash is a really good friend, so he probably won't tell.

nine

WRECKS

Bel

I'd feel a lot better about our chances at Regionals if Neelam and I hadn't argued again this morning.

"Look, I still think the spinner goes too fast, but it's fixable. I made a new spinning weapon last night," I told her, pulling it out of my backpack. I snuck out to my dad's again to make it with Luke, which was basically impossible. It's not like my mom won't let me go, but with Gabe home for Dartmouth's winter break, I can't get away from his judgy glances so easily.

"Anyway, it only has one spike," I explained at the time. "That way, we can both cause damage *and* flip—"

"You can't just change things the day of competition," Neelam snapped.

"But the bot hasn't been tested since we made new changes anyway!" I protested, before making a huge mistake and turning to Teo. "We have time to swap it out, don't we? Come on, you can trust me," I said, unintentionally pleading with him, which of course enraged Neelam and made Teo's eyes cut away from mine.

So anyway, I think I can just skip ahead and tell you that Teo's answer wasn't yes.

If I weren't feeling so crappy, I'd probably think about how unsettling it is to walk into my first Regionals, which is being held in the gymnasium of a school that, like Essex Academy, looks more like a sprawling college campus than a high school. There's a bluster of activity all the way from the parking lot to the gym, and like... okay, I knew this was a *thing*, but I didn't know it was *this big* a thing. There are people absolutely everywhere knocking into me from every angle, which is kind of annoying.

Or it would be, if I weren't too busy being filled with dread.

A lot of the teams here seem to know each other, and everyone seems to know us—not *me*, obviously, but they're clearly whispering about our team when we walk in. Teo and the others nod to some people, a select few they deem worthy of respect, but I feel distinctly like an afterthought; a loose screw somewhere, waiting to be tightened. I glance at Teo, wondering how I'm supposed to be reacting to all of this, but he won't look at me. I shake myself quickly and turn my attention to something—literally *anything*—else.

People are staring at me. No, not people. Boys. Am I imagining it? Maybe. I tug at my Essex polo and fight the impulse to check for something in my teeth. I already know it's not my clothes, because I made a point to be taken seriously today. I feel naked without dangly earrings or shiny things, but this is supposed to be about robotics, not me. I'm in costume as a Serious Person, which you would think Teo would approve.

"And this is only *Regionals*," Lora whispers knowingly to me, misinterpreting the look on my face when I walk into the packed gym. Inside, there are two main areas of competition in the center of the room and two matches scheduled to run at a time, with most of the gym's perimeter reserved for the various teams and their engineers. Our team, undoubtedly one of the largest, takes a prime spot near the bigger competition ring, which looks like a big plastic cage. While Dash and Teo immediately leave to scope out the competition, Emmett and Kai stand guard by our bots, scaring away anyone who wants to do exactly what Dash and Teo have just set out to accomplish.

Nobody seems to have anything for me to work on, so I take a seat next to our bots, figuring it'll be a long day of doing nothing. Lora is busy setting up the livestream for our social media, so for now it's just me, my hand-cut spinner that nobody wanted, and my gloom of existential despair.

"Hey, kiddo," says Mac, slipping into the seat beside me. "How's it going?"

He's trying to be all buddy-buddy with me, which I can tell is going to turn into another lesson about teamwork.

"I was just running it again last night," I repeat numbly, because I've already explained it to everyone else a dozen times. "If the vertical spinner goes as fast as it actually can, it'll damage itself. We should have used a different material to slow it down, or if we just swapped out the spinner—"

"Teo and Neelam have both competed in fights like this before," Mac says. "You'd be right if we were talking about a computer simulation, but the fact is you're up against a robot, not a computer."

Yeah, exactly. Other robots are made of material that will slow our spinner down. "I just think that—"

"Bel." This time, Mac is using his teacher voice. "It's not about whether you're right or not. You clearly understand the dynamics involved, so if this were a lab or an exam, you'd absolutely get an A." He pauses before adding, "But you're really doing your teammates a disservice by springing this on them the morning of a competition."

So that's it, then. I'm right, but because I didn't run it past them earlier, they're all getting a free pass to ignore me.

"I thought this was about winning," I say very quietly. I know it's a bratty thing to say, and Mac gives me a look like it was never his idea to have me here in the first place.

"You're a team," he emphasizes again. "In the real world, there's no such thing as an engineer who works alone. If this," he says, gesturing to our bots—the little one, Dante, and our 120-pound bot, the Seventh Circle, both named after the "Inferno," because we all had to read it the week we were reconstructing all the circuitry—"were your actual job, you couldn't just disappear and upend the whole build. You're part of a system that accomplishes more when it has strong parts that work together."

Sounds familiar. I glance up, hoping to catch Teo's eye when he returns from doing recon around the gym, but he still won't look at me. "I was just trying to help."

Mac nods. "Understood." He sets a hand on my shoulder. "But you will win like a team or you will lose like one," he says, and then he walks away to check on how the others are doing with the task robots.

I figure it's best to keep my distance for now, so I get up to wander the perimeter of the room, taking it all in. I have to say, this being my first robotics competition, it's a way bigger deal than I could have possibly imagined. I always knew we were doing a lot of work for a reason—I saw the pictures and video from last year, after all—but it's totally surreal that all of these people *also* decided to spend all their time building robots. I hadn't even considered doing it until a few months ago, and now I'm in this room with a bunch of people who are alternately running around in a panic to fix things at the last minute or crying with frustration at pieces that suddenly refuse to work.

"We passed inspection," Teo says from behind me, startling me while I'm watching one of the other teams test their weapon. (I've already been told to go away several times, but it's not like my team would listen to me even if I *did* learn something top secret about someone else's bot.)

"Oh, okay," I say uncomfortably. "Should I go back over there, or...?"

"If you want to." He's doing the thing he's been doing since homecoming and looking distractedly at everything but my face. "This is different," he comments, gesturing to my robotics polo and jeans.

"Why? It's the same thing you're wearing."

"Yeah, but like—" He rifles idly at his hair. "I thought you'd wear the bird jeans."

"Mac said to look professional," I say a little defensively, because I'm not sure if Teo said that to make fun of me or not. He always makes comments about the stuff I wear, which I know can be...a little weird. (But listen, when you can't have the expensive things that everyone else has, you start to want things that *nobody* else has.)

"Oh. Well, yeah. It's just, you know." He looks away. "I don't know, I'm nervous." He glances down at his hands. "I *think* what we have will hold, but I did the math again and—"

"I'm right, aren't I?" I know that already, because I am.

"Yeah." He shifts his feet. "Basically."

Briefly, my chest flares with vindication. But only briefly. "So why didn't you believe me?"

"No, Bel, I believed you, but come on." For the first time he actually looks up, flashing me a look of annoyance. "You could have called me. Texted me. You obviously had time to make the new spinner—"

"Seriously?" I cut in, astonished. "You're willing to lose just because I didn't ask you for help?"

He gives me something that's essentially a scowl. "Forget it," he says, and turns away just as Ms. Voss approaches me, one brow arching at what must have been Teo's parting expression.

"Hm," is all Ms. Voss says when he storms off. "Everything okay?"

"Yeah, maybe. Probably," I say. She prompts me with a glance, and I sigh. "Well, I think that in trying to claim my space I kind of...overdid it."

"Ah, well. It's a sensitive balance." She smiles at me, and I suddenly feel very grateful she's one of our chaperones. She's wearing our robotics polo and a tag that reads SPECTATOR, so I guess she's going to watch. "Are you excited?" she asks me, looking at me the way my mom does when she hopes I like whatever new thing she made for dinner. "You should be very proud of yourself, Bel. You worked hard, and no matter what happens, you've come a long way."

"I...am, yeah. I'm proud, I think." I learned a lot to get here, but I'm definitely not excited; not yet, anyway. My stomach is currently too busy tying itself in knots, and I've had the last hour to lose what's left of my patience with everyone who keeps staring like I don't belong. "But anyway, it doesn't matter, I'm not the driver. I'm just here to make repairs between rounds," I finish, without adding my actual second thought: *assuming anyone is even willing to speak to me by then.*

Ms. Voss glances around the room. "Are your parents here?"

"Hm? Oh, uh, no." I didn't tell them about it. My mom would only feel bad about having to work, and if my dad showed up, she'd feel even worse. I thought about telling Luke, but if I'm going to fail, I'd rather nobody see me do it.

Well, almost nobody.

"I'm really glad you're here," I confess to Ms. Voss. "That way," I add, "if anything goes wrong, I can remind everyone that it's your fault I tried out to begin with."

"I'll take that bet," she says, steering me toward our first match of the day.

Combat robotics is made up of short rounds of—you guessed it!—combat. The robots face off inside a very weird cage, one in a blue square and one in a red square, and each team gets points for aggression, damage to the other bot, and strategy. Teo is our team's driver, which I think was a hotly contested issue that preceded me joining the team. (Not that anybody but Neelam would have contested it.)

Every bot is weighed beforehand to make sure it meets the

competition parameters. Usually this is very stressful, but Kai, one of the most stressed-out people I've ever met, would probably rather stab all of us than allow us to fall behind schedule, and I know that almost everyone on the team's been coming to the robotics lab every spare minute they had. Lora helps a lot with keeping people on track, too. I think it's because she's so nice; nobody ever wants to be the one to tell Lora bad news, like if they used too much material or they need an extra day.

The last thing to know is that combat works tournament style, with each bot being allowed to lose two rounds before they're eliminated from competition. As with most tournament-style things, you always want your bot to have a good day—but if that fails, then you want the *other* bot to have a *bad* day. This is what I gathered about Regionals from Teo before he suddenly got "busy," which coincidentally happened after I went to homecoming with Dash. ("I know you think I'm just some spoiled rich kid, but I do have a job," Teo told me unpleasantly, like I was some kind of one-woman revolt against the 1%.)

Not that that's important right now.

My phone buzzes in my pocket just as Emmett, Dash, and Justin are setting Dante, our smaller bot, in the red square to start our first match.

Jamie: how's it going??
Jamie: wish I could be there...mock trial is killing me
Jamie: 💀💀💀
Jamie: knock 'em dead robot overlord!!!

"Bel," says Teo, looking over his shoulder to where I'm standing behind him. He has the remote in his hand, which doesn't look all that different from the PlayStation controller Luke usually plays with. "Are you listening?"

"Sorry." I shove my phone back in my pocket. "What do you need?"

He glares at me. "You to put your phone away."

Wonderful.

"So you're still angry, then," I mutter. "Cool, very cool."

"What?"

"Nothing." I glance up at him, straining to see Dante. "Do I have to stand back here?"

Teo looks like he's going to say something obnoxious, but then he changes his mind at the last second.

"No," he says, and steps to the side. "Here. You'll see better from here."

I thank him gruffly, to which he grunts something in reply, but I have to admit, the excitement is starting to hit me now that our bot is actually in the ring. Teo looks absurdly calm; his hands are relaxed around the controller and his forearms are flexed, but not tensed. I know I wouldn't look nearly so cool if I were in his position.

"You ready?" he asks me.

"Uh—" Someone bumps my other side and I step closer to him, trying to stay out of the way of the migrating blue team. "Oops, sorry, Teo—"

"This space is for engineers and drivers only," says someone from the blue team: St. Michael's, an all-boys academy. It takes me a second to realize that the kid with the remote is talking to me, because I'm wearing the Essex Academy Robotics polo that should make it obvious that I have a right to be here.

"I'm an engineer," I say, and I wish I could have enjoyed the experience of saying that for the very first time, but instead the dude gives me a blank look. Apparently to him, engineers are only identifiable by their Y chromosomes.

"Oh, right," he says. "Diversity points. Got it."

It's rare for me to get so insulted that I'm viscerally outraged, but it definitely happens. "Are you kidding me right now?" I ask him.

"Shut up, Richardson," says Teo without looking up. "You're going down."

"Whatever, Luna. Vertical spinner again? Good luck."

I clench a fist, glaring at whoever Richardson is. He's ignoring me—like I don't even matter. Like I'm not even here.

"Your bot's too big," I tell him flatly. "Gyroscopic force will send it off the ground like a helicopter. Three to one odds we shred that aluminum base in the first minute."

Richardson gives me a doubtful scoff. "You're on," he mutters. I wish I'd punched him in the face instead, but then I notice Teo looking at me.

"What?" I mutter to him.

"Nothing." He slides me another glance.

"*What*, Teo?"

"Nothing, I just…" He suppresses a laugh. "You're all…spicy."

"I'm *spicy*?"

"Yeah. You know, fighty."

"*Fighty*? Teo, speak English—"

He nudges me and I realize I missed the smell of him. Laundry detergent and boy.

(Hormones are honestly the worst thing anyone's ever invented.)

"Red team, ready?" calls the ref, as Justin, Dash, and Emmett crowd in around us. I step back to give them room, but Teo stops me.

"Hey, stay close," Teo murmurs to me, and because I'm both surprised and suddenly exhilarated, I nod. "Ready," he tells the ref.

"Blue team, ready?"

"Ready," says Richardson in a bored tone.

"Robots activate!"

A green light goes off and Teo thrusts down on the vertical joystick, sending Dante flying across the floor.

"See how fast they can go," I say in his ear, and he nods without looking away. For a couple of seconds the two bots circle each other, but then Teo slams into the side of the blue team's bot, which is named—*ugh*. Make America Bot Again. MABA.

Teo pulls away, treating Dante like a boxer in the ring; he's throwing fakes with our spinner while staying on the outside of MABA's weapon, luring them in so he can reach them where they can't touch him. I know he's worried about our weapon—his thumb hovers above the horizontal joystick for about half a breath every time—but the moment MABA turns on its spinner, it's clear their weapon is going to spin too fast.

Our bot may not be perfect, but I still know it's the better bot in the ring.

"Get it to attack us head-on," I say, but Teo's one step ahead of me. He lures MABA after us, traversing the floor and daring Richardson to pin Dante against the wall of the combat cage, a ballsy tactic that Richardson is more than cocky enough to fall for. Teo's knuckles go white and his chest fills, waiting for Richardson to take the bait and go for the kill. I do the same, holding my breath for what I hope will be my redemption.

The moment MABA tries to use its weapon at full speed, it does precisely what I said it would do: It lifts off the ground. Just slightly.

Just *enough*.

Beside me Richardson swears, earning himself a glare from the ref, and Teo gives a little half smile of satisfaction, ramming Dante forward so that our spinner shreds the bottom of MABA. It catches on one of the internal parts and somehow—miraculously—flips MABA onto its back, leaving it vulnerable to further attack. Still, rather than broaden, Teo's smile becomes a look of focused concentration, a flick of his thumb sending our weapon tearing through MABA's base where he knows the circuitry is most crucial. It's a ruthless move, arrogant, and I'm absolutely breathless. This is why he wins. This is how he does it.

Teo Luna knows how good he is, and now everyone else does, too.

"They don't have a self-righting mechanism," he says in a low voice, explaining himself to me, though I can hardly hear him over the sound of Dash and Emmett roaring in my ear.

"Oh my god, Teo, shut up, I can see that!" I gasp, innervated by the adrenaline pumping through my veins. It's impossible not to let that feeling blur with his proximity to me, because it's all the same sensation: Teo and the buzz of the fight, his control and the fruits of my hard work, him and me and everything harmonically, electric, all at once. It catches up somewhere in my throat, vibrating out from my bones until every atom in me is humming.

Behind me Lora is screaming from the spectator box and hilariously, so is Ms. Voss. "GET 'EM!" she shouts, and now I understand how Rome was able to distract everyone from destitution and starvation with gladiators. There's a real thrill to carnage, even if it's just metal parts.

"You got their battery!" Dash shouts after Dante's spinner tears once more into MABA's circuitry base, Teo's motions on the remote so swift and effortless he hardly appears to be moving. "That's it, they're out!"

Sure enough, the ref starts counting down.

"MABA, we have to see movement in ten...nine...eight..."

The rest of the room (the ones on our side, anyway) joins in.

"...three...two...one..."

"IT'S A KNOCKOUT!" shouts the ref, and suddenly there's a huge weight on my back that consists of basically our entire team shoving forward. I collide with Teo's chest, barely noticing from my personal cloud of euphoria, and he wraps one arm around me as he lifts the controller victoriously into the air.

"Oh my god, thank god," he breathes in my ear, confessing for me alone. "Thank *god*—I swear, if we'd lost to Richardson I'd have honestly thrown up in my shoes—"

I'm hysterically laughing, or maybe crying. Teo looks down at me and I look up at him and I know, I *know* it's only the first round for what's about to be a long day, but I swear, I get it now.

"I get it now," I tell him, and he smiles at me, genuinely. He smiles at me like we did this together—like even though he was the one driving, we were both equally part of this; like this win was taken from our *blood*, from our sweat and tears and angst and our hours and hours and hours of aiming for some distant, impossible glimpse of perfection—and I get it, I get it, I swear.

"I know," he says deliriously, "I know," and then he grabs the side of my face with one hand, grinning like an idiot.

"Welcome to robotics, Bel Canto," Teo shouts to me over the sound of our teammates cheering, so close I can almost taste the triumph from his lips.

At that exact moment, I know I'm absolutely wrecked.

TEO

I'm an athlete, so I'm a little superstitious. For the next round I make sure Bel is right there on my left, and even though we don't get another knockout—it goes to the judges, who give us more points for driving and aggression—it still feels like a necessity. She's pink-cheeked and breathless and reminds me of exactly how I felt four years ago, when it was my first time at one of these things.

I realize I'm watching Bel fall in love (with robotics, obviously) and it gives me a feeling that the last few competitions haven't. It's enough to remind me how much I like working with her, and I suddenly decide that the last few weeks of pushing her away have been really, really stupid.

"I don't know about this one," I confess in a low voice before our final round with Dante. The Seventh Circle's final round ended with a forfeit; the other team had a problem with their battery, which gives us a free pass to Nationals. Dante, however, is another story. "This bot's a lot better than the last two."

Bel looks at our competition, the Undertaker, which is pretty well prepared for a bot like ours. It's too stable to flip, so causing any real damage means putting us at risk for being harmed by our own spinner. It uses such high kinetic energy that a more efficient bot like Undertaker makes us vulnerable to ourselves.

I wish she'd told me sooner that she had a better idea for how to design the spinner. Not just that she planned to build one, but that she had doubts about ours in the first place. It's selfish, I know, but I hate the idea that she could have trusted me with her suspicions and she chose not to. I guess it's my fault for trying to stay away; I was trying to focus on the team, but in the end I just did them a disservice.

I'm captain. I'm the leader. I'm not supposed to let things slip through the cracks like that. I'm the one who let us down, and—

"Maybe we'll get lucky," Bel says. She looks up at me, and I wish she had on some glitter or something to distract me, because I keep having to force myself not to look too long at her eyes. I've been avoiding it for days, maybe weeks, because of how hard it hits me.

"You know what you're doing," she adds. "You won us the last round. You'll win again."

It's just a penalty kick, I tell myself silently. You do it all the time.

"Yeah, I know. Okay." Let's just get this over with. "Chances are there's something wrong with theirs anyway."

"Probably," says Bel.

"If it goes to the judges, we'll still get aggression points."

"Definitely."

"And their design isn't necessarily better just because it's harder to cause damage. We don't know how their weapon works."

"True."

"I could try to aim for a wheel?"

"That could work."

"Does it look less stable in the front?"

"I think so, maybe."

I glance at her. "Sorry. I'm babbling."

She shakes her head. "You're strategizing."

It's probably really stupid how much it unravels me to look at her right then, but I've never seen eyes that make me think about the mysteries of the universe the way hers do. It's like walking through the redwoods. Like feeling the earth beneath your feet while knowing there are things flying free above you, and things living and breathing below you, and for a moment you just feel *connected* to everything. Like there's some sort of unstoppable tide of existence and you're part of it, even for just a second.

"Luna," says Mac, startling me back to life. "You got this?"

Okay Luna, what's the right answer?

Luna, we need that point to win!

Everyone will always expect more from you, Teo, and you cannot let them down—

I shake off my distraction and face our bot. We're the ones in the blue square now, the first time we've been the blue team all day, which I try not to think of as an omen.

"Blue team, ready?"

I close my eyes, inhaling.

This is my fourth year doing this. I know by now what to expect.

(I should know by now how to win.)

This is my last year. My last Regionals. This is my chance.

(My *last* chance.)

I know what I'm doing, even if no one else does.

(I have to know what I'm doing. Because no one else does.)

I've come too far to fail. I worked too hard. I led this team.

(Failure is not an option.)

"I'll be right here," Bel says softly.

I open my eyes, exhaling.

I can't fail. Not now. Not today.

(Not with her watching.)

"Blue team ready," I confirm, thumb hovering expectantly above Dante's switch.

Bel

When it's over, I find Teo sitting alone.

"Hey," I say. "Come on. We're all getting In-N-Out."

He shakes his head. "No thanks."

"Teo. You can't stay here all night."

"I'm not." He mumbles it, so I hardly even hear him.

"You *won*," I remind him. "You *won*, Teo, miraculously. Even I couldn't believe it, but you did it. You had every reason to lose and you didn't."

He says nothing.

"Their bot broke, too," I remind him. "And you're the one who said it's not about having the perfect bot, it's about having the best bot in the—"

"We didn't have the best bot in the ring," he says impatiently.

"Okay, well, the judges obviously disagreed."

"It wasn't unanimous. Nor should it have been. If theirs hadn't—"

"Teo, honestly." I sit beside him on the floor. "You've got to be the only person I've ever seen get so upset about winning."

He stares at his feet.

"That spinner *shredded* Dante," he says, as if I wasn't there to see it happen. "It's dead."

"Okay, so we'll have a Viking funeral," I tell him. "Shoot flaming arrows at it and stuff."

He turns away, dejected. "It's not funny, Bel—"

"Why not?"

"Because I should have known better. Because there was a problem with the design, and I should have *known*—"

"Yikes," I say, forcing levity. "All this stuff about teamwork and it turns out you were the only important one the whole time."

He flinches. "Sorry, I didn't mean that. I just meant—"

"You're in mourning," I assure him. "Our bot died. It was sad and it was gruesome. It wasn't pretty. It took the judges a really long time to decide, and it wasn't the kind of win you wanted."

I reach out, tentatively putting a hand on his shoulder.

"But in fairness, I *told* you it wasn't going to work," I murmur, and when he looks up at me in annoyance, I make sure to look as sweetly innocent as possible.

But he isn't annoyed. Instead, he looks at me like...

I don't know. I don't think I've ever seen this look on his face before.

"We need a new Dante for Nationals," he says. "Build it with me."

I wish I could say I considered saying no. I wish I could say it mattered even a little bit what his question was, but it really never crossed my mind to choose anything but him.

"Yeah," I say. "Yeah, okay."

And finally, for the first time in nearly an hour, Teo Luna smiles.

ten

TRIES

Bel

Where are you always sneaking off to?" says Gabe, which is a very Gabe question. It probably says a lot that most of his friends call him Gabriel. He, unlike Luke, never calls me Ibb or any other nickname. He usually looks at me like he's forgotten I live here.

"I'm not *sneaking off*," I say, because I'm not. "I already told Mom I'm working on stuff for AP Physics."

"During winter break?" he says with a frown. "That's not the Bel I know."

Well. As much as I *love* being interrogated by my brother, I have other places to be. "Cool story, Gabe! *Bye*—"

"Hang on," he says, and rises to his feet, squinting at me. "We need to talk about this Luke thing."

"Uh, no thanks," I say, attempting to leave, but unfortunately Gabe's already talking.

"You know honestly, I think Kellan's right that we need to approach this whole thing strategically, as a family. If we're going to be able to move forward from this—"

"*Who*"—I sigh, because clearly I'm not getting out of this—"is Kellan?"

"I told you, he's my therapist. Well, he's getting his doctorate right now, but he works in counseling services, so—"

"Jesus, Gabe, you're in therapy?"

"Yes, and you should be, too," Gabe says flatly. It's impossible not to observe how un-Luke he is; they're recognizably siblings, maybe, but their expressions could not be more different. Gabe is what would happen if you stretched Luke out a couple of inches and forced him to read fifteen books a week. "Obviously there's nothing we can do about Luke. He's insisting on throwing away his future—"

"Okay, who is 'we'? You and Mom?"

"You and me," Gabe says, blinking at me. "Mom's got enough on her plate as it is."

"Okay, hang on. I know you and Luke have, like, a blood feud or whatever—"

"Mom works day and night to keep you in that private school," says Gabe. "She's set you up for the best possible future. The least you can do is pay her back by having one."

My phone buzzes in my pocket, which probably means Teo's already at school. Unfortunately, my brain is now buzzing, too. "I thought this was about Luke?"

Gabe shakes his head. "I'm trying to tell you that Luke's clearly a lost cause, but you're not. So if there's anything I can do, edit your applications or help with your essay—"

"Gabe." The mere mention of my unfinished college applications makes me queasy. "Can we talk about this later?"

"Of course. I'm here," he says, using a painstakingly fraternal voice. "I just want you to know that you have one brother you can count on, Bel."

I bite my tongue on the fact that actually, Gabe didn't take notice of me for most of his life aside from fighting with me over whether caffeine was going to stunt my growth, and yeah, Luke's not exactly a genius, but he also isn't whatever Gabe thinks he is.

But then I stop to think about how maybe Luke thinks he and I are the same, just like Gabe thinks he and I are the same. The pressure to belong to one or the other—plus the idea that my dad thinks he and I are perfectly fine, and the fact that my mom is working so hard *for me*—leaves me hurling myself out the door.

"Yeah, okay, bye, Gabe!"

I shoot a quick text to Teo that I'm on my way and sit in the car for a solid five minutes before actually starting it. The last thing I want is to fall apart in front of him—and over *what*, exactly?—so I collect myself and then head out.

"Hey," Teo calls to me when I walk into the lab, not looking up from the circuit board he's fiddling with. "Do you have the weapon you made for Regionals?"

"Oh—" Balls, I forgot it. "No." I wince. "Sorry. But I can go back and get it—"

"Nah, don't worry about it. I actually just got an email that I have to be at a game in two hours."

"For soccer?" I ask, bewildered.

"No. Well, yeah," he amends, and looks up. "I told you I ref the community games on the weekends, right? This is the last one of the year and someone bailed at the last second."

"Luckily there's reliable Teo Luna," I say, and even though I'm joking, a hint of distress flickers on his face. "No, I think it's great," I rush to assure him. "Community games? Like little kids?"

"Yeah, it's the little ones today." He seems to collect himself, summoning me over. "Can you grab that battery?"

"Hm? Yeah." I pick it up and walk over to him, dropping my school bag and positioning myself at his left. "Just working on the wiring today?"

"Yeah."

I can see he's concentrating, so in the silence that follows, my conversation with Gabe pops back into my head. I've always understood that my mom expects a lot out of all of us, but I guess I assumed that when Gabe went to Dartmouth, she'd already won as a parent. With Luke maybe dropping out of school, though, that probably goes in the loss column.

So am I supposed to even the score or something? Ironic, then, that my college application doc still has one line at the top: *I don't know what I want or why I want it.*

"You look weird," says Teo, and I startle back to focus.

"What? I'm not putting on makeup just to work on a robot, Teo." I need to start writing down some of Jamie's performative femininity takedowns for situations like this. She has very strong Alexandria Ocasio-Cortez energy (which includes both AOC's congressional-grade oration skills and, when necessary, her sorry-not-sorry red lip).

"No, I meant—" Teo rolls his eyes at me. "Your face looks fine. I just meant you looked upset. Or something."

"Oh." I feel my cheeks flush. "Yeah, no, it's just that my brother's home for winter break and we had a weird conversation." I didn't really mean to give an answer, but I think it helps that Teo's currently fiddling with wires. It's kind of soothing to watch.

"I thought your brother lives here?"

"My older brother Luke lives with my dad. It's my middle brother, Gabe."

"Your parents are divorced?"

"Yeah. Or…close enough, anyway. That's why I'm here. At this school, I mean. That's why I transferred. Because my mom moved out."

I think Teo's intentionally staring at the circuit board instead of at me, which is ideal. I don't really want to make eye contact right now, either.

"Do you still talk to your dad?" he asks carefully.

"I…do. Sort of."

"Sort of?"

"Well, I come over sometimes to use his tools. And to see my brother."

"So your dad and your mom get along then? It was…amicable or whatever?"

"Basically." I blink. "Actually no, I don't know why I said that. No, not at all."

"Do you like your dad?"

"Whoa, uh." Nobody's ever asked me that before. "I mean, yeah? Doesn't everyone?"

Teo stops to look up for a second.

"I love my dad," he says slowly. "But every now and then I forget he's my dad and he kind of looks like a stranger, so then I have to wonder what it would be like if he actually were. Like, if he randomly walked into my house and I didn't know him, what would I think of him?"

I wait, but he doesn't continue. "Well?" I prompt, nudging him.

Teo looks at me and half smiles. "I think he's probably a good boss," he says. "A good CEO and all that. He has high expectations but he's not cruel. And I think he's smart, really smart."

"Yeah, but do you like him?"

Teo sets down the pliers he's using and stares into space.

"I don't think he likes me," he says.

My whole chest crumples a little bit.

"I bet he does," I say softly, and Teo shakes his head.

"No, I mean—I don't think my dad likes kids. I think maybe he'll like me when I'm an adult. I think he assumes I'll be his employee at some point, actually, and until then he's just kind of waiting for me to be more useful."

"Teo, that's terrible—"

"No, no, it's really not. I love my mom. She loves babies, loves kids, loves fluffy things. And my dad was like okay cool, she's the soft one, she'll do the love part, and I'll just have t—" He breaks off. "Wow, sorry, I didn't mean to say that. It's not like I don't think my dad loves me or—"

He clears his throat.

"I'm…I didn't mean to make it about me," he says. "I'm fine. I'm more than fine," he says with a generic wave to his nice clothes and his expensive car, which is somewhere parked next to my very, very used one. "Someday I'll have earned all of this. Or close to it, at least."

He looks embarrassed, and something sickening bubbles up from my stomach.

"My dad cheated on my mom," I suddenly blurt out, and Teo's brows shoot up in surprise. "I've been pretending not to know that, but I'm not stupid. I don't think it was anyone in particular, I think maybe it was multiple women, which is just so gross and bad, and my mom is just the nicest, most loving person...but the worst part," I confess in an exhale, "is that I still like him, even though I know I'm not supposed to."

Abruptly my lip quivers, and I have to force a swallow.

"I like my dad so much, but he hurt my mom. And now my brothers have sides and I don't. So I don't know what to do about it."

"Bel." Teo's eyes soften, which somehow makes everything worse.

"And I know my mom totally couldn't afford to send me here but she did it anyway, and I'm supposed to go to Dartmouth like Gabe instead of doing nothing with myself like Luke, but I don't know *what* I'm supposed to do or what I'm supposed to major in or where I'm supposed to apply—"

"You haven't done your applications yet?" Teo asks with obvious astonishment, and I let out a wail.

"Oh my god, don't look at me like that—"

"Bel, they're due in, like, *two weeks*—"

"TEO, oh my GOD—"

"Okay, okay, I'm sorry. I'm sorry." By now the circuit board is all but abandoned, and we're facing each other awkwardly. "Maybe..."

Teo exhales.

"Maybe let's not work today," he says.

"Maybe not." I glance at my scuffed white Converse, watching Teo's Sperry loafers shift ever-so-slightly toward me.

"Why don't you come with me to this game? It's only about an hour," says Teo. "We can get something to eat after and talk about it. Or not. I mean, I have absolutely no idea what to say," he admits with a shrug, "but if *you* want to talk about it—"

"You want me to come with you?" I ask, surprised. We've spent a lot of time together by now, but never outside of this classroom. I assumed he liked to compartmentalize his activities: school, robotics, soccer, friends, community service (i.e., me).

"It might make you feel better," he says. "The kids are really cute. And really, really bad at kicking the ball."

"You were probably horrible at it once, too," I remind him.

"Me? No," says Teo. "Scored a goal on my first try."

"Shut *up*," I groan, but I can tell I'm smiling. "You probably did, didn't you?"

"Mostly by accident." He's smiling back, which feels like something I won.

No, not something I won—more like something I earned. Like maybe Teo Luna has a lot of different levels to him and every time I do something right, or say something real, I get to reach a new one. Collect all the keys, pass Go.

"Come on," he says. "I'll drive and take you back here later. Sound good?"

I nod.

"Sounds perfect," I say, because it does.

TEO

I sort of assumed Bel would sit on the sidelines of the park with all the insane parents, but instead she floats around. One of the girls on the third grade team tells Bel she likes her neon-pink sweatshirt, and Bel says she likes the girl's sparkly barrettes. She talks to all the kids like they're grown-ups, which is kind of funny. I can't decide whether I think she's doing it on purpose—like, if it's a proven effective strategy—or if that's just how she is.

I think it's just her.

After the game I dodge the tumbleweeds of small children and spot her where she's watching some kids whose game ended earlier. "I just have to put all the equipment away and then we can go," I tell her, and Bel looks up, disappointed.

"We can't use it?" she asks.

"What?"

"Well, I don't know," she says defensively, waving a hand at the goal. "It looked fun."

I can't help but laugh. "Do you know anything about soccer?"

"No hands, right? It's not robotics, Teo."

She plucks the soccer ball from my hand and knees it in completely the wrong direction.

"Hm," she says, frowning after it.

I arch a brow. "Harder than you thought?"

"All right fine, a little."

In the end we compromise—I put away half the field, but then we leave up the goal on the far side. It's quiet now that the kids have mostly cleared out with their parents, and on a rare gray day like this one, we don't have much competition for the park.

"Okay, I'll play goalie," I say, stepping into the goal. "You try to score on me."

"What do I get if I win?" she asks, shading her eyes. It's cool outside, but bright.

"What do you want?"

"A million dollars and world peace."

"How about just the world peace? Or ice cream." Not to be totally selfish, but personally I could use some of the latter—I'm starving.

"Done." She sets the ball on the ground smugly. "How many tries do I get?"

"Three."

"Ten."

"This isn't a negotiation."

"Fine. Seven."

"Five."

"Done," she declares, and kicks the ball into the left corner.

I tap it with a toe, launching it up to my chest and passing it back to her. "Try again."

The second ball goes into almost the exact same spot.

"Did you put a GPS in this thing?" she asks me.

"Yes," I say. "Not sure if you knew this, but I'm super good at robotics."

She sticks her tongue out at me precisely like a six-year-old and I toss her the ball again. "Come on, Bel Canto."

She rolls her eyes, then sends the ball...exactly into the same spot. This time, though, I very nearly miss it.

"I lured you into a false sense of confidence," she calls to me, hands around her mouth like a megaphone.

"Okay, so you're good on tactics." I kick the ball back to her. "Try aiming this time."

She throws her head back with a groan.

"Like, specifically try aiming for m—"

"Distraction!" she shouts, kicking the ball precisely at the moment she smacks one arm into my torso, prompting me to double over just as the ball crosses the line.

"Did it," she says breathlessly, dancing away backward. "Nailed it!" she adds, with a one-armed punch of triumph.

"That's *so* illegal," I tell her.

"Nobody knows the rules of soccer," she says solemnly.

"That's literally false."

"Oh, Teo, Teo, Teo." She sighs. "So young. So foolish."

She's hopeless. "Fine, then your last kick is mine," I tell her, maneuvering her into the goal by the hips. "Them's the rules."

"That's fair." She brushes her hair out of her eyes, grinning at me. "Try me, Luna. One shot."

"One shot," I agree, using a little footwork to wrest the ball out of her reach. "Ready?"

She drops into a power stance. "Ready."

I kick the ball into the upper right corner and it sails in, which I pretty much figured it would. She tries, but ultimately watches it go over her head.

"Hm," she says. "You've played this game before, haven't you?"

"Once or twice."

"And here I thought you'd go easy on me."

"What for?" I shrug. "You didn't go easy on me."

"You make an excellent point." She smooths her hair away from her face again, cheeks bitten pink from her herculean effort. "So do we owe each *other* world peace, then?"

I roll my eyes. "Come on, Bel Canto," I say, "let's pack it up."

In the end we get gelato and talk about the likelihood of terraforming Mars. (I think it's a definite possibility; she thinks we have no business terraforming anything. I think we're probably both right.) Eventually her phone buzzes and she glances down, which reminds me that I have several unanswered texts from Dash.

Dash: mom says u should come over for dinner
Dash: she thinks ur a sad orphan
Dash: or are u doing postmates again?
Dash: if u are then definitely get extra samosas
Dash: i can be available

"Want to come over and grab that spinning disk I made?" Bel says, looking up at me while I'm typing a response to Dash. "We could always work on it more, assuming your parents don't mind."

"Oh, they're not home," I say, about to tell Dash I'm just going to get some Thai and keep working on the bot when I catch the signs of Bel frowning in my periphery.

"They're not home?"

"They're in Geneva," I explain, looking up. "I'm flying out with my grandparents to spend the holidays with them, but I wanted to stay back and get some work done first." My dad almost always supports my decisions to work on school stuff when he and my mom travel; in his mind, every vacation day is just another chance for someone else to surpass my academic record. Plus he hates my grandma's dog. (Whatever bad blood exists between him and Latke, it's mutual.)

"Oh," I realize, startling myself into the obvious conclusion. "You could just come over to my house if you want. I have a bunch of the same stuff we have in the lab."

I don't really realize until a few seconds later that I just asked Bel to come over to my house where I specifically said my parents weren't home.

Hastily, I backtrack. "I just meant—"

"Well, I still have to get the weapon," she says, her cheeks flushing slightly. "So maybe we can go to my house first? Since I don't have my car anyway."

"Sure." I clear my throat, nodding. "Let's go."

She doesn't really say anything in the car, only humming to herself along with the music in between directions to her house. (I let her play DJ and she, thankfully, is much better than Dash, even though there is admittedly a little more Taylor Swift than I'd like.) She lives in one of those garden apartment buildings with a courtyard in the center, which she seems self-conscious about. Personally, I think it's pretty, and the glow of string lights and the smell of food complete the scene when she opens the door.

"Oh *hell* no," Bel says as I collide with her back. "What are you doing here?"

"Isabel, please," says a woman's voice. "Language!"

"Good to see you, too," says a guy about my height, though his chest is probably twice the size of mine. "Oh shit," he laughs when he sees me. "What's this, Ibb?"

"Luke," Bel groans, "this is Teo. *Please* be normal—"

"Is this your thing now?" Luke asks Bel, waving over me with a doubtful frown. "This is what you're into? That's what you get for going to private school."

"I'm Gabriel," says a skinny dude on my left, looking up from a book that says *Quantum Gravity* on the cover and standing to shake my hand. "Teo, you said?"

"Oh my god no, stop—this is Gabe," Bel says, slipping between us to knock her brother's hand away. "And Luke, please shut up—"

"It's good of you to join us, Isabel," says the exasperated woman who's obviously Bel's mom, appearing from the kitchen in a sweatshirt that reads DARTMOUTH MOM. She's fairly young—not as young as my mom, but younger than my dad—and has a round face and different eyes, although it's clear where Bel gets her smile from. "Hi, welcome to our h—Lucas, get your fingers out of there!"

Bel's mother disappears into the kitchen and Bel gives me a panicked glance.

"I'm *so* sorry," she says. "I have absolutely no idea what Luke's doing here, he doesn't even live here—"

"Doubtless our father isn't feeding him," scoffs Gabe from where he's sitting on the couch.

"—and okay well, um. Anyway, you don't have to st—"

"Teo, do you like lumpia?" asks Bel's mom, materializing again in the doorway.

"Um, yes?" I say, slightly overwhelmed, but in a good way. I'm not completely sure what lumpia is, but I think it's those little Filipino egg rolls.

"Okay good, I'll make some," says Bel's mom, and I panic.

"Oh no wait, you don't have t—"

"It's too late," groans Bel. "You live here now."

"I really don't want to trouble you, Mrs., uh—"

"Oof, yeah, don't," Bel whispers to me, grabbing my arm and pulling me out of the living room into the hallway. "And don't worry, she only has to fry them."

Aptly, the smell of garlic frying reaches me from the kitchen. I know I should feel bad about inconveniencing Bel's mom, but it does smell a lot better when the food is home-cooked.

"You'll just have to eat whatever she puts in front of you," Bel sighs, leading me through a door on the left that I realize with a jolt is her bedroom. "Filipino moms."

She flips on the light and I pause in the doorway, taking in my surroundings. I don't know what I was expecting, but it's more than I can take in at once; I mean, there's the usual things (desk, bed, dresser, window) but also many unusual ones, like the paper lanterns suspended from the corner. While Bel hurries to kick some dirty clothes under her bed, I turn my attention to her walls, looking at an art print I've seen before and trying not to stare at the photographs I haven't.

"It's fine. Jewish moms are similar," I assure her, not mentioning the way my stomach is already growling. (Gelato can only go so far.) "And believe me, so are Mexican grandmothers," I add, turning to face her.

"You're Jewish?" she echoes, surprised. She looks a little winded from her hasty attempt to clean up her room.

"I mean, my mom i—"

"Oi," says Luke, Bel's older brother, barging into her room. "Mom wants to know if he eats meat," he says when I pivot to face the doorway.

"He's right there," Bel says, gesturing to me. "You can ask him yourself."

Luke gives me a skeptical glance. "Are you like, into sailing?"

"Um, no," I say.

"So the boat shoes are what, just a costume?"

"*God*," huffs Bel, looking mortified, even though I think it's kind of funny. "You can lay off, Luke, he's just here to pick up something for robotics."

"Oh, have you told Mom about that yet?" asks Luke.

"Wait, she doesn't know?" I interrupt, turning to Bel, and she winces.

"I just…I don't need people in my business, okay? Including *you*, Luke," she growls, launching past me to shove him out of her room. Luke retreats, allowing himself to be removed up to the point of the threshold, but then he smacks out a hand to widen the door's access.

"No closed doors," he warns, jabbing a finger at me and walking away backward.

I turn to look at Bel, who throws herself onto her bed and covers her face with a pillow.

"I *swear*"—she exhales, voice muffled—"I didn't plan any of this."

It's pretty obvious that nobody in their right mind would do any of this on purpose. "It's fine, weirdo," I assure her, taking the opportunity to scrutinize her room with as much curiosity as I'd like to. "This is cool," I say, crouching down to get a closer look at her desk. "Is this an old sewing machine?"

She slides the pillow away, looking over at me. "Yeah," she says uncertainly, like she's not sure what I'll make of it.

"That's awesome." I move to her dresser, half smiling. Each of the knobs are different; she must have replaced them all individually. "I like this one," I say, touching my finger to a brass drawer pull of a bird.

"Me too." Her voice is quiet. "That's my favorite."

On top of the dresser is her jewelry collection. Her necklaces, some of them familiar, are strung across the branches of a wire tree. "Did you make this, too?"

"Yeah."

"Is this all just…for fun, or…?"

"Yeah, pretty much." I haven't turned to look at her, but her voice is unreadable. "I'm kind of fidgety, I guess. I like to keep my hands busy."

I know she does; I've watched her build things, and draw. And fidget. "Makes sense to me."

Her shelves are those illusion shelves, built into the wall so it looks like the books are floating midair. Everything here has pieces of her, down to the covers of her books. I can tell she made her own for some of them; I've seen her sketches before, so I recognize her work.

"This is so weird," she says. "It's like you're looking right at me."

I turn over my shoulder to find her watching me, brows slightly furrowed. "I've looked at you before."

"Yeah, but not like—" She stops, looking away. "Not like this."

I know what she means. My room is nothing special—it's basically the inside of a West Elm catalogue—but hers is like a museum of the inside of her brain.

"I can stop being nosy," I assure her, stepping back from her shelves, because looking so closely at all the stuff she's collected does feel a little bit invasive. I'm not sure I'd want her to see how many copies I have of the *Sandman* graphic novels, or that I still haven't touched the LA Galaxy calendar I put up when I was twelve. "Where's the—"

She nods quickly, looking relieved to have something impersonal to discuss, and reaches over to pull open the top drawer of her desk. "Right here," she says, withdrawing the spinning disk she made. "You can take it and run away now, if you want."

I reach out to take it from her fingers, noting that she's not fully meeting my eye. Obviously I'm not going to run, so instead I sit down next to her on her bed.

"Why haven't you told your mom about robotics?"

She hugs the pillow to her chest, grimacing. "I don't know. I just want it to be mine, I guess."

"Would telling her about it make it less yours?"

"I don't know. Maybe."

I can tell she's watching for my reaction, so I don't look up.

"About your college apps," I say, and she groans, throwing the pillow at me.

"Teo, don't—"

"Apply for mechanical engineering programs." I toss the pillow back to her, which she misses. It tumbles sideways to the floor and she gapes at me.

"What? *Teo*—"

"You're so good, Bel." This time I make sure to look at her when I say it. "You're a natural."

She doesn't say anything.

"You're even better at robotics than you are at soccer," I tell her seriously, and she gives me a gulp of a laugh, swallowing surprise. I pluck the pillow from the floor and hand it back to her, waiting for her reaction.

"Teo," she begins to say, and it looks like she's going to give me excuses, which as a rule I never accept.

"Bel, listen. You're good at this," I say, watching her turn away, like she doesn't believe me. Or like maybe she's afraid to believe me. "You don't have to take my word for it—you don't have to bank the rest of your life on it—but you *should* try. I don't know why you wouldn't, but it seems like you need someone to push you, so here's your push." I nudge her shoulder to prove it. "You've got until January first, right?"

She hugs the pillow tighter, shaking her head. "I might not get in."

"So? If you don't try, you definitely won't." She says nothing, so I just keep talking. "I got into MIT early decision," I tell her, and she blinks. "I found out last week. It's my dream school." Finally getting it off my chest feels like a massive weight's been lifted.

"Which is great timing, because now I can just focus on the AP tests and robotics."

"Wait," she says, her eyes wide. "You got in and didn't tell anyone?"

"I mean…" I shrug. "Kai's applying there, too, and you know how he gets." If Kai knew I'd already been accepted, he'd just stress about it.

She shakes her head, sitting upright. "Still, Teo, that's amazing— I mean *congratulations*, that's—"

"What I'm saying is you could apply there, too," I cut in, and she frowns.

"You want me to compete with Kai?"

"Who says it's a competition? I bet they want girls."

This time her laugh is slow and sweet. "Oh, right. I'm a girl, huh?"

I'm not sure what she's saying, so I brush past it. "Think of all the Richardsons you could prove wrong if you went," I point out, hoping that might tempt her.

"Easy for you to say." She bumps her shoulder with mine, adjusting so we're sitting side by side on her bed. "Do you know how many Richardsons there are in the world?" she sighs.

"Do *you* know how many fewer Richardsons there would be if there were more Bels?" I counter.

She turns to look at me, and I look at her, and all of a sudden my whole body feels aware of how close she is to me. I can smell the roses in her shampoo and the way this whole room radiates with her *exact* energy, and for the first time, I allow myself to think about how much I want to pull her closer. She lifts her chin, the tiny motion of a swallow visible from her throat, and I think she knows what I'm thinking about.

I think she's thinking about it, too.

I reach out to slide her hair back from one shoulder, tucking it behind her ear. I can see the way she softens, her pulse quickening when mine does.

"Come with me," I say.

She bites her lip before answering. "Where?"

"To Cambridge," I say. "To MIT."

"Oh."

She exhales, and I'm screwing it up, I know.

"I just think you'd be wasting it, Bel, all this talent, if you didn—"

"IBB," shouts her brother from the hallway, and Bel jumps. "MOM WANTS YOU TO SET THE TABLE."

"FINE," she roars back, and then winces when she remembers that she just shouted in my ear. "Sorry, sorry—"

"It's fine, but, Bel—"

"I'll do it." She gives me a thin smile, a helpless shrug. "Assuming I can get some letters of rec in the next week, I'll apply, I promise."

"You will?"

"Well, since you asked so nicely—"

"ISABEL!"

She sits up with a sigh, glancing at me.

"I hope you're hungry," she says, "because my mom is super definitely going to feed you absolutely everything she has in this house."

I don't tell her that actually, I think I've been starving for whatever this exact feeling is.

"I could eat," I say, letting Bel pull me to my feet.

eleven

OUTCOMES

Bel

I still look at the email sometimes. I know I should archive it or delete it the way I do with literally everything that dares to show its face in my inbox, but this one I can't seem to dismiss.

Dear Isabel Maier:

We have successfully received your application for undergraduate admission to MIT.

Holy wow. Holy *forks*. Holy mamas.

I did it. I completed a college application—to *MIT*.

It wasn't easy; for the record, I would never advise anyone to procrastinate the way I did. Ms. Voss was happy I'd finally made up my mind and my counselor seemed relieved that I wasn't going to single-handedly destroy the school's college application rate, but Mac was…less than pleased about having to submit a letter over winter break.

Still, I finally did it.

Once Teo talked me into it, the essay just flowed out of me. Talk about something that changed my outlook on the world? Easy. I talked about robotics. I talked about Regionals and about Dante. I talked about how I always thought engineering was for boys or for people who loved math or for literally anyone who wasn't me, until I realized there's only rules like that if we enforce them. Because yeah, maybe I'm right that there's lots of stereotypes and gatekeepers out there to hold us back from our passions, but Teo's right that resigning myself to their expectations would be just as stupid as letting them rule my life. It's *my* life, isn't it? Robotics helped me realize I could find a place here—or better yet, make one.

(I used better words, but that's basically the gist.)

Procrastination notwithstanding, I worked a lot harder on my application than I ever expected to want to. Even Jamie was impressed, or something like it. "I was pretty confident you were going to completely blow this one," was her take on the subject, which was honestly fair. "No offense."

"And here I thought a licentious evening of drama and carbs might make you more adoring than usual," I pointed out, waving a hand in reference to whatever hot garbage we were bingeing on Netflix.

"What? I said no offense," she reminded me before thieving an extra spoonful of ice cream from my bowl.

Now that school's in session again after the holidays, things are back to being a whirlwind. We have finals to study for, plus we're gearing up for the AP tests and Nationals, and even though those things feel positively *ages* away, time is flying by. I'm so frazzled that when Jamie and Lora show up with cupcakes, I have to ask them what the occasion is.

"Um, are you joking?" Jamie asks, at which point I realize she's holding a balloon.

"Wait, is it your birthday?" asks Teo, who happens to be walking by with Dash at the precise moment I remember I'm eighteen years old today. He comes to an exaggerated halt, like a turntable warp from a sitcom laugh track. "Why didn't you tell me?"

Jamie gives me a look that says she's *definitely* going to text me about this later.

"It's not important," I say weakly, but Teo shakes his head with disgust.

"You're the worst, Bel Canto. We're going to have to do *something*," he says, and Dash exuberantly nods his agreement.

"I'll get samosas delivered to robotics," says Dash. "We can have a party while we get Seven's weight down." (At this point we're all too lazy to call the Seventh Circle by its full name.)

"You just want samosas," Teo and I tell Dash in unison, and then we exchange a glance.

Obviously Teo and I have been seeing a lot of each other recently. For one thing, we have a bot to build, and for another he's accidentally met my whole family, except for my dad. I thought Teo would never want to speak to me again (for obvious reasons), but even when my mom did embarrassing things like making us pray before dinner, he made the sign of the cross without comment.

"I thought you were Jewish?" I whispered to him, and he glanced at me.

"I told you my grandmother's Mexican," he murmured. "You think there's an abuela alive who isn't aggressively Catholic?"

Even Luke warmed up to him a bit; just a *bit*. Gabe and my mom were won over when I told them Teo got into MIT—my mom gave him extra food as a "reward," though based on how full Teo looked, it might have been closer to punishment—but with Luke, it always comes down to one thing: the car.

"Whoa," Teo said when we walked back to his car. Luke insisted on being the one to drive me back to the school parking lot, even though I would have much rather made Teo listen to *Shake It Off* one more time (I think I caught him mouthing the words the second time). "These are nice rims."

"They're custom," said Luke instantly.

"I like the mirrors, too," said Teo, which launched Luke into an enthusiastic monologue about how difficult they'd been to get and how impressed he was that Teo had noticed the chrome detailing. At the time, I bit my tongue on saying something sappy like *Teo's really good at catching details*, even though he absolutely is.

Anyway, since then I've seen Teo almost every day. Though, as I keep telling Jamie, we're just friends.

(I think.)

"Hey," Teo says, pulling me aside when we're all parting ways to go to class. I'm loaded down with way more cupcakes than I could ever eat, but that's an easy thing to temporarily forget. "What I meant was that we should do something. Like, *I* should, I mean."

He's speaking in kind of a quiet voice, and I have to fight a smile.

"Like what, a digital robot conquest?"

"No, not robots." He rifles his hair and oh no, oh no, oh no. It looks so soft.

"So what are you suggesting, then?"

"I don't know. Let me think about it." He looks at me distractedly. "Why didn't you tell anyone it was your birthday?"

Because then I'd have to acknowledge the fact that I'm eighteen.

"Oh," he says, glancing at my face. "Yeah, okay. We'll talk later. Happy birthday," he calls to me, jogging away with a smile on his face, and oh no, oh no, oh no.

I am definitely in it now.

Shockingly, Neelam is less than enthused by my birthday.

"Can you put this away?" she asks, swatting at my balloon. "Some of us are trying to work."

"Yes, and *some* of us are trying to eat," says Dash, nudging Neelam's tools away from his spread of curried potatoes.

"Why are you even here?" Neelam snaps at him. "Go tighten some screws."

Dash rolls his eyes at me. "Yes, my queen," he says to Neelam, plucking a carton of samosas from the table for the road.

"Hey," Teo says from behind me. "Can I get your take on this?"

"Hm? Oh, sure." I turn to follow him, but not before catching Neelam's glare. As usual, she thinks Teo and I are busy flirting or something instead of working.

"What's up?" I ask him, and he sits down with our in-progress bot, which we're currently calling Thanos until we come up with a less on-the-nose name.

"I was thinking maybe we could build some sort of defense in," he says. "Make it less about our weapon and more about using *their* weapon to our advantage. It's not like we're the only ones to accidentally use kinetic energy to our detriment."

(Thank god we've been covering torque in class.)

"So are you thinking like...armor?" I ask.

"I thought it'd be cool if we did some kind of polyurethane," he says. "Then we could use a super light metal like titanium underneath."

"Oh, so that the other weapon gets damaged by cutting through our plastic?"

"Yeah, exactly. I'm just not sure how we'd incorporate it with the metals."

"We could do an overlay. Build it in some sort of hexagonal shape, like a beehive," I say, thinking. "Piece it together like honeycombs on top of the metal."

"Yeah, perfect, something like that," Teo says, nodding vigorously. "But I've never worked with plastics, and Mac isn't sure how t—"

"My dad does," I say without thinking, and immediately, I wish I hadn't.

Teo looks up at me, probably seeing on my face that I may have just made a mistake.

"Come on," he says, beckoning to me. "Let's take a sec outside."

I don't know if we're actually this interesting or if our timing was just very conspicuous, but as we slip out of the classroom, *everyone* watches us leave. Neelam shoots a look at Emmett, who immediately pretends to be busy with whatever part is in his hand.

"You okay?" Teo asks when we're outside, and I remember that he's used to always being watched. He generally seems comfortable with an audience.

"Oh. Yeah."

"Liar." He glances at me, then slides a thumb over his lip in thought. "Call me crazy, but it seems like you 'forgetting' your birthday and then getting that look on your face about your dad probably have something in common. Did he forget or something?"

No, he didn't. He never does, though I feel guilty at the knowledge that it's Teo's first guess, because it sounds like his dad has definitely forgotten about him before.

"Well no, I just..." I swallow. "I'm eighteen now," I say slowly.

"So am I," he says. "My birthday was in November. We can go vote together."

I know he's joking to keep the conversation light, but now that he's listening, I do actually want to talk about it.

"I'm eighteen, which means I'm not a minor," I explain. "So... I could choose where I want to live."

"Oh." Teo blinks. "I didn't think about that. Are you saying you don't want t—"

"No, no, I definitely want to live with my mom." I clear my throat. "It's just that, um, before I had to? And now I just...can."

He nods slowly. "And do you think your dad expects—?"

"No, no." I wince. "It's dumb, really. I was just thinking about how it's so much worse that it's up to me now."

"Yeah. Yeah, I can see that." He gives me his *Teo Saves the World* look. "What can we do about it?"

"What? Nothing." I laugh. "Not every problem has to have an instant solution, Teo."

He bristles slightly. "I know, but—"

"But I do need my dad's help." I don't know much about poly-urethanes, and I definitely don't know how to put them together into shapes. "I'm pretty sure a honeycomb design is our best bet, but in terms of figuring out what kind to use—"

"Can I come with you?" asks Teo, and I blink.

"To my dad's?"

"Yeah. I mean it's our build, right? And you promised," he reminds me.

"I promised to introduce you to my dad?"

"No." He laughs. "You promised to be a team player."

Even though I know he's talking about robotics, I think he's actually reminding me that he's on my team.

"All right," I say, and look up at him. "So is that what we're doing for my birthday?"

"Can you think of something else you'd rather do?" he asks, arching a brow.

No, I really can't. True, part of me thinks it'd be nice if he did something more, you know... *obvious*. Because I think we're just friends, but... *are* we? Doing something that's just about us rather than the team would confirm that I'm not imagining this, or that the things I feel are returned in some way—which I'm quietly hoping they are, even if we've never talked about it.

But just because Teo can ignore the way everyone inside the classroom is staring at us through the window doesn't mean I can. Specifically, I can't ignore how much it would suck if they were ever staring at anything *bad*, like a fight, or worse, a breakup. They'd be like me and my siblings trying to choose between my parents, and let's be real—*unlike* my siblings, that whole room is filled with people who routinely side with Teo. And I should know better than anyone that things don't last forever, right?

So actually, a quiet night building stuff with Teo sounds perfect. It'll be nice, easy, comfortable. Anything more than that would just get confusing.

"Let's build some armor, then," I tell him, turning to lead him back inside.

TEO

So, it turns out I got you something," I say when I slide into Bel's car, reaching over to hand her the little paper bag that's been in my glove compartment. I actually found it a week ago, but I hadn't decided how to give it to her. I guess a birthday is as good a time as any.

"What's this?" she asks, brightening with excitement.

"Keep your expectations low," I warn her, and she gives me a look.

"Okay *sure*, Teo," she says in a mocking voice, "I'll just—"

She stops, suddenly frozen.

"Oh, Teo—"

"I told you, it's nothing. If you don't like it—"

"I love it." She looks up at me and I have to swallow hard.

"Thank you," she says.

It's just another little drawer pull; nothing special, and honestly a little underwhelming as far as birthday gifts go, but my mom had been on Melrose looking for some very specific vintage dress and I found it in an antique shop.

"I thought it would go with your other bird one," I explain. "Though I guess that might be a lot of birds?" I don't know anything about…whatever this is.

"No, there should always be two." She smiles at me. "Birds of a feather, right?"

Not for the first time, I get the feeling that if I leaned in closer, it would be like magnets. Like being drawn into some sort of gravitational field where things would just magically fit. But since we're going to her dad's house—and since I'm not really sure what would happen if I let myself get sucked into whatever black hole of possible disaster this might turn out to be—I just smile and nod and she nods and smiles and we both face the road as she starts driving.

I hate to admit that some of the places we pass on the way to her dad's would make my mom a little uneasy, though the side streets eventually open up to rows of suburban-looking homes. The one Bel pulls up to looks like the sort of house people have in the movies; not mine, obviously, but it's nothing like her apartment, either. This is clearly the place she grew up, and based on the way she's determined not to look at it, I'm guessing the swing suspended from the tree in the front yard must have been something she played on as a kid.

"Luke's not home," she says, glancing at the empty driveway and knocking on the door. "He might not be here."

She looks like she might want to turn and run, so I reach out and touch her arm, trying to be reassuring. She jumps, startled, and I quickly remove my hand. "Sorry, I just thought—"

But the door opens, revealing a man in a flannel shirt and jeans. He looks like Bel and her brothers in the same distant way I look like my mom—the coloring is slightly off, since Bel's hair and eyes are dark and her dad's aren't, but the expression on his face is unmistakably hers.

"Bel," he says, surprised. "Hey, kid."

"Hi, Dad." She lights up a little, but then turns quickly, guiltily, to me. "This is Teo," she says as her father gives me the usual paternal once-over. "We were wondering if you could help us with a school project."

"Yeah? Okay. Let's head on back, then," says Bel's dad, and I know it's not actually possible to understand everything she's going through, but I think I understand a little bit more of it. Because sure, knowing this is a guy who screwed up his marriage makes you think he'd look like a villain, but he doesn't. He looks like a nice guy, and if I didn't know any better, I'd assume he'd never done anything wrong in his life.

It's immediately obvious how Bel learned to do all the weird things she knows how to do, because her dad's shed is stocked with materials I'd have killed for as a kid. Sure, I had plenty of expensive video game consoles and I messed around with robotic cars, but Bel's dad seems to have every tool under the sun. He has a home forge and soldering tools, an entire area that seems to be just for woodworking, a full vault of automotive supplies—

"I'm a hobbyist," he says, catching my glance around. "Can't say it serves me particularly well, though the kids always had stuff for the science fair."

"Did you enter the science fair?" I ask Bel, surprised, and she chuckles with embarrassment.

"I built this, um. Atmosphere? I guess you could call it? The effect of color on cognitive performance," she says. "It was a huge hassle."

"She won an award, though," her dad says proudly.

"It was ages ago. Middle school. It was nothing. So, polyurethane?" she prompts him.

That seems to be the one thing her father doesn't have a full supply of, though he has some. He shows us how to bond one panel of plastic to another, suggesting we try it out on smaller pieces.

It's my idea to scale our bot down so we can get an idea of how much we'd need. I sit down to scribble out the measurements and then return to hand it off to Bel, who glances over it and nods.

"What's this for again?" asks Bel's dad, as if he expects a specific answer.

"Class," she says without looking up, taking out a marker to measure the dimensions I selected onto the plastic. I don't correct her, though her dad looks at me for confirmation.

Sorry, I think in silence, *I'm on her team.*

Eventually we replicate a portion (a fraction, really) of what the plastic armor should actually look like at full scale, and though Bel's clearly excited, a buzz from her phone shifts her back to the same mood she was in when we arrived.

"Okay, well, we'll have to convince Mac to work this into the budget," she says in an undertone to me, "but that should be fine."

I nod. "I'll ask him."

"Good." She gives me a look; she doesn't like Mac much. I understand why, but it's hard for me not to secretly cross my fingers and hope the whole thing's just a personality clash. I know that sounds naive, or maybe even unsupportive, but it isn't. I'm definitely on Bel's side; I just don't know what taking her side is supposed to look like. I mean, it's *Mac*—he's the one who taught me everything I know about coding, about robotics. Am I supposed to just cut him off?

"Well, okay, Dad," Bel says, turning to him. "Thanks for helping, but I should probably get Teo home."

Ah, so I'm the scapegoat. "Thanks for your help, Mr. Maier."

Her dad looks slightly disappointed. "You sure you don't want to stay for dinner, Babybel?" (I tuck that away to tease her with later.) "I could have Luke bring home a cake, too—"

"No, Dad, it's fine. I should get back." She hesitates, then gives him a hug. "Thanks, though."

"Okay." He kisses her forehead, looking sad to let her go. "Nice to meet you, Teo."

"You too."

We trudge back through her side yard and into her car, where she doesn't say anything right away. I sit with the replica in my lap, but she doesn't start the engine yet. Or do anything. Or say anything.

"Sorry," she says. "Just trying to settle, you know?"

"Take your time. I'm not actually in a hurry to get home," I say, turning the plastic replica over in my hands. "This is going to be so freaking cool," I comment at a murmur, because even though I know this is about Bel and her dad, I'm still very into robots. Any spinner weapon that has to cut through plastic is going to damage itself *and* make it more difficult to land any powerful hits, which gives us a good shot at winning for design.

She turns her head to look at me, half laughing. "You're such a nerd."

"Oh, I know. My mom tells me all the time, but apparently nerds are hot now."

"Yeah they are."

I arch a brow, and she makes a face.

"Oh come on, I've seen movies."

"Yeah? You read it in *Teen Vogue* or something?"

"Ugh." She groans, shoving me away. "All nerds but you, obviously."

"Hey," I say, playing at hurt feelings even though I can't stop myself from grinning. "You realize I'm sitting right here, don't you?"

"God, your nerd energy is so suffocating right now."

"Yeah, it's like Axe body spray but more enticing."

"Oh my god, *gross*—"

"I'm surprised you can resist, honestly."

"I'm buckled in," she says, pointedly snapping the strap of her seat belt. "Otherwise, who knows."

"I'm not," I tell her.

But then we both freeze, because if this is going to escalate...

I'm not sure what I'll do if it escalates.

I'm also not sure I'm going to want to stop if I start.

I don't even know what starting would *mean*, honestly.

"Luckily I'm not as hopeless as you," she says, saving us both.

Or not. Maybe I don't want to be saved.

"Hey Bel," I say, and suddenly my mouth is dry. I think hers is, too.

"Hey, Teo," she whispers.

There's the faintest glow from the streetlight outside on her hair, and she smells like sawdust and strawberry lip balm and for a second, I really don't care what happens next. I start to understand why I got so pissed when Dash asked her to homecoming, and why I was so upset when she didn't ask for my help with our Regionals bot, and why I sprint out of practice every day just to stand next to her and poke around at wires. I get why I asked her to come to a kids' soccer game with me and why I bought her that silly little drawer knob in the shape of a bird. I get why it matters to me that she's hurting.

Because I think about her all the time. Because she surprises me, because she makes me laugh, and because this, whatever it is with her, is the only thing I ever do that's easy.

Because wherever I am, I want her close by.

I lean forward and she holds her breath, waiting. This close to her I can smell the roses in her hair, and I can see the way her lips part while she looks at me. I pause, waiting to see if she'll pull away or turn her head, but she doesn't. Instead, she tilts her chin up toward me—just the smallest inch.

"Happy birthday, Bel," I say softly, and she's so close to me that I can almost taste her reply.

"Thanks, T—"

"IBB," comes a voice from outside, the driver door suddenly yanked open as Bel and I both jump in alarm. "Oh, hey, Teo," says Luke, and I immediately return to my seat in the car, buckling the seat belt and trying to ignore the flush in my cheeks. "Oh gross," he says, observing the two of us. "Seriously, right outside my house? Where I sleep? Where I *eat*?"

"We weren't doing anything," Bel grumbles, shoving him out of the car by his face. "I'm going home."

"What, already?" Luke smirks at us. "Eh, I get it. You," he says, jabbing a finger at me. "Keep it in your pants."

"Oh my *god*, Luke," Bel groans. "We were working on our bot. There's literally nothing less sexy."

"Truth," says Luke, though he motions with two fingers from his eyes to mine. "I'm watching you," he warns, and Bel reaches out to swing the door shut. "I'M STILL WATCHING YOU," Luke shouts to me through the door as Bel starts the car, threatening in violent sign language that she can and will run her own brother over if he doesn't get out of the way.

It's obviously fair to say that the mood is pretty much shattered. By the time Bel pulls into the school parking lot for me to get my car, it's a little too far gone.

"Thanks for the birthday gift," she says, holding up the replica I'd slipped into the center console.

"Thanks for the T. Swift," I reply, turning to get out of the car.

All in all it's an anticlimactic ending. The moment I watch her drive away, I know one thing for sure.

Luke or no Luke, I should have kissed her while I had the chance.

twelve

BOMBS

Bel

I should have kissed him while I had the chance.

Why was I waiting for him to do it anyway? He obviously wanted to and I just *sat* there, frozen and not knowing what to do with my hands and wondering if he was paying attention to the zit I could feel forming on my nose. And he didn't try again later, so what if it was always going to be a one-time thing and I was dumb enough not to shoot my shot?

I should really listen to more Lizzo.

For the first few days after my birthday, I get very self-conscious around him, which I think is the result of me constantly trying to calculate whether this moment or this one or this one might be a good time to try to recreate what we had in the car, and then, because I'm thinking so much, it passes, or Dash texts us both some incredible dog video and we get distracted, or I look at Teo in full soccer regalia and remember that it would be completely absurd for him to date me. He should either be with someone like Jamie, who's going to be president someday, or someone like Elisa Fraticelli, who's already got thousands of Instagram followers and supposedly nabbed her own eye shadow palette last week. Similarly, I should not be wasting my time on high school boys when I was clearly born to be some artist's muse, which is a calling I will probably age into around my late twenties.

I mean yeah, fine, Teo and I obviously both enjoy this weird hobby we have of building robots, but come *on*, right? We're seniors, we spend a fair amount of our time arguing about math, and if I don't get into MIT, I'll basically never see him again. Even if we did get involved it would only end badly, like all high school relationships do. Like my parents did.

Still, I wish I'd kissed him. Even just the once.

After a few weeks I've mostly forgotten about it (I haven't, obviously—I think about it all the time, usually in the shower or when I'm trying to fall asleep, but let me have this one) and by early March, all of us are practically zombies. Nationals is in less than two months, and so are the AP exams. I'm so exhausted that I actually come to school in *sweatpants*, which is something I never do.

"Hey, guys," says Lora, and the rest of us groan in response. "No, no, wait," she pleads, observing that none of us have the energy for whatever she's about to recruit us into doing. "It's fun, I promise—"

"More fun than sleep?" asks Teo, who is clearly doing none of that. Unfortunately for me, sleeplessness suits him. His hair is soft and messy and his eyes are a little tormented and shadowed.

(God, I need help.)

"Okay," Lora says, preparing to launch into her pep talk, "so, as you guys know, I'm involved with planning the Holi festival again this year—"

"Holy?" I echo, leaning over to ask Dash, who nods.

"Holi. It's an Indian festival," he explains. "Super fun. People throw colored powder and it gets everywhere and all the food is vegan, but still pretty good—"

"In LA it's mostly a matter of cultural appropriation," mutters Neelam, startling me with her unexpected commentary and making

Lora go a little prematurely skittish at whatever Neelam's criticism will be this time. "You'll notice it's run by white people who think yoga is the same thing as spirituality."

"Neelam, it's like seven p.m. on a Tuesday," groans Kai. "Can you not?"

"Yeah, um, actually Neelam makes a super valid point," says Lora, who is white and does yoga (but in a very culturally respectful way!), "but it's also about drawing attention to climate change and sustainability, which affects us all—"

"And it's fun," adds Ravi. "My aunties drag me every year, so you guys should come, too."

"There's dancing," Lora adds, "and yoga classes—"

"And falafel garlic fries," says Dash.

"—right, yeah—"

"All right, Lora, we're in." Teo gives Neelam a glance that pointedly suggests *let's not spoil this for Lora, shall we?* and then turns to me. "You're coming, yeah?"

I try not to dwell on the fact that he's asked me in front of everyone. "Yeah, of course."

"Great. Put the whole team down for tickets," Teo tells Lora. "I'll take care of it. We should have a break anyway, we're clearly all losing our minds."

"Really? Oh my gosh, thank you *gobs*, Teo," declares Lora, who's absolutely delighted. "It's going to be so fun!"

"You might actually bother learning what it's about," Neelam says, still glowering behind me. "It's not just some fraternity paint party."

"Okay, so what is it?" I ask, twisting around to face her.

Neelam gives me a sour look. "It's an ancient Hindu festival celebrating the end of winter and the start of spring."

"Oh, so like the Maypole?" I ask.

She snorts. "The hyper-fixation on European history at this

school is atrocious. No, it's not like that. The Maypole is about fertility—"

"True, it's very phallic," I admit, which only annoys Neelam more.

"—and *Holi* is about good triumphing over evil. It's all about the blossoming of love and friendship and all that," she sniffs, as if these are imaginary concepts for lesser people.

"For which you are the perfect spokesperson," Teo deadpans tiredly, and I stifle a laugh.

Neelam glares at both of us. "Are you done?"

"Yes," Teo and I sigh in unison.

"Good. As I was *saying*," she continues, "it's one of the rare times in our culture that everyone is fair game for celebration. There's no differentiation between class or religion or gender. Everyone's invited."

"Which is why it's perfect for us," concludes Lora happily, and Neelam shrugs, apparently satisfied with the five seconds she was willing to be involved. "Just try to wear things that you don't mind getting colored powder on, and wear comfortable shoes!"

Teo catches my eye and makes a little face at me. I make one back.

"All right, back to work," says Neelam flatly, giving my weld an irritated glance as I roll my eyes at Teo, sliding the helmet back on.

I'm not sure what I was expecting, but the Holi festival is huge and completely packed. The park is overflowing with smells from food trucks and music and noise and there are dancers everywhere, including two who are using hula hoops in completely fascinating ways.

"Okay, I got turquoise and pink and purple," says Jamie, shoving the packets of colored powder into my hands. "No orange, please. Not my favorite."

"What if we turned it into a color war instead?" suggests Dash, suddenly appearing next to me. "We each get a color, and whoever has the most of that color wins?"

"Oh, you're on," says Kai, snatching a bag of red. "Watch out, Luna."

"Maybe we should do it in teams," suggests Teo. "Since there's not enough colors."

"Fine—I call Bel and Lora," shouts Jamie.

"Neelam," I say, spotting her behind me. "Want to be on our team?"

She glares at me. "You do realize this is missing the point," she says, though—and maybe it's just me—it seems a little half-hearted.

"But you said Holi is about friendship, right?" I remind her, forcing brightness. "So it's not really *missing* the point so much as, like, interpreting it?"

She purses her lips, which I'm pretty sure is Neelam-speak for *touché*.

"Still dumb," she says, and turns away, heading toward her other friends.

"Okay then," I sigh, turning back to Jamie as she replaces my pink and purple packets with more turquoise ones. "I tried."

"Why do you *keep* trying?" Jamie asks me curiously. "You're basically a glutton for punishment."

"If it helps, I don't think Neelam actually dislikes you," Lora adds. "She's just very intense."

This is all very on-brand for Lora, who sees the best in every person and situation whether they deserve it or not. Unfortunately, I'm pretty sure that whatever Neelam's issue is with me, it's *very* personal. Neelam's perfectly capable of amicable behavior with Lora and Jamie, plus she's over there laughing with Mari-from-Civics right now (I take it they cleared up that whole homecoming fight, which, good for them), so what have *I* done that's so unforgivable? Aside from sticking my foot in my mouth literally every time I talk to her, which...okay. Fine.

But in my defense, she doesn't exactly make it easy to say the right thing.

"Um, sure," I tell Lora, accepting the packets and looking up at Teo, who flashes me a grin as he waves his obscenely pink color packets at me. "Did Dash pick those out for you?" I call to him.

"Whatever, Bel Canto. I'm an ally," he shouts back.

I shake my head in an effort to look disapproving, but of course Jamie sees through it, giving me a little maternal cluck of her tongue.

"Girl, you've got it *bad*," she taunts me. "I'm surprised you haven't been carving your initials into the trees."

"Stop it," I tell her, cheeks burning. "It's not like that, we're just—"

"We're *just friends*," Lora and Jamie mock me in twin singsong voices.

"Oh come on," I growl, mortified and trying desperately to play it off. "You guys both said it: *everyone* has some degree of a crush on Teo Luna. It's just something in the water, or in his hair products or something."

"I don't think he uses any," says Lora, which isn't helpful.

"And besides," Jamie says, waggling a brow at me suggestively. "We might all think he can get it, but the difference is that *he* likes *you*."

"No, that's not—"

I look up to argue, but at that exact moment Teo is watching me from where he stands with Dash and Kai. He's wearing a pair of white soccer shorts and a thin white T-shirt, which somehow makes even his sock tan look absolutely glorious.

"You look cute," adds Jamie, tugging at my hair, which I left down. I glare at her, and she tosses a handful of turquoise powder directly at my boobs. "Nailed it," she says, just as Emmett runs by to streak a handful of green across her back. "Oh my *god*, Emmett, have we even *started*—"

"They're about to do the first color throw," says Lora, grabbing both our arms and pulling us into the crowd. "Are you guys ready?"

She tugs us into the center of the park's grassy lawn as we fill our hands with the turquoise color powder. On stage, a troupe of dancers shout at us to crouch down, and even though I have absolutely no idea what we're doing or if it's even safe to throw neon powder at each other, my heart is pounding with excitement.

"Ready? Count down with me! TEN—"

"Ten!" Lora and Jamie roar.

"—NINE—"

"Nine!"

I sneak a glance over my shoulder at Teo, who's got his handful of pink powder ready. "Comin' for ya, Bel Canto," he warns me. "Watch out."

I roll my eyes at him. "Just wait, Luna—"

"Oh, I will—"

"—TWO—"

"Two!"

"—ONE—"

"One!"

And then, with a burst of beauty like nothing I've ever seen before, the sky erupts in an explosion of powder, all the colors soaring up to the sun and falling back down in an embrace of laughter, love, and light.

By afternoon we're exhausted and full of falafel fries and vegan curry. Dash, who is covered head to toe in turquoise powder, drags me excitedly from stand to stand until he stops to lie down in the grass, like an overtired puppy. Lora and Jamie and I all get matching beaded bracelets to commemorate the occasion: turquoise, of course.

"There you are," Teo says in my ear, catching my arm and pulling me back just as I'm about to tag along with Lora and Ravi to one of the yoga classes on the lawn. Teo pats some pink onto both my cheeks and laughs when I shove him away, returning the favor with a smear of turquoise across his forehead. "Wait, wait, you need a little more right...*here*—"

He dumps a handful on my head and I toss some into his chest, rubbing it in like a kindergartener on finger-painting day. "Oh look, *much* better—"

He tilts his head back with a full-bodied laugh. "Okay, okay, you win. That turquoise is potent."

"Giving up so easily?" I ask, gesturing over my shoulder. "There's about to be another color toss."

"I'm almost out," he says, showing me his dwindling stash of ammunition. I'm running low, too, having used the remains of my packet on decorating his face.

"Okay, so let's do one more. No holds barred," I suggest. "And whoever walks out with more of the other color takes the W."

"You got it." He hooks his foot around the back of my knee in what seems like a very soccer-ish move and I chase after him.

"Luna, that's *got* to be a red card—"

"Oh wait, we're supposed to be dancing," he says with a frown of concentration, grabbing my hand. "Come on. This way."

"What?" I'm laughing, but mostly from exhaustion. "Wait, Teo—"

He tugs me to the left, expertly following the instructions from the dancer onstage. I nearly collide with him when he switches directions.

"Here, like this," he says, holding my hips and guiding me. "And one kick, two kicks...Geez, Bel, you're shit at this—"

"How do *you* know how to do it?" I shout. The crowd is gathering around us now to prepare for the next color toss, so naturally I've collided with at least three people in the last five seconds. Teo, on the other hand, is so into it he's even mimicking the correct facial expressions.

"Dunno. Coordination, I guess," he says, doing some extremely complex dance move just as the dancer takes the mic.

"Are we ready? You guys remember the countdown, right?"

"Oof, watch out," Teo says, tugging me out of the way of some other very uncoordinated but enthusiastic dancer, and I collide with his chest. "You good?"

I look up at him and my breath catches. Even covered in what's essentially a mix of paint and sweat, he looks so good. His hair is purple at the tips and I want to run my fingers through it. I want him to hold me, right here, for the next forty-five minutes.

No, an hour. Two hours.

"What?" I say, briefly lost in my own fantasy world.

"Are you okay?" He's honest-to-god checking me for injury, like I might have actually gotten wounded by something as harmless as a dude waving his hand around.

"Yeah, Teo, I'm fine—"

The rest of the crowd crouches around us and we both blink, remembering what we're supposed to be doing. He pulls me closer to him and squats down, pouring what remains of his pink powder into his hand as I hurry to take hold of the last of my turquoise.

"You ready?"

"Yeah, are you?"

"Maybe we should color our bot like this." He grins at me. "Just toss color bombs into the polyurethane and see how it goes."

"What would we call it?"

"I don't know. Babybel."

I smack his shoulder. "*Don't*—"

"Fine, fine. The dichotomy of good and evil."

"Oh my *god* you're the worst."

"I know." He brushes my hair out of my eyes, which I know is a tactic to cover my forehead in pink, but still. We're even closer now than we were in my car on my birthday.

Elsewhere, the countdown spirals down.

"—FOUR—"

185

"Hey, Bel?" he says.

"Yeah, Teo?"

"—THREE—"

"Doesn't matter what we call the bot," he says. "We're going to win."

"—TWO—"

"Yeah? You sound sure."

"Oh, I'm very sure."

"—ONE—"

"Why's that?"

"Some things you just know," he says, and then, in an appropriately euphoric moment, we both throw our colors into the air, watching them swirl and blend and come down in a rain of neon brightness.

Then he turns to me, but I'm already there.

"If you're sure, I'm sure," I say.

"Is that a line from *The Notebook*?" he asks me.

"Oh my god, *shut u—*"

And then he pulls me in and kisses me.

For the record, I know time doesn't *actually* stop or anything. I know the world doesn't revolve around me, but for a second it's totally cinematic, like we're the stars of our own movie and all the people dancing around us are celebrating us the same way we are. The sun is high and the joy is sharp and everything is rich and saturated and glittering, technicolor and exhilarating, us and the universe connecting symphonically in that kiss. It's like everything we've ever learned about force in physics, about materials that connect, about strong bonds and magnetic ones, about gravity and mystery. I've always believed that there's a possibility for everything in the world to collide for a single perfect moment, and that sometimes, if you're lucky, you get to have one for yourself.

This one is ours.

I slide my arms around his neck and he tightens his around my waist, and I think I always knew it would feel like this with him.

"Sorry it took me so long," he murmurs.

I'm pretty sure Jamie and Lora are gaping from somewhere, which means Neelam probably saw as well, plus Dash and Kai and Emmett and...

Whatever.

I pull Teo down for another kiss. "Sorry it took *me* so long."

"So does that technically mean I win?"

I groan. "Teo, you're the—"

"Worst, I know." He tips my chin up and kisses me once, then again and again. "Think they all saw?"

"Definitely."

"Want to back out?"

"What, like shove you away? Not sure that would work."

"We could try it," he says. "You could punch me."

"Tempting," I say, "but no."

"Might make things awkward if you don't."

"Definitely will. Why, are you backing out?"

"Definitely not. I'm just covering all our bases."

"Everyone's going to be weird."

"Yes."

"And we've really only got a few months."

"Not if you get into MIT," he reminds me, "which you will."

I feel a little shiver of portent. Is it possible it's that easy? That life just...*points* you in the direction you're meant to go? Because it definitely feels that way right now.

"So are you in this?" he asks me.

I look up at him and try to remember a time when I didn't secretly think he was the best person I've ever known.

I can't.

"I'm in this," I promise him, feeling absolutely neon-bright.

TEO

Obviously things are different now that everyone knows Bel and I are going out. Neelam, of course, does us the favor of still being kind of a dick.

"Finally," she mutters. "It's not like we didn't already know. You two are about as subtle as a brick through a window. And in this case the window is my eyes," she adds gratuitously.

"Oh gosh, *thanks*, Neelam," says Bel, exchanging a glance with me.

I like that we can do that now.

Bel and I still spend most of our time together working on our multicolored bot—which we're currently calling Battlestar Chromatica, as per the storied tradition of naming bots with corny puns—but some other things have changed. We don't have a ton of free time, given how quickly Nationals and the AP exams are coming up, but rather than studying with my usual Physics lab group, I've been doing a lot of "studying" with Bel.

"Okay, harmonic motion," she says. Our textbooks are sitting on the coffee table in her living room and our knees are touching on her sofa, hers nudging competitively into mine while we do our best to finish (read: start) our preliminary lab work.

"You're setting the curve in the class, right?" she says. "Teach me everything."

"Bel, I'm pretty sure you also have an A."

"Well, sure, but still. Ready, go." She gives me a look that has me thinking I deserve a trophy if I can make it through the next five minutes without getting distracted.

"Harmonic motion," I echo, opening my book to a random page. "It's very…harmonious."

"Excellent, I think we're done here," she says, nudging the book aside and leaning toward me. I'm more than happy to forget about the lab entirely, so I pull Bel in with one arm until she collapses on top of me on the couch.

"Hey, sailor," she says seductively.

"Weirdo."

"You like it."

"I do." She melts when I kiss her, my hand sliding under her shirt. "We should probably study, though."

"Mmhmm." She deepens the kiss, filling my nose with the roses from her hair and my mouth with the taste of strawberry lip balm. "Something about…motion?"

"Harmonic motion."

"Harmonic motion." She tugs at my shirt and I sit up, letting her pull it off me. "Wow," she exhales.

"Don't *ogle* me," I remind her. "I'm a person. My eyes are up here."

"Shut up." She kisses me again, which does the trick.

Eventually her phone alarm goes off and we both stiffen, apprehensive.

"Does that mean your mom's coming home soon?" I ask her.

"Yeah. She'll be here in a few minutes."

She sits up with a sigh, plucking my shirt from the floor and handing it back to me.

"No need to look so devastated," I tell her with a laugh, slipping it on and reaching for her again. "What are you doing tomorrow?"

"Tomorrow? I thought you had soccer."

"I do, but it's just postseason stuff I'm doing to help next year's varsity. I can duck out early." For her? Definitely.

"Mmm, I think I'm fr— Ah, no," she remembers abruptly. "My mom's got the day off, I think. So we could do something, but we can't come here."

"Ah." I tuck her hair behind her ear. "So…fifteen minutes in my car?"

"You're gross." She kisses me. "Twenty minutes."

"Done." I pause. "Or you could just come over to my house."

She gives me a curious glance. "Really? I got the feeling you didn't want me there."

"What? No way." That never crossed my mind at all. "I'm just not there very often."

"Oh. Well, I mean, sure," she says uncertainly. "Yeah, I could do that. Will your parents be home?"

"Probably not."

"Oh." She sounds a little breathy. "Interesting."

Up to this point we haven't been alone together longer than a few spare minutes at a time, like the half hour we just had in her living room. We do "date" things from time to time—we went to the movies with Dash, Lora, and Jamie last week—but I think we're still in the stages of wanting to be alone together. Whenever I kiss her in front of the others, they make a big production of it.

I run my fingers over the necklace she has on. "We don't have to do, you know. Anything you're not ready for."

"I know." She reaches down to take hold of my fingers, brushing her lips across them. "But we...could. Maybe."

I think I nearly swallow like a cartoon wolf. "Don't talk about that when your mom's about to walk in any second."

"Why?"

"Because it's going to be hard not to think about it," I grumble, "and I don't need to make my intentions obvious."

"Begone, foul beast," she says theatrically, holding her hands over her eyes, "or my mother will find me a lightskirt—"

"Lightskirt?"

"The lightest of skirts," she says solemnly.

"Seriously," I groan, "you are *so*—"

"Weird," she supplies for me, preening a little. "But you like it."

"Yeah," I tell her, and sneak in one more kiss before we hear the front door open. "I really, really do."

✱ ✱ ✱

I tell my soccer coach that I don't want to overstress my left knee and he tells me to take my time recovering, ice and elevation, blah blah, coming off a big season, take care of yourself Luna, so on and so forth. I feel bad about lying, but I already carried this team for a whole semester. I deserve a break, right?

Just one.

When I come out to the parking lot after school, Bel's already leaning on the hood of my car. She's wearing a navy-blue polka-dotted sundress that clings to her hips on a breeze, and even before she kisses me hello it's already worth the lie.

"What'd you tell your mom?" I ask her, slipping one arm around her waist.

"That I'm studying with Jamie. She won't ask questions, and if she does we've got it covered." She holds up a mini photoshoot of herself and Jamie working in the library, their books deliberately opened to the pages on harmonic motion. "I'll be home before she is, anyway."

"Assuming there's no traffic. Or that I let you go." I kiss her and she tugs me closer.

"Come on, sailor. Let's go."

I play with her fingers at red lights, pulling into my house with a new, uneasy feeling that I don't usually have when I take people here. I guess because my friends are more used to it, or I'm more used to their reactions? I mean, let's be real—it's a big house. It's hard to pretend I'm just a normal guy when Bel can clearly see the kind of life I've lived.

"M'lady," I say, opening the passenger door for her and holding out a hand.

"Oh, are you trying something here?" she asks, amused.

"Well, when in Rome—"

"—do as the weird people do?"

"That's the one." I kiss her fingers and pull her inside. "Do you want something to drink, or should we just go to my room?"

"Presumptuous," she comments.

Oops. "Sorry, I just meant—"

"Shut up, Luna. Let's go," she says, taking my hand and tugging me up the stairs.

I have to redirect her twice—there are a *lot* of rooms, and practically a whole wing of this house has always been for me and my various "objects of entertainment," as my mother calls my game consoles and stuff—but we manage to make it. I sit on the edge of my bed and she half tackles me backward, the two of us winding up face-to-face.

"Should we talk about Chromatica?" she asks.

"Later." I slide my hand around her face and pull her in for a kiss, which deepens.

And then deepens more.

Her leg slips between mine and I run my fingers below the fabric of her dress. I'll be honest, I like having her this close to me. And I'd like to do more, but I don't want to make her think I brought her here just for that.

"How are you doing?" I ask.

To my surprise, she stiffens. "What?"

"You," I say. "How's . . . everything? Physics and family and stuff."

"Oh." She clears her throat. "We don't have to talk about it."

"What if I want to?"

"There's nothing to say."

"That's fine. I can still ask, can't I?"

She sits up for a second, staring at me.

"Do you really want to know?" she asks me.

I sit up, too, mirroring her. "Yeah, of course."

"It's dumb."

"No it's not."

"It is."

"It's you. That's not dumb."

"Ugh." She closes her eyes. "You're the worst," she whispers.

I think maybe I was right to ask her if something was wrong, so I pull her into me and lie back down, this time with her head resting on my chest.

"What is it?" I ask her.

"My parents. They're fighting about who's going to pay my college tuition." She burrows her face in my shirt. "I feel so guilty."

"Why?"

"My mom is insisting that my dad should pay for both mine and Gabe's, since he encouraged Luke to drop out. I told her I could just try to get financial aid or something, but she keeps saying my dad *owes* me. And it's not that he wouldn't want to or anything, it's just—"

"A lot?" I ask.

"It's a lot," she exhales. "And I hate having to take a side."

"Do you? Have to take a side."

"I think, honestly, I've just been taking no side. Just staying out of their way." She traces little circles on my chest absently. "But it seems like such a long time since either of them looked at me like I was special to them, you know? Like I was their daughter." She sighs. "Now I'm just another burden they have to fight over."

"That's not true." I'm surprised how adamant I feel about it.

"I know it isn't *actually* true, I just..." She sighs again. "I just want to be with you and forget about all of it," she murmurs, and because I don't know what else to do, I kiss the top of her head.

"I can help you apply for scholarships and stuff for MIT," I tell her. "There's got to be loads of grants for female engineers. I'm sure if I ask my counselor for ideas we could find some—"

"You don't have to solve this for me, Teo." She twists around to look up at me. "I mean, you *are* solving it, in a way," she says, gesturing to where we're currently tangled up on my bed.

"I don't think it's solved, Bel," I tell her carefully. "But I can help you with the applications, and then—"

But I stop when she looks up at me.

"You really just...make everyone else's problems yours, don't you?" she asks me quietly. "That must be hard."

"What?" I blink at her.

"You're just...you're never like 'screw it, that sucks,' you know? It's why you take losses so hard, like at Regionals. You take everyone's expectations and their worries and fears and absorb them like a sponge, but what about you?"

"What about me?"

She shifts around until she's on top of me, looking me dead in the eye.

"You don't have to make the world perfect just so people will love you," she says.

I swallow. "That's...that's not it, I'm not—"

"Teo." She crawls up my chest until we're eye to eye, nose to nose. "I promise I'll still like you, even if I ever have a problem you can't fix," she says, and since I don't know what else to do, I lift my head and kiss her as intensely as I can.

She kisses me back, the mood between us shifting. We get so caught up in the moment that neither of us notices the sound of someone else in the house until there are footsteps coming up the stairs.

"Teo!" calls my father.

Bel rolls hastily off of me and I manage to make myself moderately presentable just as my dad walks into the room.

"Teo." My father's mouth tightens in irritation, his eyes flicking from me to Bel and back to me. "I thought you said you'd be at soccer."

"I was," I say. "I went home early."

"Why?"

"Dad, this is Bel," I say, because I hate talking about her like she's not here. Naturally, my dad ignores me.

"Why aren't you at soccer, Mateo?"

"My knee was acting up," I tell him coolly. "I thought it'd be better to rest it now rather than chance making it worse."

"And this is you resting?"

Okay, I know an accusation when I hear one. "We weren't doing anything."

My dad slides a glance from me to Bel, whose face is flushed pink with mortification.

"Teo, outside. Now," Dad says.

I flash an apologetic glance at Bel and follow him into the hallway. "Dad, listen, I know I'm not supposed t—"

"This is where it starts, Teo. Distraction." Dad gives me the impatient look he reserves for his summer interns. "Just because you've gotten into school doesn't mean you can lose your focus. You still have responsibilities as a leader."

"Dad, I'm not losing focus—"

"Who is she?"

"Bel? She's on robotics with me. She's going to MIT next year," I add, which isn't entirely true, but it's close enough. "She's an engineer, too."

Dad flicks a glance to my bedroom, then back to me.

"Don't let this happen again," he says, turning to leave.

"Dad," I say, trying to pause him. "Can you stay for dinner? Because I think if you could just sit down with her—"

"I have a meeting. And you should take her home," he says. "Now, Teo. And unless you want me to speak to your coach about what you were really doing this afternoon, I suggest you run some drills to make up for the practice you missed."

"Dad—"

"Teo, let me be clear," he says sharply. "Your mother and I afford you the privilege of responsibility because we trust you. We trust that you understand the consequences of your actions, and we expect you to behave like someone worthy of that respect. If you choose to act like a child, we will treat you like one, so take that girl home and come straight back here. Am I understood?"

There's no point arguing with him.

"Yeah, Dad." I exhale. "I understand."

"Good. Your mother will be home shortly."

Then he turns and walks away, leaving me to wonder how I'm going to explain any of this to Bel.

"It's fine," she says from behind me, and I turn with a start, realizing she must have heard everything. I guess that's not surprising, since my dad didn't bother to hide it. "I'm ready when you are."

I reach for her and pull her into me, dropping my head for a kiss, but it doesn't feel the same between us now. I think I did something wrong, but once again, I'm not sure how to fix it.

"I'm sorry," I say, and she shakes her head, giving me a small smile.

"Don't be sorry," she tells me, pulling away, but I can't let her go yet.

Not yet.

thirteen

REJECTS

TEO

Listen, Luna, I was young once, believe it or not," Mac says. "It's not completely out of the realm of possibility that I might understand why you're finding other things more interesting than robotics these days."

I shift my backpack from one shoulder to another.

"The point is your teammates are relying on you. Justin couldn't reach you yesterday afternoon to go over the driving changes to Seven, and it doesn't make your team feel good to see their captain distracted by other things."

"I'm not distracted," I say. "I was working on Battlestar Chromatica and—"

"Of course, of course," Mac assures me, with the distinct air of not believing anything I'm saying. In fairness, I *was* working on our smaller bot…at Bel's. *Let someone else figure it out for a change*, she'd said when Justin texted, and at the time I was pretty convinced she had a point.

Apparently not.

"I'm sure you can understand why it makes the others uneasy when they can't seem to track you down. Kai's a wreck," Mac says with a smirk, since we both know Kai's going to be a wreck either way, "and Dash is always the first to defend you, but anyone can see he's got his hands full."

"Dash?" I don't really know what to say to any of this, because Dash hasn't said anything to me. Did I actually miss something that big?

"I just want to be sure you're focused," Mac says. "You've got a bright future ahead of you, Teo. Unless your plans have changed—"

"Of course not." I'm going to MIT. I'm getting out. That's been the plan since...like, *forever*, and nothing about that has changed. "Bel's not asking me t—"

"I'm not saying she is," Mac says quickly. "I'm just saying I've seen kids like you get caught up in a relationship and make choices they otherwise wouldn't." He rests a hand on my shoulder. "Look, Luna, you know how special you are," he tells me. "You're the brightest kid I've ever taught, bar none. You have the opportunity to become something truly great, and I'm not just saying that because I'm your teacher."

I don't really know what to say to that. Part of me feels like I should defend Bel; it's not fair, honestly, to heap all sorts of praise on me like this when I know I haven't been doing any of this alone. Even knowing that Dash or Kai or Emmett aren't included in Mac's opinion of me makes me feel guilty.

But at the same time, I *do* understand that something about me is different. I've always been the guy who shows up first and leaves last. I'm the one who wins the MVP trophies, the one whose job it is to keep everyone else on track. I'm the guy at bat when the bases are loaded, figuratively speaking. In a crisis, you call in Teo Luna. That's the person I've been since before I even understood what it was like to have a role.

"She's not distracting me," I say eventually. "My goals haven't changed. Nothing's changed. Going to MIT is still my top priority. Winning Nationals is still my top priority."

Mac gives me a scrutinizing look, then nods.

"It's not that I don't think highly of Bel…" he says, and trails off.

"I understand." I know that I could say something to him about how Bel is actually the reason I've been doing so well in all my other classes, because every time she says anything, she changes the way I think. I can feel myself changing and shifting and thinking about things in new and different ways, but I know Mac won't want to hear that; I know that's exactly what he doesn't want.

Because regardless of what Bel says, people want a very specific version of Teo Luna. And it's not the version who spent all of last night falling into a deep internet dive about medieval English social structures because using a Shakespearean lexicon makes his girlfriend laugh. They don't mean the version who spent last week listening to her rant about how the economic model we're learning in Macroeconomics is reliant on men continuing a system of unpaid domestic labor by women. They definitely don't mean the version whose Spotify is currently paused on Taylor Swift's entire discography so he can learn all the words that make her smile, even when she doesn't want to. Especially then.

The version of Teo Luna that other people want is hyper-focused on winning. He doesn't talk about anything other than engineering and software and bots. Physics comes easily to him and he finishes his labs before everyone else; he always gets the *atta boy*, and he gets held up as an example. He pushes other people to do better because *he* is better, because he's the *best*, because without him there is no one else to rely on. Other people will cave or panic or struggle, but not him. Not Teo Luna.

Not me.

I try to tell myself it doesn't matter right now; that when Bel and I are both at MIT, everyone will finally start to think of what we have as something good and right instead of the usual teenage cautionary tale.

"I'm focused," I tell Mac again. "I'm in this. It won't happen again."

* * *

By the time AP tests are about a month away, every single one of my teachers has started giving daily practice exams and scheduling finals. Bel and I (along with everyone else in AP Physics) are essentially the walking dead. We barely do anything but study—*actually* study, not a euphemism, because at this point we can't find the time to hang out alone. Jamie's insistent on having Bel around, Dash is incapable of studying by himself, and Lora takes the best notes out of anyone we know, so the next few weeks are crammed with group study sessions at a coffee shop that has to continuously kick us out.

When we're not studying for our other classes, we're at the robotics lab. (We should probably all change our mailing addresses—as Bel likes to say, this is where we live now.) Nationals is the week after AP exams, so everything is definitely working up to a boiling point. By the time I catch Bel nearly falling asleep over the construction of Chromatica's polymer shell, I figure it's time to pull the Concerned Boyfriend card and send her home.

"Of course I don't mind," Bel says when I tell her I'm going to stay late. "It's my team, too, Teo. I want us to do well, so if you have work to do—"

She shrugs, and I'm relieved. Of course she wouldn't be mad. Anyone who thinks she's somehow distracting me clearly doesn't know her very well.

"You're awesome." I wish I had better words for her, but Justin's already at my elbow nagging me about something (Mac was right about one thing: Justin, like most people on this team, can't figure anything out without me) and nothing appropriately flowery is coming to mind. "I'm just going to work a little bit more on the circuitry problem—FaceTime later tonight?"

"Sure, yeah." She seems distracted and Justin won't leave me alone, so I kiss her cheek and follow him back into the lab.

People usually know to let me work when I'm troubleshooting something, so the rest of the night is just me tinkering in silence while

Justin and Akim slump down in lab chairs a table away. Eventually I fix the bug, we do a test run, and then we call it a night.

It's well after ten, so I'm not that surprised when Bel doesn't answer my video call. I text her good night from my car and then check my other messages.

Dash: so
Dash: i got into caltech

I immediately hit call.

"Hello?"

"Holy shit," I say. "Caltech? Dude. Congrats, that's awesome."

"Oh, yeah." Dash sounds very Dash, which means either having his mouth full or being sleepy. "Did you just get that message?"

"Yeah, I'm just leaving the lab now." I switch the phone to my car's Bluetooth system and start the engine, pulling out of the parking lot.

"Wait, you're still at school? I assumed you were with Bel."

"God, not you, too," I groan.

"Not me too what?"

I switch my voice to an imitation of my father. "Teo, it's important that you not get distracted—"

"Oh." Dash laughs. "No, dude, the opposite."

"The opposite what?"

"No, like...I think you being with Bel is a good thing. You being at school is less good."

That's not what I expected. "What?"

"Well, come on. Typically this close to Nationals you'd be a mess."

Okay, that's completely false. Or like, mostly false. "*Mess* is a strong word."

"Yeah, and a good one. You forget I've already seen it three times. You think everything falls apart if you're not there holding it together."

That's because it does, I think, but immediately feel guilty.

"Okay." I sigh. "So?"

"So I thought it was nice that robotics wasn't your entire friggin' life for once."

"Hey," I say, mildly wounded. "It's *your* life, too."

"Actually, it really isn't," says Dash, and then, after a second of hesitation, he says, "I don't really want to go."

"What?"

"I don't want to go to Caltech."

"What?"

"Are you not hearing me, or...?"

"No, I just—" I break off. "I don't get it. Why not? I thought it was your top choice."

"You think it's my top choice to go to school ten minutes away from the place I've lived my entire life?"

"More like forty-five with traffic, but I mean—"

"I got into NYU last week," he says. "Still waiting on Columbia." I blink. "Wait, New York?"

"Yeah."

"Do either of those schools even have engineering programs?" Dash is quiet for a second.

"I don't actually think I want to be an engineer," he says slowly.

"Um, what?"

"If I went to NYU I'd be, like, a train ride away from you," he says. "I've never been to Boston. You could show me the good eats."

"Dash—"

"Plus I know you've always stayed at the Ritz or whatever, but have you ever seen NYC from a shitty dorm room...? Didn't think so."

"Dash," I growl, taking the turn just before my house. "What do you mean you don't want to be an engineer? We've taken the same classes for four years. We've built robots together for *four frickin' years*—"

"Yeah, and I liked it. I thought it was fun." He pauses. "But I don't want to do it forever, man. It's not a forever thing."

"But—" I'll admit, I'm slightly horrified. I can't imagine how I would feel about never doing this again. "But then this is your last Nationals, Dash. Ever."

"Yeah, I know." He laughs. "And?"

"And then it's *over*."

"Yep."

"But—"

"Teo," says Dash. "There's passion and then there's, you know, other shit. Things you do because you like hanging out with your best friend. Or things you do just because you can, because you're good at them. But they're not the same as like…*love*, you know?"

I pull into my driveway and sit there in silence for a second, unsure what to say.

"I didn't know you didn't love it," I tell him.

He laughs. "What would you have done if you'd known?"

"I don't know, made it better. Made it more fun."

"Teo." Dash laughs again. "Dude, I had fun. I had the time of my life. And it's over now, or close." I can hear him opening and closing cabinet doors, probably hunting around for something to eat. "I don't need you to do something different."

"But if I'd known—"

"It's not like you could magically make me love it," he says. "And look, I want to be in New York. Do you know they have the most Michelin star restaurants in the country?"

"But what are you going to *do*?" I ask him desperately.

"Dunno," he says, sounding as cheerful as ever. "Learn stuff. Get a job as a server, see museums. Go to grad school, write a best-selling series of detective novels. Bartend." The sound of a wrapper from the other end suggests he's eating string cheese. "The possibilities are endless," he says, mouth full.

"God." My stomach twists. "And to think people are worried about *me* losing focus."

"Hey man, not everyone is Teo Luna."

"Meaning what?"

"Meaning some people aren't just born knowing what they're meant to be."

My phone buzzes in my hand and I stare for a second at the gigantic house my father's success built.

"Well, look, congrats either way," I tell him. "But I think Bel just texted me, so—"

"Yeah, go away," he jokes. "See you in English?"

"See you in English."

I hang up the phone and turn off the car, still staring up at my house. The lights are on, so someone's home. Hopefully it's my mom.

"Oh, hey, sweetie," she says when I walk in. Her brow furrows and she summons me over to where she's stretching on the floor of the living room. "You look sad, baby. What's wrong?" she asks, still reaching for her toes.

"I don't know, really." I sit cross-legged next to her.

"Well, I can ring up my therapist for you if you want—"

"No, I'm okay," I tell her. She offers all the time, and I actually considered it recently, since I'd like some insight into what Bel's going through with her parents' divorce. "I think I'm just sad that things are ending."

"What things? High school?"

"Yeah. And Dash is going to NYU, maybe."

"Aw, yeah, hon. People go far and wide these days, but it doesn't mean you won't still be friends."

"It's not just that, it's..." I trail off. "Do you think I'm not like other people?"

"Heck no, kid. You're as unique as they come." She grips my chin and I squirm away when she tries to kiss me on the lips.

"Mom, gross—"

"You're still my baby even if you're a hot nerd now, sweets."

"Mom." I nudge her away and she grins at me. "I mean like... do you think other people have bigger dreams than me? Or more interesting ones?"

She frowns a little, which I know she hates to do. She worries about fine lines. "Is this about your girlfriend?"

"Bel? No." My mom likes her, thankfully, and their introduction was far less awkward than Bel's first encounter with my dad. "Well, kind of," I admit. "I just feel like maybe she and Dash are more content to let life take them places."

"She's a good egg, and so is Dash. And eighteen is awfully young to be certain about anything." She reaches out to touch my hair, raking it back from my face. "I do sometimes wonder whether you ever really got to be a kid."

"Come on, Mom. I've got video games and skateboards. You did good."

"Well, the guidebook demanded it," she says solemnly.

She looks at me a little longer and then glances at the time.

"Speaking of the guidebook—get to bed, mister," she says, giving my shoulder a shove. "Sleep is important for developing minds."

"That does sound like it's in the book," I agree, rising to my feet and remembering the text I got while I was on the phone with Dash. "Breakfast in the morning?"

"I've got early Pilates, so sure, honey. Give Mama a kiss."

I drop a kiss to her cheek absentmindedly and she squeezes mine. "Night, baby."

"Night, Mom."

I pull up my messages and see that it isn't Bel, but Kai.

Kai: OMFG I GOT INTO MIT
Kai: MIT 2024 BABYYYYYYYY
Teo: yesss, congrats!!

But then I stop to think about it, because if Kai got into MIT today…

That means Bel should have found out today as well.

Bel

"H ey, hija," says my mom, creeping into my room in the morning. "Are you feeling any better?"

She has a glass of orange juice in her hand for me, which is cute. Sorry Mom, but I'm not actually ill. I had other reasons for going straight to bed last night.

"I'm okay, Mom." I sit up slowly. "Shouldn't you be at work by now?"

"I'm leaving in ten minutes." She reaches out and checks my temperature. "You don't feel hot."

"I'm okay. I'll be fine for school." I don't want to go, but since I have a nurse for a mother, I've never been able to fake sick. Besides, I have a bot to finish. (Though, thinking about showing up to robotics makes me feel supremely unwell, so maybe it wouldn't be a total lie.)

"Okay." My mom smiles at me and I think again how unfair it is that I keep so many secrets from her. I mean, what exactly am I afraid of?

(Disappointing her. Failing her. Giving her hope and then taking it away.)

"Have you heard from any schools yet?" she asks me, rising to her feet. "My coworker Marilou told me last night that her daughter got into UC Santa Barbara."

"Oh, yeah, I think the UCs are a little ahead of everyone else," I say thinly.

"Yeah, probably." She leans over to kiss my forehead. "Have a good day at school, anak ko. I love you."

"Love you, Mom." She slips out of my room and I collapse back against my pillows, glancing at my phone screen.

Teo: did you hear from MIT yesterday?

My stomach gives another brutal twist. I hold down his earlier good night message to "love" it and then pause before answering.

The thing is…I've been really happy lately. Sure, I'm dying a little bit from all the studying for finals and AP exams and Nationals, but things have been so good that I probably should have known they'd end soon. Chromatica's been coming together beautifully, Teo is basically the most thoughtful boyfriend ever, Jamie's so stressed that I don't even have time to worry about anything because she's already fretted enough for the both of us, and even Neelam's so distracted she doesn't talk to me unless it's to give me actual productive advice. She even asked me a question the other day—yes, *me*, she asked *me*—about the best way to fix Seven's spinner, so, like, this should really be the time of my life.

Unfortunately, I'm not sure Teo's aware that I've heard a little bit more than I was meant to from his private conversations recently. I heard him telling Mac that his future was his top priority, and I heard him tell his father that I was going to MIT—which, sure, was probably a lie meant to ease the situation, but I also heard the little layer of truth underneath. He's qualifying the time he spends dating me by focusing on the fact that I'm a detail that fits perfectly into his life. I'm going to be an engineer, like him, and I'm going to MIT, like him, and the only way he can make room for me is if… he doesn't actually have to make room. So unless I go to MIT, I'm just a complication in his plans.

What sucks is that for the first time in my life, I actually *like* the way my future looks. It's the first time I really understand what it is to even *want* a future. The possibility of a major or a career never seemed exciting to me until I realized that this, building and designing things that did whatever I wanted them to, was an actual job that some people got to have. For the last month, I've been able to exist in an imaginary future where Teo and I lived on the same campus and took over college robotics together. And then maybe he'd work in AI or virtual reality or something and I'd be the head of a design team that does some good in the world and we'd collaborate occasionally but mostly he'd have his thing and I'd have mine, and we'd just keep doing exactly what we do now: arguing about what happens when you fall into a black hole in between periods of making out.

But it turns out that I only had one shot for a future like that, and needless to say:

I blew it.

Bel: haven't heard yet, why???

"Is there any way to appeal the decision?" I ask Ms. Voss at lunch. I'm not actually sure if she's going to be able to help me, but better I stay out of everyone's way. I've been avoiding Teo all morning and now even Jamie's starting to pester me, so this is as safe a place as any to hide.

"You could," Ms. Voss says slowly, looking at the MIT rejection email on my phone screen. "But I don't know that it'll do you any good. I'm really sorry to tell you, Bel, that most often people who appeal their admissions results only change things by making a massive donation."

I wince. "Oh."

"I'm sorry," she says, handing my phone back to me and looking like she means it. "This school sends a lot of people to MIT every year, so it might just be luck of the draw."

"Yeah." I glance at my hands. "And I guess my application was pretty last minute."

"Your previous academic record may have been a factor as well," Ms. Voss says hesitantly. "Your old school didn't offer many AP classes, so your GPA was...not as competitive."

"That's so unfair," I say, because it's just easier right now to blame this on the system. "That's so elitist."

"It is," Ms. Voss agrees. "Some students start earlier and are better prepared than others, so I'm afraid both the boys who got accepted from your robotics team might have appeared to be better options on paper."

I can feel my eyes welling up with tears, which I hate. "Because they knew they wanted it sooner? Is that it?"

Ms. Voss gives me a look that makes me so much more sad. "I find that many math and science teachers are quick to point boys in the direction of engineering careers. I had hoped to do the same for you."

"You did." I rise hurriedly to my feet, not wanting to cry in front of her. "I…thank you, Ms. Voss. I wouldn't have tried at all if not for you, and I'm sorry I—"

I'm sorry I let you down is definitely my breaking point.

"Oh, Bel," she calls after me, "please don't apologize—"

"Sorry, sorry, I just have to…"

I don't even finish my sentence. I just push open the door and hurry to find some obscure corner of this stupid school so I can wallow in my own disappointment before I have to face Teo and the rest of AP Physics.

I nearly collide with someone, barely missing them. "Hey, watch it—"

"Sorry—"

"Bel?"

I wince, recognizing Neelam's voice, but keep walking. "Not now, please—"

"Ugh," she says, sounding bored. "*Please* tell me this isn't about Teo Luna."

I spin on my heel, ready to scream in her face about how unfair it is that she's always so mean to me, but instead…the dam breaks.

Neelam stares at me in total shock as I promptly and humiliatingly burst into tears.

"It's not *fair*," I sob, hurrying to hold my hands over my mouth. "It's not fair that I'm supposed to know everything at eighteen, it's not *fair*—"

"Oh geez," says Neelam with a long-suffering sigh, taking hold of my elbow and hauling me behind the band room. "Get it together, Maier."

I yank out of her reach and slide to the ground, crumpling against the wall. "Just leave me alone."

"So you didn't get into your dream school. Is that it?" she asks me, and glares at me for another minute before grumbling to herself and taking a seat next to me. "It's not the end of the world. I didn't get into Yale either, but you don't see me having a meltdown."

"It wasn't my dream school, it was my—"

I break off, sniffling and suddenly hyperventilating.

"Oh geez," Neelam says again. "Don't tell me you only applied to one school?"

I say nothing.

"Bel, what the *hell*," she says, which is probably the first time I've heard her come close to swearing. "Didn't your counselors talk to you about applying to safety schools?"

"I didn't have time." I can tell it's difficult to understand me right now, but thankfully she doesn't snap at me to enunciate. "Teo convinced me to apply at the last second, and I didn't...I wasn't thinking—"

I break off and for a second Neelam says nothing.

Then, eventually, she says, "I'm guessing you applied to MIT?"

I nod.

"You realize that's one of the best engineering programs in the entire country."

"I'm *aware*, Neelam—"

"As in, there's hundreds of thousands of kids doing the same crap we do who all want to go there. And not only do they want it more than you, they also have better grades than you do."

"Okay *wow*, I get it—"

"You want to know why I don't like you?" she asks, and I glance up, startled and still sniffling. "Well, okay I don't *not* like you—look, whatever. The problem I have with you is that you walked into robotics and got a spot without even trying. You don't know how to do the work," she says flatly. "And you don't understand how hard it is to be a girl competing with boys who don't even realize that they, unlike us, are perceived as more competent no matter what they do."

"That's not even true," I protest, furious. "I got plenty of crap at Regionals—"

"You got a *taste* of what it's like," Neelam says. "But I've been competing in math and science my whole life. I've been told girls can't win math competitions or can't built robots my whole *life*. My brothers are all pre-med, but I've been told every single day to act like a lady, to smile and be polite, to be pretty and dainty—and what boy ever has to hear that? Not *once*," she snaps, "and what you don't understand is that when you come into this world unprepared and unfocused and without even a *fundamental* understanding of what you're doing, you have nothing to fight back with. Take Mac," Neelam says, suddenly adamant. "You saw how much he favors Teo and Dash, right? But when you pointed it out he called you a bad teammate, he told you to work harder. I work hard because no matter what I do, people will always tell me I should have done more. So I do the *most*. Because I understand that it doesn't end here!"

Neelam rises to her feet, agitated, and starts pacing in front of me. "If you really want to be an engineer, then get ready," she says with a glare at me. "Get ready to hear *no*. Get ready to hear *you can't*. Get ready for *I just don't like her* or *she's not likable*. Sure, you're lucky, you're pretty and bubbly and people like you," she adds with another look of annoyance, "but you're even worse off than I am for that, because they won't take you seriously. This team? This team only takes you seriously because Teo Luna did, and lucky you." She practically spits it at me. "Lucky you, because he doesn't take *me* seriously, and thanks to him nobody on our team ever will."

"I tried to—" I tell her, and she cuts me off with a shake of her head.

"I'm not asking for your help. I don't want your help."

"But if you just—"

"What I'm saying is you don't get it." She falls back into her seat beside me. "It's not about liking you or disliking you. It's not like I hate you." Her mouth tightens, though she doesn't look at me. "It's that I know you're not ready. You didn't earn the shot you got, and you're not ready."

All my arguments feel flat, because in a way, she's right. I definitely work harder than she's giving me credit for, but she's still right. I got placed in this class and on this team *because* I didn't do the assignment I was supposed to do in the first place. I got lucky when a teacher saw potential in me; potential that another teacher—even a good teacher, or a teacher like Mac, who can't understand what Neelam and Ms. Voss instinctively know from their own experience—might never have seen.

And Teo did pick me. For whatever reason, he picked me.

But just because a boy picked me once, that will never be enough. If I want the world to recognize what I am truly capable of, I have to show them.

I start to cry again and Neelam groans. "Okay, what now?"

"Nothing, I just…" I sniffle and hide my face behind my knees. "I get it. Of course I didn't get in," I realize with a little sob. "Of course not. I'm not qualified. I don't actually know how to do any of it." I wipe my nose with my sleeve, hoping she won't say anything about my hygiene.

Neelam is quiet for a long, long time.

"So learn," she says eventually.

Just then the bell rings for sixth period and Neelam gets up, giving me another semi-unpleasant glance before holding out a hand for mine.

"You're not stupid or anything," she says. "To be honest, you're smarter than most of the boys in our class. You just need a solid foundation. And to, like, figure out if you even really want this."

I roll my eyes but accept her help up, letting her pull me to my feet.

"What am I going to tell Teo?" I ask.

She makes a face. "I literally do not care," she says.

"Fair enough." I give her a half-hearted smile. "Thanks, I guess."

"Whatever. Don't mention it."

She starts walking away from me, which I guess means we're going to make our way separately to the same classroom. Which is fine, because I have a lot to think about on my own.

Teo might be off the table. I think part of my sadness is knowing that in some ways, his dad and Mac are right. I don't want to hold him back, and even though I don't think he'd make any decisions based solely on me, I also don't really want to hear him say that.

But Teo isn't the only thing I fell for this year, and it's not like my life is over at graduation. I pull out my phone and send a text to the only person who might understand.

Bel: do you think you'll ever go back to school?

There's a bubble of typing, and then Luke responds.

Luke: idk maybe
Luke: i signed up for a class at santa monica community college
Luke: figured i might want to learn some more carpentry and stuff

The second bell rings, indicating a minute left to get to class, so I shove my phone back in my pocket and hurry to AP Physics, wiping away the smudges of my eyeliner and doing everything I can to hold my chin up high.

fourteen

DISTANCES

TEO

"I just think maybe we should take a breather," Bel says.

Needless to say, this is not what I thought would happen when I asked her if she wanted to come over after studying for finals. To be honest, I thought things were going to go in completely the other direction. Not that I lured her here for sex or anything, but this time I made sure my parents weren't even in the same state, much less likely to come home anytime soon.

I sit on my bed and try to process this. "Um, what?" I say, which means the processing isn't going well.

"It's not that I don't...it's—"

She falters, then squeezes her eyes shut.

"Never mind. I should just...I should go. I can't...I don't know how t—"

"Absolutely not." I shoot to my feet and start walking. "Come on."

"Where are we going?"

"Car," I say. "Isn't that where you have discussions like this?"

She lingers in the doorway behind me. "What kind of discussion is this?"

"I don't know," I say honestly, "but it feels heavy to me."

She nods slowly, then follows me. It feels a little bit silly to be getting in my car right now, but at least it gives me a second to think.

"Okay," I say, pulling the driver door shut as she climbs into the passenger seat. "Let's talk."

She leans her head against the back of her chair and exhales deeply, staring straight ahead.

"So, I lied to you," she says. "I already knew last week that I didn't get into MIT."

I wish she didn't turn to look at my face, because I'm pretty positive the look that immediately crosses it will determine how the rest of this conversation will go.

"It's fine," I say. "It's totally fine, we'll just…it's okay, we can—"

"Don't try to fix it." She stares straight ahead again, but then twists around to face me. "Okay?"

"What? No, I wasn't…" I *could* fix it. I could probably make a call. I mean, what is the point of having this much money if I can't use it to make my life easier? I've never been frivolous with spending by any means, but I should think having my girlfriend with me at college is a reasonable expense. "I mean, if you wanted, I could try t—"

"Jesus." She exhales. "Teo."

"Bel, I'm just trying to help—"

"Help who?" she asks me, and I'm a little taken aback by the coldness in her voice. "Help you?"

"What? Bel, come on—"

"Look, I get it," she says bitterly. "I get that I'm worth a lot less to the people in your life if I don't go to the same school you do, but if your first instinct is to try to *force* it—"

"Hey, Bel, no," I say, reaching for her hand, which she grudgingly lets me hold. "I'm really not trying to…" I don't know. "I just meant that I want to help. *You*," I add hastily. "Because if you really want to go there—"

"I do, actually," she says. "I got really excited about the program."

"Okay, then perfect, I'll just see if I can get my dad to make some c—"

She shakes her head, pulling her hand from mine.

"You're unbelievable," she murmurs, and I...don't think she means it in a good way. "You still think you're the only one who can do things right, don't you?"

"Bel," I say, because I can feel the way the conversation is taking a turn. It's funny how that works, the way you can feel yourself sinking deeper and deeper, but it's like some kind of cartoon quicksand thing where you can't get out.

"Do you not think I could get in on my own?" she asks me, which even I know is a horrible warning sign.

"I didn't say that. I just thought—"

"It's like you want *so badly* for me to be something I'm not."

"What? No, Bel, listen to me—"

"You think I'm just like everyone else in robotics, don't you? That I can't function without your help?" she says, and I can hear it, my voice being echoed back at me, my own words suddenly repurposed and twisted. "I heard you lie to your dad about where I was going to school. And I heard you tell Mac that going to MIT was the most important thing to you."

"Bel, that wasn't real. I was just saying that to get him off my back—"

"Were you?" She sounds skeptical, impatient, and it makes my frustration spike. "You're always trying to *push* me—"

"That's because if I didn't push you, you wouldn't even *move*," I snap.

The car goes deathly quiet, and even though I know I screwed up, I can't help it.

I'm mad.

"I'm not trying to change you," I tell her, "but I *am* trying to make you live up to your potential. Is that seriously so wrong of me to do? To want you to make something of yourself?"

"So I'm nothing if I don't," she says flatly. "Is that it?"

"I really believed you'd get in, Bel. I really thought you were going to. It wasn't a lie, because I honestly, genuinely, one hundred percent thought we'd both be going there—"

"So you really didn't wonder for a *second* what would happen if I didn't?" she says. "It never crossed your mind that you might have to leave me behind?"

I know the right answer is no. I know the best thing I can say is that I would never have left her behind; that I was planning on us being together regardless of where we were at this time next year. I open my mouth, intent on assuring her that of course it doesn't matter what she does next or where she goes to school, and for a second, I'm absolutely positive I mean that.

But I wish she didn't see whatever she sees on my face.

"There's my answer," she says, and glances at her hands. "Can you take me home?"

"Bel." No, no, no. This can't be happening. "Bel," I try to plead with her, "we're not done with our bot. We still have t—"

"Don't worry about it. We can still work together and study together, it's fine." She won't look at me. "And look, people are going to talk, so maybe we just shouldn't mention any of this."

"Are you serious?" Okay, now I'm pissed. "You want me to just pretend everything's okay when you're basically telling me you don't even want to try?"

"Oh, that's *such* a cop-out," she says irritably. "Look, we both know you're not going to want to do some sort of long-distance thing when you're at MIT and I'm still here. So what's the point pretending?"

"So this is all just nothing to you," I say, feeling sick to my stomach. "The last month, you're just throwing that away?"

This time, it's Bel who says the wrong thing.

"Yes," she says.

It's probably best that we're already in the car. When I drive her home, I can't even look at her.

I don't know how to process that the girl sitting next to me is someone I swear I've never even met.

Bel

I wish I could say I wake up the morning after my fight with Teo to find my message screen filled with apologies and emoji hearts, but I didn't sleep all night, so I already know there's nothing there. Not that I blame him; I'm the one who broke it in the end, but in my defense, it was for his own good. As much as I don't consider myself the distraction that everyone else seems to think I am—nor do I think it's fair to make it sound like Teo has some magical "potential" that I don't have, just because it took me longer to figure out what I was good at—I also don't want to hold him back. I know what kind of guy he is, even if I did get really freaking frustrated with him last night, and I know there's no point giving him the stress of trying to make a relationship work from literally across the country.

Better we both just...move on.

Bel: teo and i broke up
Bel: i don't want to talk about it
Bel: i'm fine
Bel: i just wanted to tell you
Jamie: ☹
Jamie: girls' night?
Bel: yeah
Jamie: okay girl just leave it to me
Jamie: love you xx

* * *

At school Teo doesn't look at me, and I don't look at him. I can't decide if it would be worse to see him sad or if it might break me to watch him act like nothing happened, so instead I just don't look his way at all.

I'm dying to know if Teo told Dash anything (Is he sad? Does he miss me?), but also, I'm prepared to be furious if he did (Dash is my friend, too!). I want everyone to know that we broke up (if anyone tries to make me talk to him right now, I *swear*—) but I also want to tell no one, say nothing, because maybe if I keep it to myself the whole thing will just disappear. (He's going to call me and try to make up...right? Right??? This can't possibly be the end!)

My heart hurts from the back and forth. I don't hate him, I want him to be happy, but I'm angry and I want him to feel what I'm feeling, to suffer a little, because he hurt me and I hurt him. I knew this would happen—I *knew* I should never have gotten involved with him—but I can't stop reliving our old moments, rereading his messages just to punish myself, like jabbing my finger in a bruise.

Ultimately, the worst part is that life goes on as normal. That everything else is the same, so I have to miss him even though he's right there. On the outside nothing has changed, but somehow, everything is different. The songs we used to like are ruined. The places we used to go are haunted for me now. Do I wish I'd never met him at all, or that I'd never joined robotics? Sometimes yes, but most of the time no. I miss him, but I need those things, those memories of how I felt and the way he used to look at me, because without them I just feel empty. I feel absolutely nothing at all.

Part of me wants to call him and tell him I was wrong—that I should never have done what I did and that I didn't mean the things I said—but what would be the point? I *did* mean them. I wasn't wrong. Our problems haven't changed and neither have we. As good as it felt at the time, I know the little game of pretend we were playing when it came the future is no longer going to work. Ms. Voss is right about me—and so is Teo, though I can't thank him for it yet. They both saw the same thing in me: that I've never really known how to reach for what I want.

I need to take up my own space. I need to be my own push. There's a secret, desperate part of me that wants to follow Teo Luna anywhere, to let him fix everything for me so that I never have to lift a finger, but I know I can't live in that delusion.

Whatever Neelam and I didn't get right about each other, she saw one thing about me that was true: I got lucky. I didn't have to learn to succeed on my own because for most of the year, I've had Teo on my side. If I followed him now, I'd never stop doing it, and then what would happen to me? I like myself most when I'm with him, but that's exactly the problem. If I'm still not enough *with* him—me, truly me, the MIT reject whose parents will never have a mansion, not ever, even if they work sixty hours a week until they die—then I'll never be enough without him. And just because he chose me once doesn't mean he'll choose me every time, especially when I'm no longer so convenient.

So all I can do is miss him, even though he's right there in front of my face.

Like with all breakups, it's really, really hard at first, and then eventually it gets easier. I stop checking my phone expecting to see his name. Lora and Jamie are very helpful, texting me memes and GIFs all day to distract me. I get used to the feeling of looking up at him and seeing that he's looking somewhere else instead of magically meeting my eye like he used to. Dash treats me exactly the same as always, so even though I'm not squished on the sofa cuddled up with Teo anymore, we all still study for finals as a group and act like everything is normal. After two weeks, Teo and I develop a system where we just don't talk unless we have to, which is easy enough.

He spends most of his time working on Seven, so all I have to go over with him about Battlestar Chromatica is the drive controls and what we're going to cut to make weight.

Finals go by in a blur. So does the AP Physics exam, which we take on the first day. Jamie and Teo and the others have way more exams than I do, so for a while I hardly see anyone at all.

"Everything good with you?" says Luke, who seems to have patched things up with Mom since moving in with Dad. He's in the habit now of coming over a couple times a week to have dinner with me, so I'm back to helping him with the car.

"Well, I told Mom about community college," I say. I talked to Ms. Voss and she suggested I get all my general credits and basic drafting out of the way so that I can transfer wherever I want after two years. Community college is free in California, so that way I'm actually saving a ton of money while still being able to get a degree from one of the top engineering schools. "Mom was a little disappointed, I think, but she gets it."

"You should give her more credit," says Luke, which is a surprising thing for him to say. After all, he's the one who moved out because our mom supposedly expected too much out of him, but maybe that explains why he has wisdom to impart. "She just wants us to be happy."

"I know," I sigh.

He finishes reconnecting the battery in his car and reaches for a rag, wiping the grease from his hands. "You should really tell her about robotics," he comments, and I shrug.

"She thinks it's a Physics field trip."

"And you're not telling her the truth because . . . ?"

"I don't know. I don't want her to be there or anything. Seems stressful."

"What if I want to be there?"

"Whatever," I say ambivalently, and he tosses the greasy rag at me. "Oh my god, *gross*, Luke—"

"Listen, nerd," he says. "It's not like anyone expects you to do anything cool, like, ever. But if it makes you happy, then that's something we should be part of."

"Ew, Luke, you sound like a self-help podcast—"

"You don't have to keep stuff like that a secret, that's all I'm saying."

I wish I could say that my brother annoying me distracts me from not having Teo, but unfortunately it just makes me think about him more.

"Where's Teo been?" Luke asks me, reading my mind.

"He's moving to Massachusetts next year, Luke. No point trying to drag it out."

The more I say it, the weaker my explanation sounds.

"Yikes," says Luke, looking at my face. "That bad, huh?"

"Whatever," I say.

But the truth is that even though it gets a little easier every day, it still really, really hurts.

There's a scramble leading up to Nationals that causes another shift between Teo and me, because while we've been cordial so far, he's well into crisis mode now. At this point, I don't think he can even distinguish me from anything else robotics related.

"Did you finish the spinner?"

"Yes, it's right here—"

"It was an ounce over yesterday, we need to fix it—"

"I fixed it, Teo, we're good—"

"Thanks, Bel Canto," he says, rubbing his head and turning away without realizing what he's said, though of course I do. I suffer it like an arrow in my chest, though luckily Seven's not quite finished, so Neelam is barking at all of us like an army general and demanding all hands on deck.

Traveling with robots is obviously a challenge. On the bright side, Nationals this year is being held at the convention center in

Downtown LA, so even though we'll have to stay overnight after our weigh-in for competition, it's practically local. We take a charter bus over to the hotel where the weigh-in is happening—seriously, this school is unnecessarily luxe—and file into a line to get our room keys from Mac. As the only girls, Lora, Neelam, and I are assigned a four-person room, having already agreed to let Neelam be the one not sharing a bed. We figure it's best to put her in a good mood before everything goes to hell, which it does almost immediately.

"The weapon on Seven's not working and we're totally screwed," Kai announces in typical Kai fashion during our testing period. I'm a little bitter about Kai these days since I know he's going to MIT with Teo instead of me, but in this case, he's not exaggerating. We're last in the queue for weigh-ins, but we can all feel the pressure of the officials gradually circling toward us. This last-minute issue could mean failing to qualify for tomorrow, which would be a disaster, and the other teams are here trying to get a look at what weapons they're competing against, so Seven and Chromatica have to be concealed under blankets while we work. "Something's wrong with the mechanism, it's not reacting—"

"Did you charge the controller?" Teo and I ask at the same time. We glance at each other and then swiftly look away.

"*Yes*," Kai snaps. "I'm not stupid!"

"Okay, give Teo the controller," I say, taking it from Kai and handing it over my shoulder to Teo. "Dash and I will look over the circuitry, maybe there's something you missed—"

"We have to rebuild this piece," Neelam says, popping up from somewhere else and glaring at someone who's trying to use a yardstick from a distance to measure Seven's base. "I think it must have gotten damaged somehow on the way over."

"Oh Jesus, okay—" I offer a silent apology to my mother for my usual blasphemy and grab Dash's arm to pull him over to Seven, only I notice that for some reason, Teo's standing stock-still. "Teo," I call to him, "you have the controller, right?"

"Mmhmm," he says without moving, which is unlike him. Normally he would be the one shouting orders, not me.

"Teo, we have to get moving," I remind him, though everything I know about Teo suggests he shouldn't have to be reminded. "Weigh-in's in less than five hours—"

"Mm." He shuts his eyes, steadying himself, and I realize he looks...sweaty.

I may have learned most of what I know about robots from my dad, but my mom's a nurse. I know what this looks like, and if it's what I think it is...

"No, no, no—take this," I say, letting go of Dash and sprinting over to Teo. I pull the controller from his hands and shove it at Emmett, who looks at me like I've just slapped him. "Okay, come h— NOT NOW, KAI," I bark before Kai can complain to Teo about something else. "Jesus, you guys are such babies...okay, Teo, talk to me," I say, feeling his forehead and swearing in really bad Tagalog under my breath. He's burning up and now that I look at him closely, his eyes are definitely a little glazed over. "How were you feeling when you got on the bus this morning? Any aches, fever?" If it's the flu it could be really bad—he'd miss all of Nationals.

Dash materializes at my side, looking worriedly at Teo. "He took a Dramamine on the bus. I think he was feeling nauseous."

"It's nause-*ated*, not naus-*eous*," corrects Neelam from afar.

"Read the room, Neelam!" I growl over my shoulder, motioning for Dash to go help with whatever it is Kai needs. "Teo, are you with us?"

"I'm fine," mumbles Teo, who is at least putting words together now. "I'm fine. Just have to shake it off."

If that's a Taylor Swift reference, we're worse off than I thought. "You're not fine, Teo—LORA," I shout, turning over my shoulder to look for her. She pops up from somewhere like a meerkat. "Can you bring over some water?"

Teo, meanwhile, is adamant. "I'm fine, Bel. I have to drive the bot, I'm—"

He breaks off, swaying a little, though I'm still holding on to him as I continue bellowing across the room.

"Lora, water! Ibuprofen if you have it, and— OH SHIT," I announce, accidentally drawing everyone's attention directly to our little corner of the massive hotel ballroom as Teo whirls around and hurls into the nearest trash can, thereby signifying that all our hard-fought plans are about to take a turn.

fifteen

GIRLS

Bel

"Teo wants to talk to you," Dash says, appearing over my shoulder when we finally clear our bots for competition, which happens *three hours* after they told us it had to be done. In all honesty, I'm not convinced the spinning weapon we scrambled to fix on Seven is going to work in combat, but at least it made weight. We'll just have to fix it between rounds tomorrow—if (cough, *when*) anything breaks.

"How's he doing?"

I straighten and touch my hair self-consciously. It's been tied in a ratty bun on the top of my head all day and looks terrible. (Though probably not any worse than Teo, considering he's been throwing up in the bathroom of his hotel room since he got sick this afternoon.)

"He's, uh…emptied of fluids at this point," says Dash. I can tell he's phrasing it that way to keep from being gross, but I've heard my mom say worse. "He says it's important."

"Okay, um. Sure." I wish I didn't look disgusting, but it's not like it makes a difference. "Did he say why?"

Dash shakes his head, which means maybe yes but the bro code has sworn him to secrecy, so for all intents and purposes that's a no.

"Oh, okay. Thanks, Dash."

"No problem." He hands me his key, offering me a courtly bow. I reply with a curtsy and make my way upstairs to his and Teo's room.

"Hey," I say when I slip inside, catching sight of Teo where he's buried under the blankets. "You okay, slugger?" I add, pantomiming something of an old-timey baseball maneuver.

"You're so weird," Teo sighs thinly. Then he sits up, or tries to, but I dive straight for the edge of the bed, holding him down.

"Don't get up. You've got to rest for tomorrow."

He shakes his head. "I'm not gonna make it, Bel."

"Nonsense, sweet prince, this isn't the Sweat—"

"I'm not going to *die*," he groans, rolling his eyes at me. "I'm just not going to be able to drive tomorrow."

He's probably right, but I'm not going to be the one to tell him that.

"Well, who knows," I say optimistically. "We'll see in the morning—"

"Bel, listen, you gotta drive the bots." He lets out a dangerous-sounding retch-cough that unsettles us both. "Yeah, maybe sit a little further away," he agrees when I not-so-subtly shift in the other direction. "Sorry."

"Don't apologize, Te— *Ooohhhh*, wait. What did you say?" I ask, belatedly processing what he just asked of me.

He shrugs. "You have to be the driver, okay? You're the only person I trust to do it."

"That's crazy," I say instantly, because it is. "Have Dash do it, or Kai—"

"Dash doesn't have your instincts. And Kai panics."

"Fine, Emmett, then—"

"Bel, listen to me. We won Regionals because you were in my ear." He manages a look of sternness despite being pale and clammy and generally unable to stand. "Our bot was flawed, but thanks to you, we won anyway."

"Yeah, because *you* drove it—"

"Because we got lucky, technically," he corrects me, "but also because you were there."

"It wasn't me. It was you," I say firmly, looking at my hands. Something about being alone with him for the first time in a month is making my chest hurt, especially because this conversation is giving me very strong flashbacks to the day I realized I had feelings for him. (I was so happy then, and so was he, and this sucks and it hurts and I hate it.)

"Bel, don't argue with me, I'm sick," Teo says.

"But—"

"I drove, sure, but you told me what to do—"

"Then it still wasn't me, it was *us*," I blurt out, half startling him. "I'm only good when I'm with you, Teo," I say, and then, because it's so pathetically true, I swallow hard. "I'm at my best when I'm with you."

If he knows I'm not just talking about our robot, he does me the favor of not making a big deal of it.

"Bel, I picked you for this team because you have vision," he tells me. "Because you've got an eye. Because you see the way things work and the way they don't work. That's all it takes to be a driver."

"But I've never driven in competition before!" I protest.

"Yeah, but you'll know what to do. I trust you."

"Teo—"

"It's your bot," Teo tells me. "They both are. Chromatica and Seven could have been catastrophic failures. We could have settled for imperfect parts, but you kept us from that. You fixed them. You pushed us. Our team built winning bots this year, Bel," he adamantly declares, "and that's because of you. I'm proud of that. Of you," he says.

I have to admit, it's not the romantic moment I imagined when I was on my way up here. I sort of thought maybe Teo was going to tell me that it was stupid for us not to be together and who cared if long distance was hard, we could do it. I thought maybe he would miraculously not have a stomach flu anymore and that he'd kiss me and tell me he missed me; that he'd wanted to talk to me just so he could say that he wanted us to be together no matter what.

But in a lot of ways this is better. Because I feel like I've been waiting a long time to hear that I deserve something, and knowing that my teammate is genuinely proud of me—that my team *needs* me—is the validation I never expected to get. It's something I never thought I'd hear, and suddenly I wish I had told my parents about it, because Luke is right.

It *is* worth celebrating.

"Thank you," I tell Teo, which is sort of underwhelming and not really an answer. He nods, but then goes slightly green, fumbling for the covers.

"Sorry, sorry—"

"No, go ahead," I say, keeping all my limbs out of his way while he runs to the bathroom.

Once he's gone, I finally have a chance to think about what he's asking me. As much as I appreciate what he's saying, something about it feels...wrong. Sure, it'd be cool to drive the bots tomorrow— *especially* since I've just sat through another day of boys looking at me like I don't belong there—but I don't know that I could defend the possible arguments against me.

I don't have any experience driving in competition: check. I've only driven the bots in practice, just to see what was moving and what wasn't, or to test out the weapons to make sure they worked. That's not the same as being in a fight against an actual opponent.

I haven't practiced driving Seven at all: check. Chromatica is my baby. I know the sum of Seven's parts, sure, but I only ever worked on it when there was nothing else for me to do.

This is my first year of robotics, my first time at Nationals, and

I don't know what caliber of competition to expect: check, check, check. I don't have the benefit of knowing the things Teo knows.

But just as I think it, I realize there *is* someone on this team who does.

I pull out my phone; the whole team's on speed dial, so with the push of a button it's ringing.

"Hello?"

"Neelam, hey," I say. "You done downstairs?"

"Yeah, just finished. Where are you?"

"I'm checking on Teo. And hey, listen, before you say anything," I add, because I know she's been stressing all day while everyone else was crossing their fingers for Teo to get better, "he asked me to drive the bots tomorrow, but um...I think I'm gonna pass."

Neelam says nothing for a moment.

"He doesn't have a right to just *assign* the driver," she mutters, obviously annoyed. "It's a team decision, first of all, and he can't just—"

"I was thinking you should do it," I cut in. "I was actually going to ask if you wouldn't mind taking over for me."

Silence.

"The thing is, I didn't earn it," I say. "But you did."

More silence.

"Which doesn't mean I *couldn't* do it," I tell her quickly, because I want her to know that I'm not totally inept. "He's right that I *could*, but I think you're the right person to do it. So if you don't mind me being in the drive box with you, then I think the two of us can make it work."

She doesn't say anything.

"So...is that a deal?" I prompt her. "Or...?"

Silence.

I glance at my fingernails.

I'll give her a few more seconds.

Like, three more seconds.

Maybe five.

Five…four…three…

"Yeah," Neelam says. "Yeah, fine."

"Okay," I exhale, relieved. Finally, I did something right. "I mean, it's not exactly enthusiastic," I joke, "but I'll take it. See you in a couple min—"

"Bel," Neelam interrupts me. "Thank you."

I know it's kind of a big deal for her to thank me, so I try not to let the awkwardness stick. Neelam isn't Jamie or Lora—she won't want gushing, and she hates anything sentimental.

"Well, hey," I say in a lighthearted tone, "we have to stick together, right?"

"Don't make this weird. Bye." She hangs up and I roll my eyes, putting the phone away just as Teo sluggishly returns to curl up on his side in the hotel bed.

"Did I just hear you give it to Neelam?" he asks me exhaustedly, and even though I know I probably shouldn't touch him while he's full of germs, I smooth his hair away from his forehead.

"Yeah," I say. "It was the right thing to do, Teo."

I brace for an argument—I'm familiar with his compulsive need to solve problems, after all—but he only closes his eyes, burrowing deeper under the covers.

"Fine, whatever. I trust you."

Not a very Teo response, but I guess he's not very Teo at the moment. I figure with all this dehydration he should probably sleep, so I rise to my feet and turn to leave the room.

"Bel?" Teo calls after me.

I turn. "Yeah?"

"I miss you," he mumbles into his pillow.

I think he might be a little delirious from all that vomiting and illness, so I try not to let my chest fill up too much with hope.

"Me too," I say quietly, slipping out to get some rest before tomorrow.

I want to feel like myself today, so I pull on my bird jeans with my robotics polo and throw on a little glitter. Last time I was trying to blend in and be taken seriously, but now I feel like the way people perceive me should be based on a lot more than whatever I choose to wear. There's no rules saying I can't have birds and ribbons on my pants and still be a great freakin' engineer, so I fix my hair and makeup until I feel good about the version of myself looking back at me in the mirror.

"Are you done yet?" demands Neelam, who rolled out of bed and threw on the same thing she always wears. True, there's a lot of ways to be a girl and hers seems much more practical, but at least I feel like me with all my usual armor on. And I really think I'm starting to like the person I am.

"Yeah," I tell her. I'm more nervous than I've ever been, so Lora grabs my hand and squeezes it. "Let's go fight robots, shall we?"

We stumble down to the hotel's continental breakfast bar to shove some food into our mouths ("You have to eat *something*," Lora says, coaxing me with a piece of toast while Dash pours every single kind of cereal into a single bowl) and then we load the bus. By now the team knows both that Neelam's the driver and that Teo had given it to me first, which I can tell rankles a few of them. Kai, though, looks relieved when he falls into the seat across the aisle from where I'm sitting next to Lora.

"I'm just glad it won't be my fault if something goes wrong," he says, and while I hear the implied lack of faith in Neelam, I ignore it.

"How's Teo?" I ask him instead.

"Basically a zombie. We all hoped he'd at least be able to operate the remote, but—"

"Dude," I say with a roll of my eyes, "he's had, like, zero

nutrition in the past twenty-four hours. Even if he *could* stand upright, I don't think that counts as being in top form."

"Yeah, well, given the options..." Kai's eyes drift to Neelam.

For the first time, I understand how hard it must have been for Neelam to love something so much despite being on a team full of doubting blowhards. I don't think I'd come into school in a very sunny mood either if I'd had the same four years she had.

"Hey, she can take the pressure," I tell Kai in Neelam's defense. "She does it every day."

"Yeah, shut up, Kai," says Lora, which honestly shocks me. It was hardly obscene but still, it's *Lora*, who never gets angry. Like, ever.

"Geez, whatever," says Kai, and then Dash drops into the aisle seat, nudging him aside and shoving a plastic baggie full of Lucky Charms into his backpack. I'm not sure if Neelam heard us, but I can tell her chin lifts a little from where she's sitting a few rows ahead.

We already know from the weigh-in yesterday that there are tons of teams here from all over the country, but it looks *way* different when we get to the convention center. The building is flat and massive, like a spaceship, and though I didn't really expect it, there are a lot of cars trying to enter the parking lot.

"Whoa," I say, looking out Lora's window from the aisle seat.

"I know, right?" says Dash, who gets a little misty-eyed. "Can't believe it's my last time doing this."

I reach over to pat his knee. All the seniors have been getting a little nostalgic; me included, even though I never really got attached to this school. Still, something about the friends I made while building robots makes me feel like the people on this bus will stick with me a lot longer than the three years I spent at my old school.

Mac and the other chaperones herd us off the bus and start directing us to the area reserved for our team. I'm recruiting Dash and Emmett to help Justin with Seven when I feel a tap on my shoulder.

"Bel?" says Ms. Voss, and I throw a distracted glance at her before doing a double take. "I brought some guests with me this time."

My heart stops when I realize that both my mom and dad are standing beside her, looking a little stiff and overwhelmed. My brother Luke is trying to see under the blanket we have over Seven, but mostly I'm stunned by the fact that I haven't seen my mom and dad standing next to each other in close to a year. The last time I did, they were fighting.

"Oh, um. Hey, guys," I say. "How did you, uh…?"

Ms. Voss arches a brow that suggests she must have had some part in this.

"We'll talk later about why you kept this from us," my mom says, and though I wince apprehensively, she steps forward and pulls me into a tight, mama-bear kind of hug. "So proud of you, anak," she says in my ear, and to my surprise, my dad steps forward, too.

"Get 'em, Bel," he says, and my mom almost flinches when he joins our hug, but she hides it quickly. "We can't wait to see you win."

"Uh, we'll see." I pull away feeling dazed, belatedly recalling that I'm supposed to be working on some last-minute tests to Chromatica. "I have to, um—"

"Go ahead," says Ms. Voss. "I'll show 'em the ropes."

"Ibb, this is wild," says Luke, jogging over to us. "There's, like, hella robots here."

"Oh god, hi, Luke—"

"Where's Teo?" asks my mom. "He's part of this, right?"

"Oh, um—"

"Hey," says Dash, materializing at my elbow. "Can you look at this?"

"Sure." I exhale, relieved. I give my parents a last glance over my shoulder, but already my apprehension is fading. They both wave back, looking nervous but excited.

I have a weird feeling that my parents are going to be okay

together today, since it seems like they finally have something in common that isn't totally wrecked. Maybe that's the credit I never gave myself before, come to think of it. Luke is like my dad, Gabe is like my mom, but I'm the mix of both of them.

I wave them off and return to our team with Dash. "Thanks," I whisper to him.

"No problem. Those are your parents?"

"Yeah."

"That's my mom," he says, pointing at a woman in the crowd with dimples and a carbon copy of Dash's dreamy expression. "She's really embarrassing," he adds, though he's smiling broadly when he catches her eye and she points to a T-shirt that reads DARIUSH'S MOM.

I wave even though she has no idea who I am, and then we both allow Mac's booming voice to corral us back to order. Our first fight is soon, against a team from Florida.

"Oh shit," says Emmett, looking down at the list. "Did you see who's in the wildcard round?"

"Ugh." Dash and I both look down and see Richardson's name as the driver for St. Michael's.

"Whatever. We beat them before, we'll do it again," I say.

"She's right." Neelam's at my elbow with a nod. "I hate him," she mutters to me.

"You hate everyone," I whisper back.

"Yeah, but especially him." She and I exchange a glance that means he's said the same things to her that he said to me at Regionals.

"Maier, Dasari," Mac shouts to us. "Let's hustle, kids, let's go!"

"You ready?" I ask Neelam, who gives me a steely nod.

"Yeah," she says, looking nervous but not afraid. I get that.

"Good. Let's go kick some robot ass."

Our first fight is close. Neelam's definitely comfortable driving Seven, but she's had less practice in this environment than Teo; I can see she's second-guessing her instincts. Still, she shoots out from the red square—we're red again, which I allow myself to believe is a sign—and I know it takes the blue team's driver by surprise. (He and his teammates were staring at us earlier, and it wasn't a polite stare. It was a *what do they think they're doing here* stare, which never gets any easier.)

Their bot has a really powerful flipper, and their driver is definitely experienced. He keeps approaching Seven from the back corners, which leaves Neelam to play defense. That's not a great way to get aggression points, so I'm staring at the other team's bot (Shredder, which, given the Ninja Turtles nickname, is *so* obviously built by a team full of boys) trying to figure out where our vertical spinner can do the most damage.

Neelam does a quick retreat to get away from Shredder's flipper that almost gets us in trouble with their horizontal spinner, though I notice theirs has the same problem ours did before we fixed the spinning weapon. Once Shredder's spinner gets moving, it's going to heat up right next to their battery.

"Get them to use the spinner," I say to Neelam, who balks. She doesn't have Teo's instincts for goading her opponent, which in fairness probably comes from the inherent swagger of being...well, Teo Luna.

"Bel, are you joking?"

"Get them to turn it on, just keep away from it," I shout at her. "We have to get under the—"

"Oh, got it." She's seen more of these than me, so she understands before I'm forced to shout out loud what our strategy is. She darts in and weaves, using our weapon for the first time nearly a minute in. If this goes to the judges, we might lose points for not adapting a workable strategy quickly enough. Our best bet is a knockout, which means doing damage—a *lot* of damage.

Getting Shredder to use the horizontal spinner is a good start, because Neelam and I both see at the same time how their bot lifts slightly off the ground once it turns on.

"There, find a weak spot!" I say half hysterically.

"I'm *trying*—"

She slams the base of Seven into Shredder so that it pops up in the air at an angle, and then she turns on our vertical spinner just in time for our single sharp tooth to catch. It rips through the bottom of Shredder's titanium base and throws Shredder into the air.

"Oh my god, oh my god, oh my god!" I scream, not even caring that my mom's behind me somewhere in the crowd to hear my blaspheming. "NEELAM, OH MY GOD!"

Shredder lands unsteadily and Neelam *goes* for it. This is where she shines; everyone knows she's got plenty of killer instinct. Seven shoves Shredder into a corner and uses the spinner to force Shredder upright, tearing through the circuitry again. Within seconds, Shredder's horizontal spinner cuts out, and I look to my left to realize the blue team's driver has gone tellingly pale.

"We have to see movement in ten seconds or it's a knockout!" shouts the ref. "Ten...nine...eight..."

Behind me, I can hear the crowd join in.

"...four...three...two..."

"Oh my god," whispers Neelam, who looks close to tears.

"One...THAT'S A KNOCKOUT!" shouts the ref, and Neelam turns to me in shock, her face frozen. I stare back at her, unsure whether to cry or laugh, and she steps forward to hug me, I think, until we're broken apart by a crowd of thundering boys.

"YEEEEESSSSSS," roars Emmett, wrapping Neelam in a monster hug, and Dash throws an arm around my shoulders from behind me.

"Hell yeah," he says, exuberant. "That was *sick*, dude—"

We celebrate limitlessly until we're interrupted.

"Good match," says the driver from the blue team, stoically holding out his hand for ours. Neelam, Dash, and I collect ourselves in the name of sportsmanship and shake in return.

"Yeah, you guys were great," I say. Which they were, obviously. (Even though we were better.)

"So, uh, this is my sister," says the driver, nudging a girl toward me who looks like she might be in middle school. "She thought you guys were pretty dope."

"Oh, thanks, girl." I lift my fist for a bump.

"I like your jeans," she tells me shyly.

"Thanks." I glance up at the blue team's driver, who shrugs.

"She didn't think girls built robots," he explains.

"Oh, well they do," I tell her firmly. My team is dragging me away to make repairs and get ready for our next fight, but I figure it's a good time for some wisdom.

"I mean come on, boys can do it," I call out to her. "So how hard can it be?"

Okay, so it wasn't wise and the blue team driver rolls his eyes, but hey. His sister smiles brilliantly, and I think that maybe if Neelam and I helped one girl believe she could do it—and that girl helps another girl—and then *that* girl helps someone—

I glance over my shoulder to where Jamie and Lora are sitting with Ms. Voss, who holds up a glittery sign in my direction.

WHO RUN THE WORLD?

In that moment, Mac inadvertently catches my eye; we're both looking at the same thing.

"I see you, Maier," he calls to me, lifting a fist in triumph. No—in solidarity.

I see you. It floods me, head to toe, like the release of a year's worth of tension.

Good thing I don't have time to cry, because I would absolutely bawl my eyes out with pride right now if not for having to go kick some more robot ass in fifteen minutes.

sixteen

CHANCES

TEO

I wake up like I'm coming out of a coma and realize I'm alone in our hotel room. Dash, Kai, and Emmett left behind a hurricane of stuff this morning, and a glance at the clock tells me I'm missing what's probably their third round of combat.

Assuming they didn't lose before now, that is.

I glance at my phone to see that Dash is texting me every five seconds, which in this case I'm relieved about. I hit play on Lora's Instagram story and watch Bel and Neelam get a knockout, ending with the two of them facing each other in astonishment. Bel has on her jeans with the birds and my whole chest aches while I watch her; she's somewhere between laughter and tears, and I suddenly remember that it was only a few months ago that I was pulling her in for our first victory hug.

So much has changed since then, but the way I feel when I look at her...that hasn't. That's just as fierce and proud as it's always been.

The video is focused on the knockout itself, obviously—which for the record I *do* care about—but being on the outside of my final Nationals competition is...not like I thought it would be. I'm sad, yeah, and I wish I were there, but I'm actually kind of relieved that it's not my responsibility to drive the bots right now. It's been my job to carry everyone for so long that part of me suspects my whole body physically revolted at the thought of doing it again. When I was swimming in and out of Kai's argument with Emmett about whether I should still be able to drive, I was really torn, because I know it's on me to be the person who never lets anyone down. If they'd agreed that I should do it anyway, I would have gotten myself out of bed. I wouldn't have questioned it for a second. But truthfully, I'm glad it was out of my hands in the end.

Even if Mac was right about what I owe this team, Bel was more right, and so was Dash. I'm not the team; *we* are. We built those bots together, and it shouldn't have taken twenty-four hours of continuous vomiting for me to realize how much I trust them—*all* of them. Because even if they couldn't have gotten here without me, I wouldn't be anywhere without them. They have everything they need, a whole year's worth of tireless work, and I'm relieved—no, I'm *glad*—that now, for sure, I know it: they don't need me to win.

So what's sad for me isn't that I'm not driving, but that I'm not part of it, win or lose. The people in this fifteen-second video that I've been watching on a loop are my best friends in the whole world. They're my team. We've spent the last however many weeks and months and years building shit together that we let other people destroy, and somehow the only thing that never gets broken is the bond that we have with one another.

Even—I hope—the one between Bel and me.

There's a sound at the door and I sit up slightly, thinking maybe someone came back during the break for lunch to let me know how the competition is going, but it's my mom who slips inside. I'm assuming Mac had to call her.

"Hi, honey," she says, creeping into the room on tiptoe as if she expects to find teenage boy cooties on the floor, which is definitely the case. "You awake?"

"Yeah, I'm up." I drag myself upright. "Still kinda iffy, though."

"Ah, okay." She sets her purse down and sighs. "Bad timing, huh? You never get sick, baby boy."

"Yeah, I know. Not awesome." She's right. I never get sick. "You didn't have to come, though."

"Of course I did." She reaches over, testing my forehead. "I think the guidebook says to do this," she murmurs, frowning a bit, "though I can't say I know what I'm looking for."

I can't help it. I laugh.

"You're good, Mom," I say. "I think the guidebook probably has a lot of subjective advice."

"True, it can be somewhat contradictory," she admits with a sigh. "Scoot over, will you? I left a Thai massage for this."

"Dad's not coming, is he?" I ask, obliging her as she settles in next to me. She slips an arm around me and leans my head onto her shoulder, which is comforting.

"Do you want him to?" she asks.

Honestly, it'd just be a waste of his time. It's not like he's usually here for this sort of thing, and I really don't mind it. His time is limited, and since we're not that close to begin with, I'd really rather not worry about whether he's itching to get back to work or not. I mostly just feel guilty whenever he's obligated to fulfill his paternal demands.

"It's fine," I say, wondering why I have to force myself to mean that. "I mean it's not like I'm actually competing or anyth—"

I break off as Mom's phone buzzes in her purse. She reaches over and, surprisingly, my dad is FaceTiming her.

"Well, speak of the devil." She hits answer and holds up the screen so we both fill it. "Our baby bird is still alive, Mateo," she trills to my father, ruffling my hair. "We're still killing it at this parenting thing."

"Excellent," my dad says with a chuckle. Nobody makes him laugh like my mom, but he turns his attention to me anyway. "You feeling okay, kid?"

Okay, so I know I said I didn't want my dad to drop everything just for me, but that doesn't mean I don't like hearing that he still wants to talk to me.

"Yeah, Dad," I say, burrowing a little deeper into my mom's side. "I'm fine."

Bel

Has Teo said anything?" I ask Dash before we slip out of our fourth round of competition. We're in the winner's bracket, so at this point, one more win will clinch it. I've never seen my mom look so excited and terrified at the same time—I even saw her covering her eyes when Chromatica took a hit that punctured its multicolored polymer shell. Luckily my dad leaned over and explained something to reassure her; probably about how we'd built it with metal underneath.

(I know they're not getting back together or anything, but still. It's nice to see them lean on each other, even if it's just for one day.)

"He just sent me a bunch of emojis," says Dash, his thumbs flying over his screen. "See?"

He shows me what is indeed a mess of modern hieroglyphics.

"Oh, okay." Not like I expected Teo to be transmitting me secret messages from his sickbed, but—

"Here, this is for you." Dash shows me a new message on the screen, which says:

tell bel to take it easy with the srm

"Oh." He's reminding me about the self-righting mechanism he built, which is finicky. A self-righting mechanism is something you can choose to add to your bot; just in case your robot gets flipped onto its back, the mechanism flips it back upright again. With the weight of the plastic armor on Chromatica, we had to limit our battery system to keep it below fifteen pounds, so our self-righting mechanism might take some time to rev up if we do have to use it.

It's a helpful reminder, but since he didn't call me Bel Canto or anything…

"Yeah, okay, thanks," I tell Dash. "He's just talking about one of the parts. It's fine."

"Oh, okay cool. I was worried he meant his 'super regrettable moment' or that he was a 'sorry remorseful muppet'—"

"Dash, you've been doing robotics for a hot minute, you know what SRM means," I say, but then I blink, registering what he said. "Wait, what are you saying?"

He slides a glance at me. "He misses you," he says simply.

Hearing that kills me a little, but it's not like Teo and I didn't break up for a reason.

"Honestly, Dash, it was for the best—"

"No it wasn't." He kind of paws at my head the way Luke would. "You miss him, too. Admit it."

I grimace. I'd love to deny it, but he *did* just see my face when he told me Teo had a message for me. It's not like Dash is a total idiot.

"I'm not saying I don't miss him, I just—"

"That's all I needed to hear. Hey, focus," Dash adds to me, giving me a nudge toward Neelam, who's frantically signaling me over. "Go win us one more, okay?"

One more.

One. More.

"Yeah, yeah, I'll try."

I shake any lingering thoughts of Teo from my system and jog over to Neelam. I'm about to open my mouth and remind her there's nothing to panic about when I stop short, realizing who our competition is.

"Heard Luna's out," drawls Richardson, materializing with two of his cronies like the villain in a really bad James Bond film. "This is gonna be a quick three minutes."

"How are you even here?" I ask him irritably. "You couldn't even win Regionals."

His eyes drift down to the embroidery on my jeans.

"Super cute pants," he comments in a high voice.

I'm 100 percent going to punch him in the face.

"Bel." Neelam nudges me. "Ignore him."

"What's your deal?" I ask Richardson, making sure to look his teammates in the eye, too, so they know they're part of this even if—*especially* if—they choose to say nothing. "I mean, I get it, losing is embarrassing," I add with a lift of my chin, "but hey, we're just glad that boys are getting the opportunity to try."

"Look, congrats on the diversity points," Richardson drawls, "but we don't need them."

He flicks another glance at Neelam and me and turns away, stepping into the—gulp!—red square, which means we're blue. (Ugh, I'm totally just as superstitious as my mother is.)

"Make him sorry," I mutter to Neelam, whose hands tighten around the remote when we step into our team's designated area.

"Oh, don't worry. I'll make him cry," she murmurs back.

I wish I could say it doesn't bother me to hear Richardson mock us for being girls, but it's totally frustrating. Not because it's wrong—which it is—but because it's exactly the sort of thing that prevents most girls from trying. The girls who get ahead are the ones who can let stuff like that just roll off their backs, but that's not the easiest thing in the world to do. There's a lot more kinds of strength than just being outwardly tough, and it's a lot to ask of anyone to succeed when most people in the room are waiting to see you fail.

I sneak a glance over my shoulder at Jamie, who's basically the smartest person I know and almost definitely our valedictorian, and Lora, the most ambitious out of all of us, who's still always gracious, who never sinks to negativity or cynicism. I think about how much I want them to succeed in life; to go far, as far as possible, until every girl who succeeds is like a beacon of light for all the others.

Then I shake myself again, because I'm ready to let this moment be about me.

"Blue team, ready?" asks the ref.

Neelam hits the start button without hesitation. "Ready."

I don't bother looking at Richardson. Instead I look at his bot, which is a redesigned version of the bot he brought to Regionals.

MABA's Second Term. Seriously? What a little—

"Focus, Bel," says Neelam, nudging me. "What do you think?"

"Uh…" There's no real way of knowing whether they fixed the gyroscopic force problem just by looking, though they've taken a little off the bot's height. From what I can tell, there's now a lever from the top to prevent them from losing the same way they did last time. They haven't taken anything but superficial nicks and scratches in previous rounds of today's competition, which means they must not have any obvious weaknesses.

I wish now that I had made an effort to see their weapon in action earlier today. Ravi and Emmett gave us a vague report from what they happened to see between rounds, but I don't know if anything they told us could measure up to seeing it myself.

"I don't know," I tell Neelam honestly. "You'll just have to test them and see."

"Fine." She sets her jaw. "I've got this."

"I know you do." She doesn't know Chromatica's intricacies as well as Seven's, since Teo and I built this together. Still, she's been driving it all day, and I know she learns as she goes.

"Let's do this," I say, just before the ref calls out for the start.

Right from go, MABA—I am *not* calling this bot by its full name—comes roaring out of the red square, making a beeline straight for Chromatica. Neelam is pretty quick to respond, just barely missing when MABA's spinner tries to dig into our plastic shell.

"You just have to stay upright," I tell her, glancing over at the judges. We won the last round in a judging decision, so I already know they're impressed with the way we designed the armor. I'd prefer a knockout, obviously, and I'd really like to personally make sure Richardson watches his own bot go up in flames, but until we know what MABA's weaknesses are, we're aiming blindly.

Neelam sort of grunts something at me in concentration. MABA dives in again and she turns on the spinner, which successfully does some damage.

"Nice. Keep getting after it," I say, and she nods, going in for another hit.

It goes on like that, back and forth, for over a minute. By the time we pass the one-minute remaining mark, neither bot has a lead. I glance at Richardson, who's sweating it a little, obviously trying to do more damage to Chromatica than our colored shell will possibly allow.

Neelam, losing patience, goes in for the kill, but the timing of her attack means momentum isn't on our side. Chromatica flips from the impact and my hands fly up to my mouth, catching a gasp when it lands on its back.

"It's not flipping back," Neelam says, slamming down on the self-righting mechanism.

God. It's like Teo had a premonition or something. "I know that, just keep working it—"

"Bel, it's not moving—"

"I know, I know, just wait—"

Richardson takes advantage of our momentary stillness and slashes up the underside of Chromatica, tearing through our thin titanium base.

"Bel, what do I do?" demands Neelam.

"Crap, crap, crap," I say, trying to think. "Look, keep trying—"

"Should I turn on the spinner?"

"No, no, we need to reserve all the circuitry for flipping it upright—"

"We need to see movement from Battlestar Chromatica!" yells the ref as MABA spins, doing a little victory dance for the audience.

"Any movement at all! You have ten seconds, blue team. Ten... nine..."

No, no, no. Not this. Not this bot.

Not *our* bot.

"Bel," gasps Neelam, jamming her thumb down on the mechanism. "Are you sure?"

"I'm sure, Neelam, I'm sure." I'm not sure. I have no idea. Teo built this piece, not me. I know it has weaknesses—I know it *should* work—but this is high school robotics. It's not a computer simulation. In real life, things don't always go the way they should.

"Just wait, okay? Just keep trying—"

That is my bot, my brain screams. This is my hard work, this is my blood, sweat, and tears, this is mine and Teo's, this is *everything we worked all year for*—

"But if I used the spinner, I could—"

"No you can't, please don't give up, Neelam, *please*—"

"...six...five...four..."

I glance desperately over my shoulder and see that Jamie and Lora are clutching each other. My mom has her hands over her eyes, and Mac has one hand over his mouth. There's a lot of jeering coming from the red square; all the St. Michael's boys are celebrating prematurely and staring mockingly at me, which I do my best to ignore.

"Just trust me," I plead with Neelam, hoping she'll remember that I trusted her last night.

She says nothing, but the position of her jaw says clearly: *you'd better be right*.

I know it'll be on me if this goes wrong. This isn't even about Richardson anymore, even though I can see him smirking from my periphery. I'm asking Neelam to take a leap of faith based on calculations that Teo and I made *in theory*, and I'm the first person to know that the real world doesn't always act according to our expectations. Turning our weapon on will count as movement, it'll keep us in this fight, but it won't be enough to save us. We'll have to power up the self-righting voltage again at some point, and at this rate, we won't have time to do it.

It's now or never. Do or die. Neelam's never trusted me before—she's not the only one, and I can hear the boys behind us shouting to do something, *anything*—but I know this like I know my own heartbeat: it *has* to work.

I can't even breathe, and the sound of the ref's countdown is swimming in and out.

"...three...two...one—"

Just then the mechanism activates and Chromatica launches up from the ground, springing up from nothing as the voltage finally powers up. Richardson's smirk wipes away, his teammates' mouths clamp shut, and in that moment, I know.

This is what it feels like to have built the best bot in the ring.

"I'm absolutely going to strangle Luna for the heart attack I just had," mutters Neelam through gritted teeth, diving straight for MABA as I burst into tears of relief, all other sounds in the arena drowned out by the screams from the crowd at our backs.

seventeen

BIRDS

TEO

I expected the team to go celebrate after their day of competition, but instead they all pile into my hotel room. I'm still not feeling 100 percent, but it was an easy decision not to go home with my mom when she offered to take me with her. I want to be here with my team, win or lose—though judging by the looks on their faces, I think it's a win.

"Seven *crushed* it," Dash tells me, pumping a fist into the air with a whoop. "All the new stuff we added freaking *killed*. The juniors basically won't even have to do anything to make it a three-peat next year," he declares, flushed with victory at the legacy we left.

"That's awesome." I'm relieved to hear it. "And Chromatica?"

"Did you think we only won one weight class?" asks Emmett, grinning with his arm slung around Kai. "Dude, we killed it, man."

"You should have seen it when Bel handed Richardson back his own battery," Kai adds, crowing with laughter. "She was stone cold, it was hilarious. Richardson looked like he was gonna puke."

I crack a smile, ignoring a little twinge of longing at hearing her name. "I no longer wish that on anyone, believe me, but it's great to hear." Then I look around and spot Neelam, who gives me a sort of half shrug.

"Hey, you did good, Dasari," I call out to her. I wish it had been my idea to ask her to drive, but...okay, to be honest I had my doubts. Clearly I was wrong, and I'm not mad about it. "I'm glad you were the one to take over," I tell her.

"Duh, Luna. I already know I'm better than you." She rolls her eyes and wanders out of my eyeline, checking out of the conversation. Same old Neelam, I guess.

"You should have seen it," Dash continues, launching into a description of one of the knockouts I missed. Several people chime in, too, to the point where I can understand basically nothing.

(Talk about FOMO.)

"Man, I just..." I look at everyone's faces of exhaustion and feel a little pang of sadness. "I hate that I wasn't part of it," I comment, but then I hear a little throat-clearing sound from somewhere near where Mac's standing at the door.

"Actually, you were," says a familiar voice.

I blink, spotting Bel in the room, which suddenly goes quiet.

"Uh, hey, kids," says Mac, straightening as Bel takes a hesitant step toward me. "Let's all give Luna some space, okay? Germs," he adds, giving Dash a nudge.

Everyone else files out kind of slowly, and Mac pauses next to Bel once the room is almost empty. She, I notice, is currently holding something behind her back, out of sight from where I'm waiting.

"Not too worried about me catching Teo's germs, Mac?" Bel asks, irreverent as always.

"You get ten minutes, Maier," he tells her. "Then you're checking in with one of the chaperones outside. Got it?"

She nods.

"All right. Oh, and Maier," Mac says, pausing before he leaves us alone. "You really taught me a lot this year."

"Me?" She frowns.

"More than you know, kid." He pats her shoulder and then slips out of the room, leaving Bel alone with me.

"See? Progress," I tell her.

She rolls her eyes and comes closer, revealing whatever she's holding behind her back.

"I made the others promise not to spoil it because I wanted to do a cool reveal, but…" She shrugs. "Take a look."

It's a trophy. Not a super nice one by any means, but I look down and see the engraving:

BEST ENGINEERING AWARD

"For which bot?" I ask, running my fingers over the engraved letters.

"Take a guess." She's grinning at me.

"Ours?"

"Yep." She looks up and her eyes hit mine full force. "So you get it now."

"Get what?"

"That you *were* part of it. No—not just part of it." She takes the trophy back from me and I stifle a laugh; she's obviously having trouble letting it go. "You're the best engineer, Teo. The driver, the leader. You're the backbone of this team." She grudgingly puts the trophy back in my hand. "You can have it." She sighs. "I mean, I was there to witness all of it, so…"

"You can keep it," I assure her.

She doesn't even think twice. "Okay, cool," she says, hugging it back to her chest. "Sorry, I'm still kind of emotional about it. I mean, I know we have more money than other robotics programs"—she sighs again—"and I basically just built on the success you guys had last y—"

"Bel." I reach out to cover her hand with mine. "You earned this. Nobody gave it to you."

She glances at where my knuckles are resting on top of hers and swallows.

"Are you going to tell your parents?" I ask her.

"Actually, Ms. Voss told them," she says, laughing a little. "They came to watch."

Wow, that's huge for her. I check to see if she's stressed about it, but she seems…happy, I think. "Both of them?"

"Both of them." She smiles distantly. "I'm probably grounded, to be honest. But at least they seem to understand why I decided to do community college next year, so—"

"You did?" I ask, surprised. It's obviously been a long time since we talked.

"Yeah, I…" She clears her throat awkwardly. "I just really want to do this, you know? To keep doing this. And who knows, maybe I'll apply to MIT again two years from now, or possibly next year, if I can get a bunch of general credits done." She blinks, mortifying herself. "Not that you need to…Not that I meant—"

"Bel." I can't fight a smile. "That's awesome."

"Yeah?" Her eyes widen.

"Absolutely. I'm…is it cheesy to say I'm proud of you? I'm so proud of you."

Her cheeks flush. "Okay, slow your roll, Luna. I haven't even *done* anything yet—"

"Bel, come on. You know I'm proud of you all the time," I tell her honestly.

She gives me a long, vulnerable look, and I realize it's about time I just told her everything that's been going through my head. If high school is good for anything, it's proving that nothing lasts forever.

"This was never about where you went to college," I tell her. "I know I made you feel like you had to be something you weren't, but I swear, it wasn't ever like that for me."

"I know that now." She hangs her head slightly. "I think I was just embarrassed and…I didn't have a *plan*, and you always make things look so easy—"

"Bel, nothing is easy for me. Before you, I felt like I was drowning." I've never told anyone that before, but I mean it. "Before you, nobody in my life was really trying to see what I actually was, good or bad. They just wanted parts of me, the leader or the captain or the—"

"Obedient son?" she asks quietly.

"Yeah."

We sit in silence for a couple of minutes, our hands still wrapped around our trophy.

"So listen," she says, "about prom—"

"Bel, I just really miss—"

We both stop.

"Were you going to ask me to prom?" I ask her, fighting a laugh.

"Well, I mean, as a practical matter…" She trails off, blushing furiously. "I mean come on, these are modern times, girls can ask boys—"

"I miss you," I say, getting the whole thing out this time. "I miss you so much. I will absolutely go to prom with you, I'll go anywhere with you—"

"Oh my god, shut up." She bends her head and lets out a little sob-laugh. "Teo, Jesus. I miss you, too."

I look down at where she's doubled over on my lap and don't know what to do.

"What are you laughing at?" I ask, totally bewildered.

"Just…everything." She gives another hiccup of something and drags herself upright, exhaling, and all I can think about is how glad I am to be near her. How much better everything feels when she's close to me. I keep thinking how dull everything's felt over the last month without her, how empty it was compared to all the months before it, and I don't even care how far away Massachusetts is. Even just the sound of her voice feels more like home than my parents' gigantic mansion ever has.

"Okay, sorry." Bel sighs. "It's been a weird day and I'm just—"

"I think I'm in love with you," I say, and when she freezes, so do I. I wasn't expecting to say that, but at the same time, I know it's true. "Sorry, you don't have to say it back or anyth—"

"I love you," she says, and blinks. "Wow, I didn't even have to think about that, did I?"

I'm pretty sure she and I are both considering how nothing definitive comes easily to her. She told me once that she never understood how people could be so certain about their futures, or about anything, but now she sounds sure about this. She looks it, too.

"Well, it's not like it's college," I say, hiding my relief, even though I'm absolutely soaring. "It's just, you know. Me."

She rolls her eyes. "Sure, Teo. Just you."

She scoots closer to me on the bed, and suddenly I hate that her ten minutes are going to be up soon, because I don't plan to let go of her ever. I tuck her hair behind her ear with one hand and pull her closer until it hits me like a record scratch.

Oh yeah. There's a reason I've been in this bed for, like, thirty-six hours.

"Wait," I say, pausing just before her lips meet mine. "Germs."

She ignores me, closing the distance between us without a moment of hesitation.

"Eh, it's not like I have a bot competition to worry about," she says, and I go in for another kiss, laughing as I pull her closer.

Bel

I ended up being too sick to go to prom, which was fine with me. Teo showed up at my house in his tux and held my hair back for me for most of the night, which Luke took several pictures of from the doorway. I think he plans to use them as blackmail at some point, but I don't even care. If your boyfriend can watch you sprint for the bathroom in your prom dress and still insist that he loves you, I think that's probably a good sign. (Not that I recommend trying it at home.)

Luckily I'm all recovered now, and after a couple of weeks of squirreling around waiting for the school year to end, the time has finally come for graduation. The last week of school is finals for everyone else, but since most seniors had to take them before AP exams, we're free to do things like wander around nostalgically signing one another's yearbooks.

By now we all know that Jamie's our valedictorian. She's committed to Stanford, which is also where Neelam is going. They're not going to room together or anything, but I have a feeling they'll see each other from time to time.

Lora gets a merit scholarship from USC's Annenberg School of Communications and Ravi decides to go to UC San Diego, a cool two-and-a-half-hour drive away from her (assuming traffic behaves). Dash decides on NYU, Emmett picks UC Berkeley, and Kai and Teo are of course both going to MIT.

People ask me what my plan is all the time, too, and I'll admit I was a little embarrassed at first. Saying I'm going to enroll at Santa Monica Community College is…not exactly the thing you want to say when your best friend is valedictorian and your boyfriend is a genius. Still, I eventually get used to saying it, because I know it's the right choice.

Neelam is right. Life is long, with plenty of chances to start over. I didn't get a solid enough math foundation from high school and I'd like a few more skills going into a competitive mechanical engineering program. The first class I decide to sign up for is a computer-animated drawing class, plus I add in a drafting class. I'm also scouting out jobs for the fall, which Mac has been surprisingly helpful with. He introduced me to someone he knows at a program providing STEM-based tutors to underprivileged kids.

By the time I do end up in an engineering-focused program—which I will—I plan to be fully prepared without having wasted a cent of my parents' money.

"So how does it feel to have a plan?" Teo asks me.

"Not bad, actually." I've been really holding on to these moments of strolling across the quad with my hand in his, because as excited as I am about the future, I know I'm going to miss him like crazy. "How does it feel knowing that your plans are all perfectly in order, as always?"

"Actually, MIT doesn't let you pick a major right away," he says with a laugh. "I'm going to have to be sort of aimless for the first couple of years, which will be...a first."

I can't help it; I laugh. "Whoa. You sure you can handle that?"

"Eh, I've learned a thing or two about letting go," he says, giving my hand a squeeze before we drop onto the benches of our lunch table.

It's hard to believe there was ever a time that I didn't feel this close to someone. Teo's seen the most disgusting, secret, uncertain parts of me and I still can't believe he wants all of it, good and bad. But then again, I've seen all his fractures as well, and I wouldn't give those up, either. I guess that's what being in love is—though, what do we really know about that? We're still young enough to be as dumb about each other as we want to be.

We've agreed that we're going to take things easy while we're apart. I don't want him to feel like he has to talk to me all the time or anything, even though I know that's easier said than done. I don't want him to lose out on any of this experience, just like I don't want to pine for him while I have my own stuff to figure out. So, for right now, we're going to have the best summer ever with all of our friends, and then...

We'll take things one day at a time.

"Hey, before everyone gets here," Teo says, "I got you something."

"What? *Teo*—"

"It's small, don't worry." He pulls something tiny out of his backpack, and I can't help a little gasp of delight when he hands it to me.

"Oh, it's another bird for my collection," I say with excitement, taking the little antique pin from his fingers. "It's so pretty, Teo—"

"My mom's still shopping at that vintage place, so the owner set it aside for me. I figured you could use it in your hair or something," he tells me, "but also, I don't really understand what you wear, so...up to you."

"Well, it's perfect. *Becauuuuse*," I say, pantomiming a drumroll on the lunch table, "I have something for you as well."

"Really?" He lights up like a Christmas tree. Silly boy.

"You really love presents, huh?"

"I mean, I've been very deprived in life," he says, "so, you know..."

I punch him lightly in the arm. "Shut up. I wasn't going to give it to you yet, but since you're sitting here empty-handed—"

"Yeah! Give it to me." He grins.

I roll my eyes and pull out something only slightly larger from my bag.

"Close your eyes," I say.

"Whatever you say, Bel Canto." He closes them and I reach for his hands.

"Okay, now."

His eyes flutter open and he looks down at the thing I made for him, which is basically a tiny animatronic sparrow I built using a watch battery and some of Luke's spare auto parts. I've been spending a little more time at my dad's lately, so he's given me free range of his tools. I started working on this right after I was too sick for prom, though I wasn't sure what I was making or who I was making it for until it was finished. And then I knew.

"It's, you know...because there should always be two birds," I explain, feeling a little silly, because I don't actually know if boys are sentimental like this. Teo kind of stares down at it, then immediately starts tinkering with the circuitry to figure it out.

"It flaps its wings if you do this," I say, showing him the connectivity in the mechanism. "I didn't want to make you take something stupid to your dorm, but I thought, you know. It was small enough that you could tuck away in your desk, or—"

"Are you kidding? Bel." He leans over and swipes a kiss across my cheek without direction, still too fascinated by the bird in his palm to look up. "First of all, I want to know everything about how you made this. Secondly, I'm putting it on *top* of my desk. Or my nightstand. Or you know, whatever I look at most."

"Well, if you want," I say, though of course I'm pleased to hear it.

"Birds of a feather, right?" he says with a grin, and for a moment, my chest tightens.

I'm going to miss him a lot. So much. There are moments like this when I feel totally in sync with him, which I know is going to feel like I'm missing a piece of myself when he's gone.

Still, it's not that often in life that you meet someone you get to share moments like this with, and I know it would be terrible to waste it.

"Birds of a feather," I tell him, like I'm promising him something big.

Any second now Dash is going to show up and eat part of Kai's lunch. Jamie's going to appear and tell us some hilarious story about what happened during the AP Gov wiffle ball tournament this morning. Lora and Ravi are going to compare checklists about what they're planning for their dorm rooms—Lora and her roommate already have a shared Pinterest board for their decoration ideas—while Teo's friends on the soccer team argue about who's got the best chances in the next World Cup. Emmett's going to let us tease him about how close Berkeley is to Neelam at Stanford, all while pretending he doesn't care.

But for right now, it's just Teo and me. And as quiet as this moment is compared to some of the others we've had together, I still get that rush of being in exactly the right place at the right time. Like when we won that first knockout together at Regionals, or when we did that first color throw at the Holi festival. I've felt myself careening toward him all year, crashing into him again and again for months.

Maybe life hasn't always pointed things out to me the way I was expecting, but if I was lucky enough to let the universe catapult me here, then all the hard stuff along the way was worth it.

Just before Teo pulls me closer, my phone buzzes in my pocket.

Jamie: you better not be making out with teo when I get there
Jamie: you will not BELIEVE what just happened in wiffleball

I toss my phone into my bag with a chuckle and tug Teo in by the collar.

"How much time do we have?" he says, already leaning toward me.

"Oh, just enough," I tell him.

And then I kiss him, in a moment that feels like all I'll ever need.

epilogue

Bel

TWO YEARS LATER

So...I didn't go to MIT.

Actually, I didn't even finish the two years I'd planned to be at SMCC. After the first year of kicking ass at drafting and getting in my basic calculus requirements, I got a call from Neelam. I'd heard from her every so often before then, maybe every month or so when we chatted over text, but this time she was calling with an unexpected opportunity: Emmett's robotics team at Berkeley needed someone with an eye for design, and had I considered applying? Apparently Neelam had a professor in her Biochem program who'd seen our bot in action, and since her professor was married to the engineering director at Berkeley, well...she happened to know there was space for someone like me.

Like, specifically me.

After talking it over with Ms. Voss, who I'd been seeing once a week to help with the club she started at Essex for girls interested in STEM, I started at UC Berkeley a year ago in August.

I do miss the work I was doing at the tutoring place Mac found for me—and I *definitely* miss biking down to the beach during my afternoon breaks in Santa Monica—but being at Berkeley is basically like my senior year of robotics on steroids. Being close to Jamie and

Neelam is great, too, though I've been so busy this semester I've barely seen anyone in weeks. Thanks to all the time I spent getting good at different design programs, I've been able to convince my teammates and professors to let me take a lot more risks, which led to me taking on more responsibility in our component builds. All the work I've put in over the past two years has allowed me to really grow and improve, and now there's no question that I'm one of our team's best designers.

Which is why when my team asked me to drive the bot, I didn't hesitate. I know I've done the work, tirelessly. I've led this team the best I could, and at this point I have more experience under my belt than most of them. I've earned the right to say I know this bot better than anyone, so today, I'm stepping into the driver's seat at a National Collegiate Robotics competition for the first time.

I won't pretend that doesn't mean the world to me.

I pull out my phone when it buzzes, glancing over the messages from my parents and brothers. My mom and dad are definitely grateful I picked a public university, though with work study and the money I saved from my year of community college, I was able to get a pretty good financial aid package. More importantly, their acknowledgment that they both contributed to the generally successful person I am now seems to have helped ease the tension between them. They'll probably never be the same as they were while they were married, but I no longer worry about them so much.

Luke called me this morning, too. After a couple of years working with my dad, he's back at school finishing up a degree in construction management. I shoot back a few heart emojis in the family group chat and then turn my phone off, shaking out the jitters and trying to get a good view of our competition.

"Hey, Maier," says a voice behind me while I'm craning my neck to see into the ring, and I whip around to face the driver on the MIT robotics team.

"Hey yourself, Luna," I say smoothly. "Sure you're ready for this?"

"Oh, born ready. Sure about the height on that spinner?" he asks.

"Surer than you should be about that hammer. How long does it take to react?"

"Wouldn't you like to know," he says with a smirk, which I am more than happy to return.

All this smack talk is purely for the benefit of our rival teams, of course. (Some boys still can't take the idea that a girl in sparkly Doc Martens belongs in robotics, but I'm always happy to prove them wrong.) Teo and I both know that this is going to be one of our toughest rounds of competition—I know *exactly* how good of an engineer he is, and likewise, his team's already heard about how our bot broke a collegiate record during testing—but there's no real animosity here. This is just like the time we spent in Mac's robotics lab, challenging each other and pushing each other to our best, only this time he's in his MIT crew neck and I'm in my Cal T-shirt.

We've known for ages that we would be facing each other today, and as luck would have it, we're facing off in the first round.

"I'm red," I tell him, a little smugly. "You know what that means."

"Superstition is for the birds, Bel Canto," he says. He knows I've got a bird pinned into my hair that means when this round is over—when I've won, obviously—my boyfriend still owes me a kiss.

Yes, we're still together. We tried to keep things simple for Teo's first semester, neither of us holding the other to anything, but we talked every day and never stopped saying we loved each other. By the time he came home for winter break, Teo told me he wanted complicated. I said I did, too.

So yeah, going to two different schools across the country isn't the easiest thing in the world to manage, but we FaceTime for at least a few minutes every day while trying very, very hard not to accidentally spill any secrets about the bots that have taken over our lives. We also make sure to see each other in person about once a month, which means my roommate is as familiar with seeing Teo as Kai is with seeing me. (Dash, too, spends a lot of time on Teo's couch, and I try to time my visits for when he's just leaving. My favorite thing is digging into the leftovers from when Dash goes on a pierogi cooking spree.)

It's been a little hectic, definitely. On the bright side, Teo and I applied and got accepted to the same engineering program in Edinburgh for next fall, so we're finally going to get more than a few spare days in the same place. Both of us are looking forward to exploring the world together in just a couple of months, but right now...

Right now is about the fight.

"Red team, ready?" calls the ref, and I step into the red square.

"Ready," I say, hitting the button that activates our side of the ring.

"Blue team, ready?"

Teo steps up a few feet away from me, controller in hand.

"Ready," he says.

Teo and I exchange a glance, openly competitive. I'm pretty sure no one could tell by looking at us that we were making out, like, fifteen minutes ago, or that we're probably going to be rehashing the whole fight tonight in one of our rooms.

(Well, okay. We might do other things, too.)

The lights in the ring flash, temporarily blinding us. I'm nervous, I'll admit. But not afraid. I can feel my pulse in my throat and I know this will be the longest three minutes of my life, even though it'll go by in the blink of an eye. Life is like that sometimes, but I'm determined to make the most of it. I let my thumb hover over the forward control, bracing myself for the start command.

"Hey. Bel." I glance over at Teo, who winks at me. "See you on the other side."

"You're the worst." An easy shorthand for *love you*.

"Yeah, yeah." He smiles, and I know that win or lose, Teo Luna and I are made of a strong foundation. What he and I have together is the best thing we've ever built.

As we turn to face our bots in the ring again, the whole world goes quiet. I breathe in, slowly, and exhale out. Ms. Voss once told me that I needed to take up my own space in this life, and as right as she was then, I think I've managed to take it a step further. It took me some time, but I think I finally know the secret: that you can stand up without standing alone.

You know what else I know? The guy on my right loves me. The ones standing next to me trust me. I won't notice until later this afternoon because my phone is off, but Neelam and Jamie are with my roommate Rachel behind me. A year ago, I had nothing but a computer animation and some spare parts, but now there's a robot of my own design sitting in front of me.

My hands tighten on the controller and I'm nervous, but not afraid. This is my comfort zone.

"ROBOTS," the ref shouts, "ACTIVATE!"

I'm in my own space now.